BURNING AMBITION

MARGARET THOMSON DAVIS

BURNING AMBITION

B&W PUBLISHING

First published 1997
by B&W Publishing Ltd
Edinburgh

ISBN 1 873631 64 2

British Library Cataloguing in Publication Data:
A catalogue record for this book is available from
the British Library

Cover illustration:
Wishart Preaching Against Mariolatry
by Sir William Fettes Douglas (1822-1891)
Courtesy of
the National Galleries of Scotland

Printed by Biddles Ltd, Guildford

PART I

SCOTLAND
1546

— I —

THE old town of Haddington was alive with rumour. Although a bone-chilling February wind was whistling through the town, the market square was packed with people going about their normal business. But there was only one topic of conversation that day—the news that George Wishart, the notorious heretic, was amongst them and would preach that very afternoon at the market cross.

As the great bell of St Mary's church tolled in the background, and the afternoon wore on, anticipation grew in the crowd that filled the square. Then, appearing seemingly from nowhere, Wishart was there, standing on the uppermost step of the market cross. A wave of excitement passed through the crowd—it was not every day that their quiet little town witnessed such bold defiance of both the church and the law of the land.

In a calm yet powerful voice Wishart began to preach.

'My friends, how good it is to see so many gathered together here today to listen to the *true* word of the Lord. For so long you have been deceived by the lackeys of the anti-Christ of Rome. Now, at long last, the time has come to overthrow them—yea, just as our Lord cast out the money-lenders from the Temple!'

A few scattered cries of 'Amen to that!' rose up from among the crowd, but many looked apprehensive, fearful to be seen to agree with such dangerous sentiments. At the back of the crowd, two figures on horseback—a tall, broad-shouldered young man and his companion, a young woman with fiery red hair—stood out from those around them. Their expensive clothes and fine horses marked them out as members of the nobility, and even the preacher seemed to notice them. They appeared to be engaged in a heated discussion.

'Marie, why will you not listen to me?' asked Donald McFarlane. 'I keep telling you—it's too dangerous for you to be seen anywhere near this man, especially now that they are calling him a heretic!' He gestured towards Wishart, while his eyes raked the crowd, searching for any sign of trouble.

'You worry too much, Donald,' his companion replied. 'Why should we care about what he may or may not be? Let's just enjoy the spectacle. God knows, there is little enough excitement in our lives.'

'If your father finds out where you have been and who you have been listening to, then you'll understand why I worry about you,' Donald told her in an exasperated tone.

Marie looked petulant. 'I only want to listen to the man. Where's the harm in that?'

'You know perfectly well that Wishart is preaching reform of the Catholic clergy as well as the Catholic church. For God's sake, Marie, have you forgotten your own father is the Bishop of Moray!'

'My father . . .' Her voice filled with bitterness. 'How could I ever forget him? But tell me why should I take any notice of an old lecher like him? He treats my mother like a mere plaything, and he takes precious little notice of me!' Her mother, Effie Dalgliesh, was one of the Bishop's concubines, and Marie herself was only one of his many illegitimate children.

4

Her voice was raised with the passion of her feelings and Donald hissed a 'Wheesht' at her.

'No, I'll not wheesht,' she said in a louder, more defiant tone, clearly intending those around to hear. 'I think Master George Wishart talks a lot of sense!'

A few of the crowd were beginning to look round at the two young riders.

'For God's sake!' Donald hissed. 'You don't know what you're talking about, and if you carry on like this, you'll get us both thrown into the Cardinal's dungeons.'

'Are you afraid?'

'Of course not. As ever, my only concern is for you.'

Immediately Marie felt guilty. Donald had been a good friend since childhood. She knew he was no coward. His problem was the intensity of his love for her. And that was her problem as well. He wanted them to marry and settle down in some cottage or other on his father's land. But, as the youngest son, Donald would never have any claim to the McFarlane estate or to the big fortified house on the hill. Even so, it wasn't Donald's lack of money or prospects that discouraged Marie. At least, she didn't think it was. She told herself that she just didn't want to settle down. She was only sixteen and in a restless, vague kind of way, knew that she could and would do better and more exciting things with her life.

The dominie, Mr Fraser, who taught her with such dedication at the village school, had told her she was destined for better things, and she was determined to work hard at her studies and make the most of her opportunity to learn. Her education was one of the few things for which she felt some gratitude to her father, for it was Patrick Hepburn, the Bishop of Moray, who financed the school and the dominie.

The dominie! Now there was a man she could look up to and admire. Mr Fraser spoke his mind without fear or favour and seemed to have earned some measure of respect from the Bishop, and he had certainly earned Marie's intense admiration and complete devotion. There was no doubt that Marie was his favourite pupil, for he spent so much extra time with her. Recently he had even suggested that she came to live in the schoolhouse.

Jeannie, Mr Fraser's wife, had been outraged. Marie had overheard her yelling at her husband, and his patient reply,

'But she could work for her keep. She could help you in the house when she's not attending to her studies. I worry about her living with that stupid harlot of a mother and that old lecher the Bishop. She's in moral danger, Jeannie.'

'She *is* the moral danger,' Jeannie had screeched, 'and she's in our house too much as it is. She's far older than any of your other pupils. Why is she still here at all? That's what I'd like to know.'

'She's a gifted child, that's why. . . .'

'She's no child! She's sixteen and could pass for twenty with those brazen eyes of hers.'

Marie could just imagine Mr Fraser's pained expression at his wife's ranting, but his voice remained patient.

'She's gifted, Jeannie. Her grasp of Latin and mathematics, and now her Greek—'

'I'm sick of hearing about how wonderful that bastard is. Don't ever forget that's all she is—just another of the Bishop's bastards. . . .'

That had brought Marie near to tears. Because it was true. She *was* just another of the Bishop's bastards. Yet, at the same time, it had only made her all the more determined to get the better of this millstone that hung round her neck.

Marie's gloomy thoughts were interrupted as George Wishart's voice rose to a crescendo.

'My brethren, you must exhort your Prelates to repent of their wicked ways, or they will feel how terrible is the wrath of Almighty God!'

'Aye! Especially those damned sinners Beaton and Moray!' came a harsh shout from the crowd.

Marie looked round to see who had spoken against her

father. She did not recognise the face, but the man who had spoken was a tall, imposing figure with a long unkempt beard and a wild look in his eye.

'Who's that?' Marie whispered to Donald.

'Take no notice, it's only Knox—he's a local trouble-maker. Just ignore him. Everyone else does.'

But Marie felt something strangely compelling about the stranger dressed in black. As she stared at him, he turned and caught her eye, and scowled back at her. She couldn't help thinking that he looked like a dangerous man to cross.

As Wishart continued to preach, Knox kept interrupting, denouncing Marie's father and Cardinal Beaton again and again, but then a sudden commotion at the far end of the market square silenced everyone for a moment, as they turned to see what was happening.

'Damn!' said Donald. 'I knew this would happen. It's the Cardinal's soldiers.'

As the horsemen rode into the square, the thunder of hooves, the cloud of dust, and the sunlight glinting on weapons and armour created instant panic in the tightly packed crowd. Marie and Donald's own mounts reared and pawed the air in fright as women screamed and everyone struggled this way and that, desperate to reach safety.

As the soldiers crashed through the crowd, men, women and children were knocked aside. A few unfortunates who fell in the path of the horses were trampled under iron-shod hooves, but the horsemen seemed oblivious, intent only on seizing their prey—the heretic, George Wishart.

Donald and Marie managed to stay on their horses, but they were carried helplessly along by the crowd. Suddenly, Knox pushed roughly past them and ran towards Wishart, shouting loudly at the soldiers as they seized the preacher.

'Unhand him, you spawn of Satan!' he bellowed.

The soldiers ignored him, and Knox, picking up a large stone as he ran, hurled it at them. The soldier he hit cursed loudly, drew his sword and turned round to face his attacker, but Knox was no fool—he had already melted back into the anonymity of the crowd.

'Come on,' Donald urged Marie. 'The quicker we're away from here, the better.'

Marie seemed transfixed by the violence that surrounded them, looking on in horror as the soldiers struck down Wishart's few remaining supporters.

'We must do something. . . .' she cried.

'Don't be a fool. This has nothing to do with us! And there's nothing we can do—except get ourselves out of here.' Marie had lost sight of the preacher now, but she knew that if these were the Cardinal's men, then they would be taking Wishart to the Cardinal's castle at St Andrews. Her father, along with a multitude of other members of the clergy and the nobility, was staying there at the moment, and the Cardinal had no doubt organised the arrest of the notorious heretic as a way of impressing his guests.

Marie turned her horse to follow Donald. She was trembling.

'What harm has that man ever done to anyone? I must speak to my father. I'll speak to the Cardinal if necessary.'

'Are you mad?' said Donald. 'All that will do is let them know you were here, listening to a heretic preaching. Who do you think ordered all this anyway? It was the Cardinal himself, no doubt with the full support of your father!'

'I thought you sympathised with people like Wishart,' said Marie.

'You know I do,' Donald replied. 'But now is not the time for heroism. Even the bold John Knox has flown.'

They had a long journey ahead of them, and as they rode in silence away from the chaos of the town, Donald had time to reflect on what they had just witnessed.

If only he could tell Marie just how much it had all meant to him. She knew nothing of his true involvement with Wishart and the underworld of secrecy and deceit in which he moved. Only a few short months before, Donald had stumbled into that world, and it had seemed as though nothing would ever be the same again. At first, he had attended a few of Wishart's secret gatherings. Gradually, the preacher had taken Donald into his confidence until one day, after all the others had left, Wishart had taken Donald to one side.

'I have been watching you closely, my friend,' Wishart said, 'and I think you are the sort of man I can trust. Am I right?'

Donald was puzzled, but replied,

'Of course. I would never betray you.'

'I am glad to hear it, Donald, for now I am going to tell you something that you can never repeat to another soul. Do I have your word as a gentleman?'

'You have my word.'

'Excellent. Until now, my friend, you have seen me as nothing more than a simple preacher, have you not? Well, I have to tell you I am much more than that. I am an agent of his Majesty King Henry VIII of England, and I came to Scotland to work for the benefit of both our nations. Your country is in grave danger from the plots and schemes of the French, and only an alliance with the might of England can save this land from civil war.'

Donald was stunned by what he was hearing. Wishart continued,

'As you know, the greatest ally of the French in this land is that old fraud and lecher, Cardinal Beaton. If he were to be . . . eliminated . . . then the French influence in Scotland would be at an end. To put it as simply as I can, I am here to bring all this about. But I need help, and I think you may be the man I have been looking for.'

Donald knew there was much sense in what Wishart was saying, yet what he was suggesting would mean becoming involved in treason and murder. But Wishart had been very persuasive.

'And remember this, Donald. King Henry does not forget his friends. If you join me in this business, it will mean

9

wealth and position for you in the new Scotland. I know you are unlikely to inherit much as a younger son, and this may well be the best chance you will ever have to make your way in the world. Think hard, Donald, think very hard before you turn it down.'

Donald's mind had been in turmoil. But one thing and one thing alone had finally decided it. He had always known that without wealth and property he would never be able to marry Marie. Wishart was right: this was an opportunity he could not refuse.

'I think you have found the man you are looking for, Master Wishart,' Donald said, and the two men had shaken hands. Then Wishart began to tell him how they would proceed.

Now, as he rode beside Marie, Donald wondered what would become of Wishart, but more importantly he wondered if Wishart would betray him. So long as Wishart maintained the façade of being a simple preacher, then Donald would be safe. But who could tell what Wishart might let slip, under the inevitable torture he would undergo as a heretic in the dungeons of Cardinal Beaton?

Their journey back to St Andrews passed without incident, but Wishart's fate was still on Marie's mind. As they arrived, Marie turned to Donald,

'I *will* speak to my father,' she said stubbornly.

He looked round at her with a sigh.

'Oh, Marie . . .'

He looked so familiar, so dear to her in his dark cloak, and his hat with its low flat crown hidden by a halo-like brim and small horizontal ostrich feather.

But she wouldn't capitulate.

'I only want to help the preacher.'

'I know,' Donald said with another sigh. 'And I suppose nothing I can say will stop you so I might as well save my breath.'

Marie dismounted with a smooth agile movement despite

the restrictions of her long skirts, and Donald led their horses away to the stables.

❖ ❖ ❖

As Marie crossed the courtyard she passed Magnus Hepburn, the only other of her father's illegitimate children she had actually met and who, like herself, had been allowed to adopt the Bishop's surname.

He gave her a cursory greeting. They had never been friends. On the contrary, he had always taken every opportunity to play cruel tricks on her and torment her. Until the last time when she'd fought back, nearly scratching his eyes out, as they rolled about on the schoolhouse floor. Even Mr Fraser had been shocked at her behaviour.

But Magnus Hepburn had never tormented her again.

She remembered Magnus's mother pouncing on her later and dragging her before the Bishop in an absolute fury. Alice McNeal had always been jealous of Effie Dalgliesh of course, and any favouritism the Bishop might show to Effie or Marie.

'Do you know what this wicked red-haired fiend has just done?' she had screamed at her paramour.

'Wicked red-haired fiend?' the Bishop echoed. 'That is surely something of an exaggeration.'

'No, it is not,' Alice insisted. 'She set upon your son, scratched him, kicked him and actually rolled about on the ground punching him black and blue.'

The Bishop tutted, secretly amused at the thought of that tedious boy Magnus being beaten by a mere slip of a girl.

Then he'd tactfully smoothed Alice's rumpled feathers with the promise of a new gown.

He'd also promised to punish Marie. This punishment had consisted of ordering the dominie to give her extra work, which was no punishment at all. Indeed, it only increased Magnus's jealousy of her.

11

* * *

Nellie, Effie's maid, met Marie in the corridor and said,

'The mistress wis lookin' for you. She's up in her bed-chamber.'

Marie nodded, and reluctantly climbed the narrow stairs.

'Where have you been?' her mother demanded as soon as Marie entered the room. 'I told you to stay here in the castle and help me entertain the Cardinal's important guests.'

'Entertain the Duke of Glasgow, you mean,' Marie said contemptuously. Effie had been attempting for some time to persuade Marie to marry Machar McNaughton, Duke of Glasgow. The fact that he was a repulsive, fat old man did not discourage Effie at all. Her only thoughts were for the material advantages such a match would bring.

'All right, all right. And what's wrong with that? It's about time we took our proper place in society. And this is our best chance.'

'Our proper place in society?' Marie laughed. 'And what might that be?'

Her mother fluttered her eyes heavenwards as if appealing for help from the Almighty.

'The Duke has a castle in Glasgow. He is one of the most well-liked and respected men in the country as well as one of the wealthiest. We could be living there in the lap of luxury. We'd never need to worry about money again.'

'I'd have plenty to worry me if I was tied to that pig of a man.'

'Oh, you wicked lassie. How dare you speak about the Duke like that!'

'I don't want to marry anybody but if I had to, it would be Donald McFarlane that I would choose.'

'Oh *him*.' Her mother flapped her hands in a gesture of dismissal. 'What could he offer us? Is that where you've been?' she cried out, the truth suddenly occurring to her. 'Stravaiging about with that useless creature.'

'We weren't stravaiging about. We went to hear George Wishart preaching.'

'The heretic?' her mother screeched in dismay, collapsing back into a chair. 'Did anyone see you? Oh, dear Jesus, I hope no-one saw you. If the Bishop or the Cardinal found out, that would be the end of us. We'd be finished. If your father turns against us we will be penniless, left to starve. You'd be lucky not to end up at the stake—'

'Oh mother, be quiet. I was only listening to the man preach. They dragged him away. . . .'

'Yes, I know. I saw him brought here. He'll be tried of course, but that is merely a formality. He is *certain* to be executed.' She brightened a little. 'I imagine it will be quite an occasion, no doubt with a banquet and all sorts of entertainments afterwards.'

Marie had stopped listening.

Just then Nellie came into the room.

'Miss Marie, your father wants to see you. He says it's urgent.'

Effie instantly feared the worst.

'Oh no! Surely he can't have found out about your stupidity already? Promise me, Marie, promise me you won't let your father know you've been anywhere near George Wishart!'

But Marie had already left the room. Walking along the lantern-lit passageway, her heart pounding, she reached the library where she knew she would find her father.

He was sitting at a table lit by a silver candelabra, his quill scraping laboriously over a scroll of paper. He looked up.

'Marie.'

'Yes father?'

He laid down the quill, leaned back and clasped beringed hands over his scarlet robe.

Marie drew a chair over so that she could sit facing him.

13

In a voice seething with suppressed anger, the Bishop spoke.

'I am greatly displeased with you. Mr Fraser is always telling me how quick-witted and intelligent you are, and I believed him. Until today. Is it true that you have been consorting with heretics?'

'If you will only let me explain—' Marie began.

'How can you explain defying the church and everything I stand for in so flagrant a fashion? I tell you my child, you should consider yourself fortunate indeed not to be sharing the heretic's cell after what you have done!' He paused for a moment, then continued,

'But you are young and naïve in matters of religion. And indeed of life. The lion cub looks attractive and harmless enough. But he is still a dangerous animal. So it is with the heretics. It is not just their wicked heresy that is the problem. They favour an English alliance and the king of England is a deadly opponent of the true faith. They are tearing this country apart like the lion tearing at the body of its prey.'

Marie was listening intently, her brilliant green eyes fixed on her father's sallow face. Now she said,

'But the way that man was treated was *so* cruel. Donald and I only wanted to—'

The expression in her father's eyes hardened and she recognised in them a man who would show no mercy, not even to his own flesh and blood. When he spoke again there was cold anger in his voice.

'So young McFarlane was with you, was he? Well, I shall have words with him. I had heard that he was keeping bad company. By God! When I have finished with him he will curse the day he ever heard the name of George Wishart!'

Marie had lowered her head and begun to weep. Against his better judgement, her father took pity on her.

'Marie, you poor child, you must understand, these heretics feed on innocent fools like you. You must never forget that the punishment for heresy is death. However, on this occasion I choose to overlook your questionable actions. Let us call it a . . . childish error of judgement. But I warn you, if you disappoint me again, you may not find me so merciful a second time.'

The Bishop rose from his desk and walked over to the window. Looking down into the courtyard in the gathering dusk, he could just make out the shapes of workmen piling wood around the stake. He turned back to Marie.

'Tomorrow, the heretic will be condemned, have no doubt about that, and I expect you to attend the execution and see justice done.' He paused for a moment. 'Perhaps that will cure you of your dangerous *naïveté*. Now, leave me, I have much work to do.' And with that the Bishop turned once more to the window.

Marie walked out of the room in a daze. How had she ever become involved in all this? Why on earth had she made Donald take her to Haddington? But she still felt sorry for the poor preacher languishing in the dungeons below, imagining the dreadful tortures he was he suffering at that very moment. And then a shiver ran down her spine as she remembered how she had blurted out Donald's name. Her father had been merciful to her, but as for Donald . . . ?

II

WISHART slipped and stumbled as the guards hustled him downwards. Ahead of him, the steps of the narrow winding staircase fell away steeply, disappearing into the darkness, deep underground. Each crudely carved tread sparkled feebly as the smoky torchlight reflected off the damp stone steps. At the bottom stood a heavy oak door of rough hewn planks and rusting ironwork. One of the guards flung back the bolt, opened the door, and shoved Wishart roughly forward into the darkness of the dungeon.

As the door slammed shut behind him, a fetid smell rose like a wall in front of him, a reminder of all the other poor unfortunates who had occupied this cell in the past. With a grimace Wishart realised he was standing in the residue of years of human effluent. Although there was little light, there was enough for him to recognise a stone pallet to rest on. Thankfully he found it free of the disgusting mire that covered the floor. He looked round for the source of light. It was coming from high above his head, at the end of a narrow stone niche. Suddenly Wishart felt terribly weary, and he slumped down onto the cold stone. Lying on his back in the gloomy damp of the cell, he stared upwards, hypnotised by the beauty and purity of his own tiny patch of sky, and wondered what tomorrow would bring.

✤   ✤   ✤

In the blackness of his cell, time soon ceased to have any meaning for Wishart. Sometimes, if he listened intently, he could hear the distant sounds of life outside continuing without him. The faint echoes of girlish laughter brought the beautiful face of the striking young woman at the market cross to his mind's eye. He had seen her with Donald McFarlane at that last meeting, and although he had never met her, he had heard much about Marie Hepburn, daughter of the Bishop of Moray. Having seen Marie, with her proud bearing and glorious tangle of red hair, Wishart could well understand why Donald was willing to risk so much for her. Many times, as they hid from the Cardinal's men in dark attics and damp cellars, he and Donald had spoken of her.

But more often, they had spoken of the plan to kill Beaton. Donald had accepted Wishart's assurances that it had to be done, and he had put any doubts he may have had firmly to the back of his mind. Everything had been ready, and the conspirators were just about to put their plan into action when Wishart was arrested.

As he paced up and down his cell, Wishart reflected ruefully on how close he had come to succeeding. If only he could have evaded the Cardinal's men for another few days! But he had no-one to blame but himself—ignoring the advice of his friends, he had insisted on going to that last meeting to maintain the appearance of being a simple preacher. What a fool he had been! He had been playing a dangerous game, and now he was undoubtedly going to pay the price. And he could expect no help from his friends in

England. By the time they heard of his predicament it would be too late. In any case, he knew only too well the ruthlessness of King Henry's spymasters. They would probably find it more expedient to deny all knowledge of him and let events take their course. For a brief moment he considered the possibility of Donald and the others finding some way to get him out of the Cardinal's dungeons, but he dismissed the idea as hopeless. Then another thought struck him. What if Donald could persuade Marie to use her influence with the Bishop? If only he could find some way of getting a message to Donald . . . Perhaps all was not lost just yet.

✤　　　✤　　　✤

It turned out that Donald had already tried to slip in to see Wishart secretly, but had been intercepted by the Captain of the Guard, a polite and decent kind of man, according to Donald. Nevertheless, he had been adamant about not allowing anyone near the heretic.

'I'm under strict orders from the Cardinal,' the Captain explained. 'No-one sees Wishart. And if you're a friend of his, I advise you to keep it to yourself. This castle is a dangerous place for anyone who sympathises with heretics.'

'I've only made things worse,' Donald told Marie when they met later. Then his voice dropped to a whisper and Marie was barely able to catch his words. 'But if we can't save him, at least we can avenge him and carry on his work.'

'Never mind that now, Donald, there is something I have to tell you. My father knows you were at Wishart's meeting, I think he means to do you harm.'

'I'm not afraid of your father,' Donald replied.

'Well perhaps you should be. At least try to keep out of his way until all this is over.'

'You may be right,' said Donald. 'After all, I will not be much use to Master Wishart if I too am locked away in the dungeons. But I swear, if they kill him, I will make them pay for it!'

Marie looked away. Then she spoke.

'I don't think I can bear to watch him being executed.'

'You have no choice. The Cardinal has ordered everyone to attend, and your father will be expecting to see you there. You cannot afford to anger him any more than you already have.'

* * *

Later Marie told her mother,

'I will not stand by and watch that poor man being burned. It's too horrible. I refuse to be any part of it.'

Effie's small face crumpled with anxiety. In panic she fluttered about the room like a trapped moth, golden skirts seesawing over their wide pannier.

'But your father commands it. What would it look like if you didn't obey him? I'll tell you. It would look like you were sympathising with the heretic. And with all the highest dignitaries in the church here to witness your heresy! Do you want to be burned next?'

'You wouldn't care. You'd come along and enjoy the spectacle like the rest of them,' Marie said bitterly.

'You're a wicked ungrateful lassie, Marie Hepburn, and I wouldn't be a bit surprised if you end up tied to a stake with the flames licking around your feet. Oh, dear Jesus, it doesn't bear thinking about. . . .' Effie staggered back into a chair, half fainting, desperately waving her fan. 'What is to become of us? How can you do this to your poor mother?'

Marie hesitated, biting her lip. There was some truth in what Effie said. And if she defied the Bishop, it might only make things worse for Donald. She was prepared to risk the Bishop's anger, but she couldn't be responsible for anything happening to Donald.

'If you insist, then I'll go,' she said reluctantly.

19

'Oh, thank you, thank you, Marie. The Bishop would have blamed me, you know, and I can't bear it when he's displeased with me.'

Marie felt a pang of sympathy for her mother and she wondered momentarily what Effie saw in the Bishop. He was a cold and ruthless man. But at the same time she knew her mother revelled in the excitement of life at the palace of Spynie. There, Effie could mix with the highest in Scottish society. And then there was the cottage in the grounds of the palace that the Bishop had provided as a home for her mother and herself. He also provided a modest sum every now and again on which they could live and keep Nellie, the maid, and John, the groom and general handyman.

But the Bishop also supported Alice McNeal and Magnus Hepburn, who lived only a few miles away from Effie's cottage. No doubt there would be other female calls upon his purse as well, and Marie knew it was a constant worry to Effie that a day might come when 'her' Patrick would no longer feel obliged to provide for her. She never tired of reminding her daughter of this dreadful possibility.

— III —

THE morning of the execution dawned bright and clear, and from first light, a buzz of excitement filled the castle.

'Everyone who is anyone will be here!' Effie told Marie, as she hurried along, dragging her daughter with her. But because she was a petite woman, she had to keep raising herself on tiptoe. It was the only way she could see all the people in the crowd and give them her customary bright smiles and waves of greeting. She soon became quite dizzy with delight as they moved among the elegantly painted and richly clothed ladies and gentlemen.

Everyone was chatting and laughing, filling the castle with excited noise and Marie could scarcely hear herself think. Then she noticed Magnus and Donald arrive, along with her cousin, James Hepburn, the young son of the 'Fair Earl' of Bothwell. Magnus's mother Alice waved cheerily to them. Although Alice was jealous of Effie and told all sorts of tales about her to the Bishop whenever she could, in public at least, she was bright and friendly. Effie, to her credit, was too good-natured to be jealous or spiteful to anyone, and warmly returned her greeting.

Soon the babble of conversation was hushed, as a trumpet blast heralded the arrival of George Wishart. His face, the colour of alabaster against his sombre clothing, looked strained but resolute. He walked calmly if a little rigidly, eyes fixed on a distant horizon. As the Captain of the Guard guided Wishart towards the pyre, the preacher smiled kindly at him and seemed to bestow on him a look of gratitude.

Not that the poor man could have anything to be grateful for, Marie thought.

'There will be a lovely banquet after all this is finished,' her mother whispered. 'You'll enjoy yourself, you'll see.'

Effie could never accept the fact that her daughter did not enjoy such occasions. Marie had been spared from attending most of the Bishop's orgies at the palace of Spynie, but it was usually by feigning some indisposition or other. Magnus and Donald were always roped in to take part mainly because their parents, like hers, loved to attend.

Now, at the castle of St Andrews, Marie was reluctantly impressed by so many guests dressed in such splendour. The gentlemen, in huge puffed and slashed sleeves, and elaborate codpieces, and the ladies bedecked in a striking panorama of all kinds of rich velvets. Some were in satin, others in taffeta, others in damask, all of them decorated with gold buttons, fur linings and ruffs. But most magnificent of all were the bishops and the Cardinal, their robes emblazoned with huge scarlet crosses.

'Laud's sake,' Effie hissed at Marie as they walked up the steps of the east tower, from where whey would get the best view of the forecourt below. 'Can you not raise one wee smile? What'll folk think? You look so miserable.'

No-one could accuse Effie of looking miserable. She made a vivid impression in her orange coloured dress with its wide skirt supported by wooden hoops. Its enormous cuffs were set above the elbow and spilled in deep luxuriousness to below the hips.

Effie liked clothes that showed off her neat little figure to advantage, and she was fond of flashing a shapely ankle when she climbed the stairs or was enjoying the dance. She favoured dresses that forced her breasts upwards to bulge above the square *décolletage*, and she wore bodices that fitted closely at the back with a trained skirt set in deep pleats behind. She often tried to make her daughter dress in exactly the same fashion. But Marie, although taller than her mother, never carried off these embellishments with the same *joie de vivre*. As often as not, she ended up wearing underlinen, finely pleated and held closely and high round her throat with a neat frill. And she absolutely refused to have her dresses made in the same garish colours as her mother's.

As they reached the parapet, Marie was struggling desperately to think of anything that would take her mind off what was about to happen. Her eyes wandered over to where Cardinal Beaton sat, flanked on either side by the bishops. She met her father's stare and wondered if he could see the contempt in her eyes.

Finally, she could no longer avoid looking towards the place of execution. As Wishart's guards strapped him into a long black coat and led him to the stake, the two executioners were already waiting by the stake with packets of gunpowder to tie under his armpits.

Men in armour stood nearby to foil any attempt at a rescue, and gunners with artillery at the ready lined the walls of the castle, their eyes scanning the crowd for any sign of dissent.

The trumpets blew once more, and Wishart's chains were made secure.

The expectation of the crowd was now so strong that Marie could almost feel it physically washing around her. Down below, people pushed and jostled to get a better view. The odour of their unwashed bodies assailed Marie's nostrils with an unusual vigour, and as people were pushed first one way then the other, the clamour of their raised voices swelled to a meaningless babble. Suddenly, a yell went up and she knew the fire was lit. Unwillingly she felt her eyes drawn, as if in a trance, to the smoking pyre. There was a gasp from the crowd as suddenly the flames caught and leapt skywards. At first Wishart just kept looking up and above the crowd, his eyes focused on the patch of powder blue sky high above the grey stonework that enclosed the courtyard.

As the flames caught hold, his face contorted with the anguish that tortured his lower limbs. Just as the executioner stepped forward to tighten the rope around his neck and end his suffering, Wishart summoned all his remaining strength for one last desperate proclamation. His words were aimed at Cardinal Beaton.

'God forgive you! But you will not wait long before the wrath of the Lord descends upon you in this very place!'

Donald had assured Marie that Wishart would not suffer. He said that heretics were usually garroted before the flames got going properly. But Wishart had obviously suffered terribly. As the flames licked hungrily higher, the crowd, which had been in such high spirits, suddenly began to get restless. Many seemed to feel that, whatever his crime, Wishart did not deserve the unspeakable cruelty he was suffering.

Then, above the noise of the crowd, a voice cried out 'It should be Beaton who burns today, not Master Wishart!' and Marie turned to see the agitator John Knox shouting and gesturing towards the Cardinal. His supporters joined in with angry shouts of their own, and Beaton started to look nervous. He turned to the Bishop of Moray who sat next to him and said,

'My Lord Bishop, this rabble is getting out of control. I sincerely hope—' But before Beaton could finish, a shattering explosion came from the direction of the stake, and those nearest the pyre were showered with the heretic's blood. Clearly, the gunpowder had exploded.

Mercifully Wishart had already lost consciousness as the heat, the smoke and the pain overcame him, and with a great crash the pyre collapsed around his smouldering remains in a cloud of smoke and sparks. Feeling sick at heart, Marie ran down the steps of the tower, an acrid, sour taste rising at the back of her throat to mingle with the stench of burning meat.

She quickened her pace and ran out of the castle and on into the town, finally stopping in an alleyway. As she gasped for breath, the conventional smells of human excrement and rubbish were, for once, welcome to her nostrils.

✤   ✤   ✤

Later that evening, when the celebrations were in full swing, Marie discussed George Wishart's prophecy with Donald, Magnus and young James.

'After what I saw today, I hope Beaton suffers just as Master Wishart did,' she told them.

Magnus just shrugged and said,

'He was out of his mind. He wouldn't know what he was babbling on about.'

Marie ignored his sarcasm and James said,

'I for one don't think he deserved to die like that.'

'Keep your voice down,' Donald warned.

'I don't care who hears me.'

Donald glowered at the boy.

'Have you forgotten it was your father who gave Master George up for the Queen's smile and the Cardinal's gold?'

James flushed and Marie felt sorry for him.

'For goodness' sake!' she protested. 'James is not yet twelve years of age. There's no point in blaming him for what his father does.'

It was then Marie remembered she'd eaten nothing since the night before. She'd been so upset at the thought of Wishart's execution. Now she felt faint with lack of sustenance. Starving herself would not bring George Wishart back, she thought as she followed the others over to the long table illuminated by dozens of candles in many-branched silver candelabra.

Magnus and James filled their plates with greedy enthusiasm. Donald ate absent-mindedly, but Marie could only pick at a little fish.

Already her mother was prancing about at the dance with complete and shameful abandon.

'Would you look at my mother!' Marie groaned, but James laughed and said,

'Och, she's having a grand time. The three of you are old before your time!'

Effie's green velvet shoes and stockings were catching everyone's eye. Or at least, every man's eye. Her frizz of fair hair was escaping from her gable hood and straggling, wet with sweat, over her brow. Her partner of the moment, the Duke of Glasgow, was sweating even more profusely. A stream of moisture was running down his face and soaking his moustache and beard. Eventually, bellowing with laughter and clutching at his oversized belly, he managed to roar out,

'Enough, enough, Effie. I've a wheen more flesh than you to heave around.'

To Marie's annoyance, Effie dragged the great bull of a man across to her.

'Ah, my favourite lady!' the Duke addressed her.

Marie felt sure the whole of the vast concourse of people must be listening.

'My dearest one . . .' he continued, grabbing her hand and pressing thick wet lips against it.

Marie immediately jerked away.

'If you'll excuse me, sir.'

Then, clutching up her skirts, she took to her heels.

'Marie,' her mother called after her, 'come back here at once! At once, do you hear?'

Marie reached the shadowy passageway and sped swiftly up the stairs. The high candles flared and fluttered in the draught making quivering patterns on the stone walls. The light hardly reached the stairs and a couple of times she missed her footing and stumbled.

In the bedchamber, the candles had already been lit and a fire burned smokily in the hearth. Nellie must have been watching for her coming because within minutes she appeared and helped her mistress undress. She was a talkative girl not much older than Marie and she immediately began gossiping about the celebrations. She was eager to know who was dancing with whom. Marie, however, was in no mood for chatter and cut her off abruptly. Nellie left in an obvious huff, and Marie retired to bed.

But she couldn't settle to sleep. The big four-poster bed was cold and lumpy and the bedcovers pressed heavily down on her. As she drifted off to sleep, a nightmarish vision of George Wishart seemed to appear in the flickering flames of the bedroom fire. She heard his doom-laden voice and she knew with fear in her bones that, one way or another, no good would come of this day.

— IV —

MARY of Guise looked out of the window and across the lawns to where her young daughter was playing happily. She was glad that winter was nearly over—it had never been this cold in her beloved France, and the freezing Scottish snows depressed her. But today the sun was shining, and she was determined to make the most of it. And like any other four-year-old, her daughter loved to play outside in the sunshine. The only difference was that her daughter was Mary, Queen of Scots.

Since the death of the child's father, James V, life had not been easy for them. Henry VIII had sent his army to Scotland several times, and wanted to unite England and Scotland under the Protestant banner. But Mary of Guise would have none of it. Until her daughter was old enough to rule alone, Mary was determined to guard the young Queen and her inheritance with her life. And now, as she watched the child at play in the garden at Stirling Castle, the cold hand of depression descended on her as she thought of the future.

There was a loud knock on the door, and her old friend Cardinal David Beaton was ushered in.

'Your Royal Highness,' said Beaton, bowing low to the ground.

'David, it is so good to see you, *mon ami*.' Mary of Guise felt as if she had known the Cardinal all her life. Indeed, he had been Ambassador to France many years before, and, when she journeyed to Scotland to marry, it had been David Beaton who had accompanied her. She remembered his arrival at the French Court so long ago. Although so young, he was eager and clever, a born diplomat and an amusing companion. He had worked hard and made many powerful friends in France and in the Vatican, but as the years had passed he had also made powerful enemies. He was hated in England, and it was rumoured that Henry VIII now wanted him dead.

'And it is good to see you, your Highness. It has been too long. And our young queen seems to be growing up so fast.'

'*Oui*, that it so, but perhaps not fast enough for Scotland's sake, I fear. The English have spies everywhere. It can only be a matter of time before they come for my Mary again.'

'You are both safe here in Stirling Castle, your Highness.'

'For the moment, perhaps, but for how much longer?'

'That I cannot say. You received my letter about the spy Wishart?'

'*Oui*. You said he was in the pay of the English?'

'That is so, your Highness. Posing as one of these so-called 'reformers', he has been preaching rebellion. But we shall have the last laugh, I assure you.'

'What do you propose?'

'We have the names of many of Wishart's fellow conspirators. Soon they will meet the same fate as their leader, and that should stamp out their unholy treason once and for all.'

Mary rose from her chair beside the fire, and walked over to the window. How different life was now, she thought. When she had arrived in Scotland, she had been only twenty-three, so young and innocent. Her first husband had been French, but had died tragically young, and when she came to Scotland to marry the king, she could speak very little of the language. And then her beloved James had died, leaving her to cope with a newborn child and a kingdom in disarray. Yes, life was a terrible struggle. Her mind drifted back to her guest.

'The heretics are not the only problem, though, David. Many of the nobles seem to be taking the side of the damned English.'

'Most are still loyal, your Highness. As far as I can tell. It is only when they get a sniff of English gold that their loyalty seems to disappear.'

At that moment, the door burst open, and the young Mary, Queen of Scots, ran into the room. A flash of red hair, she rushed up to her mother and embraced her. A second later, her flustered nurse appeared and started to apologise for the intrusion.

'Do not worry, Janet. Leave Mary with us for the moment. After all, what we say concerns her, though she is too young to *comprend*.'

Janet Sinclair closed the door, and Mary turned to her daughter. 'Mary, say *bonjour* to your Uncle David.'

The young Queen had not noticed the Cardinal sitting in the far corner of the room, but immediately ran to greet him, before skipping back to her mother's side.

'Our Queen has much energy,' the Cardinal laughed. 'I fear she may need it in the future.'

'You are right, *mon ami*. And it is up to us to make sure she has a future in Scotland. But what of Governor Arran? I fear that he still has English sympathies, and that the Lords of Scotland will follow his lead.'

'He is loyal for the moment, your Highness. As long as his son is under my, shall we say, *protection*, his hands are tied. And he seems more interested in gold than politics or religion.'

'We must see that it stays that way. I trust you will inform me if the situation changes.'

Cardinal Beaton was to stay overnight at Stirling Castle before returning to St Andrews, and the Queen Mother welcomed the company of such a civilised old friend. Indeed, it was such a refreshing change to be able to talk with him in French. And he was, as ever, an excellent companion at dinner.

The next day they said their goodbyes, and the Cardinal and his *entourage* departed. From her chambers high on the castle rock, she watched as he disappeared slowly into the distance. And despite his reassurances, she still worried. Henry of England was a powerful enemy even for this prince of the church. If the king of England wanted him dead, it would surely come to pass, and if anything happened to Cardinal David Beaton, her staunchest ally, she dreaded to think what would become of herself and her daughter, Mary, Queen of Scots.

V

A FEW days after the heretic was burned, most of the guests, including Donald McFarlane, his older brother Hamish and their father, left St Andrews Castle to begin their long journeys back to their respective homes. Nobles on horseback, resplendent in satins, furs and scarlet feathers, bobbed along, their ladies riding beside them in gleaming satins and rich velvets. Following them were trains of servants and mountains of luggage.

Only a few of the Cardinal's close friends in the clergy and some ladies remained. These included the Bishop of Moray, Effie and Marie. Alice McNeal and Magnus had also stayed on. Magnus, however, was poor company for Marie. He was too busy trying to make a good impression on their father. Marie would far rather have had the company of young James Hepburn. At least he was entertaining and always ready for an adventure. However, even James had eventually left when his father, the 'Fair Earl', had returned to Bothwell where there was urgent business to attend to.

She missed James. But most of all, Marie missed Donald McFarlane. She took to wandering about the draughty corridors on her own or huddling over a book, giving herself a headache trying to read in the flickering candlelight. Sometimes she just hid away in her bedchamber. Her mind was forever drifting back to Donald. She had grown up with him. He had been her constant companion for as long as she could remember.

'When are we returning home?' she began pestering her mother who was perfectly content, continuing to enjoy the Cardinal's lavish hospitality. And of course there were still enough ladies and even a few gentlemen left with whom she could chatter.

'You're more depressing than a dreich day,' Effie told Marie. 'And you can just put that Donald McFarlane out of your mind. He's not the one for you and the sooner you realise that, the better. If it wasn't for the fact that his father's such an old friend of the Bishop, we would forbid you to see him altogether. There's absolutely no comparison between him and the Duke of Glasgow.'

None indeed, Marie thought.

'The Duke has already spoken to your father. He is serious, Marie. He is!'

Marie tried to be sensible. She would discuss the problem with Donald as soon as she returned home. They would work something out. Donald had always kept her out of trouble before.

Then a welcome yet puzzling thing happened. She received a message written in French from Donald—no doubt to prevent the servant from reading it. It said that she was to tell no-one, but was to come to the castle gate at midnight.

She was looking forward to seeing Donald earlier than expected, but why was he coming back to St Andrews? And why did they have to meet at dead of night?

Unless . . . an exciting thought struck her. Had he decided the only way out of her predicament with the Duke was to kidnap her and carry her off from under the very noses of her father and mother? Would he gallop off with her, insisting that she must marry him? She felt an unexpected thrill at the thought.

Nellie came as usual to help her undress but Marie told her to go away and leave her alone.

'I'm gonnae clipe on ye one o' these days,' Nellie warned. 'Aye, one o' these days, I'll tell yer mither what a cheeky lassie ye are.'

Marie laughed.

'No need to clipe, Nellie. My mother already knows all my faults. Away you go and enjoy yourself, then get to your bed early. I'll see you in the morning.'

'Ye're up tae somethin',' Nellie accused darkly. 'I can tell.'

'Just get out of here and mind your own business.' Marie's voice sharpened with impatience.

'Aye,' Nellie muttered, turning away. 'Ye're up tae somethin' all right.'

Marie paced the floor until the time came for her to don her hooded cape and race along the corridor. Down the dark winding staircase she hurried, until she reached the courtyard with its lanterns glowing like embers.

It was just before midnight when she reached the guards on duty. The two men greeted her in surprise. She explained that she had an assignation with her sweetheart, Donald McFarlane, and they laughed and winked conspiratorially. It was common gossip that the Bishop and his mistress were against the match and were planning to marry the girl off to the Duke of Glasgow. It amused them to think that they could do something to help the path of true love.

They opened the gates but were immediately taken aback to find not only Donald McFarlane, but several other men stepping out of the darkness into the yellow light of the lanterns. They were dressed as workmen and carried leather stonemason's bags. Nevertheless, the guards drew their swords.

The men explained very humbly that they were masons who had much work to complete in the castle, and to save them getting up and travelling at the crack of dawn, they had decided to snatch a few extra hours' sleep in the castle before starting work bright and early.

There had been a great deal of rebuilding work going on in the castle for some time, and the faces of the men, now that the soldiers could get a better look at them, seemed vaguely familiar. Their good humour returned, and the men were allowed in. For a few minutes the guards indulged in teasing banter with Donald and Marie, before bidding them goodnight and sweet dreams.

'I thought we were meeting at Spynie,' Marie began once she was alone with Donald. 'So why have you come back to St Andrews?'

'Trust me, Marie,' Donald said. 'I'll explain later.'

Before she could say any more he had hurried after the workmen. Marie walked slowly back along the corridor. Her romantic dreams had been dashed, and all her original uneasiness had returned. In the deathly hush of her bedchamber, she wondered what it could all mean.

— VI —

CARDINAL David Beaton lived in the most luxurious fashion possible and his many mistresses revelled in his lavish hospitality. But Marion Ogilvy was his favourite. They and the few other ladies and gentlemen remaining in the castle had eaten well that evening and supped a great deal of wine. Then the Cardinal and Marion had left the other guests and gone, none too steadily, hurrying as fast as they could in their sexual urgency, to the Cardinal's private apartment. It was at times like this that the Cardinal lost much of his dignity. He was soon to lose even more.

Before he was able to disrobe, the door of his bedchamber burst open and Beaton was horrified to find himself facing a gang of armed men, swords and daggers at the ready. Marion Ogilvy screamed in terror, and ran from the room.

'What's the meaning of this?' Beaton addressed the first man he recognised. 'Donald McFarlane, your father and I are like brothers.'

While he was speaking, he made a desperate lunge for the two-handed sword he always kept beneath his bed, but he never reached it, and the intruders pinned him against the wall.

McFarlane flung the Cardinal's sword across to the other side of the room, saying grimly, 'You won't be needing that where you're going!'

The Cardinal was trembling now but whether with fear, or fury, or both, his enemies neither knew nor cared.

'Repent the shedding of George Wishart's blood!' one of them commanded.

Beaton ignored him, crying out defiantly 'You dare not harm me. I am a prince of the church.' But even as he spoke he realised the futility of his words.

'Great prince of the church,' another of the men intoned sarcastically, 'for the good of your immortal soul, be quick about it and repent the shedding of George Wishart's blood!'

'George Wishart was a heretic. His was the fate of all who defy the true church. I had no choice.'

'Then nor have we,' he said, running the Cardinal through with his sword.

Swords and daggers flashed in the candlelight as the others joined in the slaughter. Finally, as Beaton's blood-stained corpse lay twitching on the floor, one of the men undid his trouser flap and sliced off the Cardinal's genitals. Then he dangled them from the dead gaping mouth. After-wards they hung his body from the foretower of the castle for the edification of the people.

When Marie heard the screaming and shouting, she rushed from her room just in time to see Donald disappearing like a shadow down one of the dark stairways. She called out to him but he ignored her. Then she was caught up in the general panic that followed the realisation that the Cardinal had been assassinated. Both her father and mother were in a state of shock at first. Then her mother suddenly became hysterical. Marie tried to calm her, but nothing could stop Effie screaming and wildly thrashing about until Marie, in desperation and fearful that her mother would take a seizure, struck her a hard blow across the face. At least that quietened Effie, who fell silent, staring wide-eyed and ashen-faced at her daughter. The Bishop also looked shaken.

'Go to your room, Marie. I'll see to your mother.'

Marie returned to her bedchamber, her whole body trembling with fear. She stayed in her room for what seemed an eternity, listening to the commotion outside.

It was some time later when Donald came to see her, and told her that the conspirators had managed to take the castle.

'George Wishart's death had to be avenged,' he explained. 'The world is a better place now without that fornicating hypocrite.'

Marie's apprehension was not allayed. She felt confused and afraid. Donald seemed like a stranger to her now. He had become a murderer, and she didn't know what to say to him. Yet she welcomed the comfort of being held in his arms. For the first time she clung to him and allowed him to make love to her, and in doing so, her body awakened to a passion that blotted out thought. They lay in each other's arms until morning. Then he kissed her and said,

'It's time I went to help organise our defences. As soon as the news of the Cardinal's death gets out . . .' He shrugged. 'Our enemies will descend on us like ravening wolves.'

❖   ❖   ❖

Once she was alone, Marie still couldn't fully accept that Donald could have had a part in committing murder. But later, she had an even greater shock. The two guards who had been on duty at the gate the previous night had also been murdered. She found Donald and asked him what had happened, and to her horror, she learned the awful truth.

'I had to stop anyone finding out that you helped us. It was to save you. Now no-one will ever suspect that you were involved in all this.'

'But I *didn't* help you. I mean, I never realised, never in my wildest dreams did I think that you—'

'I know. But who else would believe you? I couldn't take the risk, Marie. You mean so much to me.'

Marie's emotions were in turmoil. Gazing at Donald's lean, sensitive face, she felt he was still a dear and totally familiar part of herself. Yet at the same time, her perception of him had completely changed. She shuddered to think what the future might hold for them, trying desperately to banish the words murder and murderer from her mind. After all, men—good men—were killed all the time during a war. Cardinal Beaton had certainly been at war with the Protestants, and now they were fighting back. Donald was only one of many fighting for what they believed was a just cause.

The problem for Marie now was, although her loyalties were with Donald, did she feel any real loyalty to his cause? She could see much truth in what George Wishart and now Donald stood for. Nevertheless, she had been brought up in the Catholic church for sixteen years and she had so often found comfort there. Her emotional nature responded gratefully to the singing of Mass, to the rituals and to the beauty of what the Protestants were now calling papist idolatry. Could she turn her back on everything she had known before? It was a question she couldn't answer.

✤   ✤   ✤

The next morning the situation in the castle became clearer. The assassins and their supporters had seized the castle, and although they were holding some hostages, most of those who wanted to leave would be allowed to do so. The Bishop of Moray was fortunate that Marie was his daughter—he might well have shared Beaton's fate had Donald not intervened, allowing him to flee along with Effie and Marie. Marie had not wanted to go, but Donald had insisted.

'This is no place for a woman,' he told her. 'It's only a

matter of time before we will be besieged, caught here like rats in a trap. Once Arran gets word of this it will be a fight to the death.'

'But I want to stay here with you Donald,' Marie pleaded.

'It's out of the question. The danger would be too great. Now, hurry, you must go!' And with that he led her to the gate, where the Bishop and the rest of those about to leave had gathered.

'Take good care of her, my Lord Bishop,' Donald said.

'I will indeed,' replied the Bishop. 'And very shortly, I hope, the Earl of Arran will take care of you and the other murderers hiding within these walls!' Without waiting for a reply, the Bishop dragged Marie and Effie away. Mounting their horses, they rode out of the castle.

Marie slumped in the saddle, hardly able to take in the impact of the events of the last few days, no longer able to hold back the tears that streamed down her face. Turning around to look back towards the castle, she could just make out the lonely figure of Donald standing in the gateway.

❖   ❖   ❖

Safely back at Spynie, Effie at least seemed to have recovered her composure. One thing was certain: there was no question of Marie ever marrying Donald McFarlane now. As she told Marie,

'That's the last you'll see of him and a good thing too. Now maybe you'll come to your senses and agree to have a good man who's worth something.'

Marie made no answer. She was in a daze of grief. She couldn't eat. She couldn't sleep. She couldn't even weep any more. She didn't know what to do. Nellie, although much the same age as Marie, was forced to treat her like a child, dressing her, undressing her, putting her to bed each night, hauling her out of bed each morning, trying to cajole her to eat or drink. Marie remembered hardly anything about the long ride from St Andrews to the palace of Spynie and then to the house she shared with her mother.

Returning to all the familiar scenes of the childhood and youth she'd shared with Donald, the wave of grief broke and flooded out, and she wept broken-heartedly. Later she rode over to the palace to beg her father for news of Donald.

'How dare you even mention the name of that damned murderer in my presence!' the Bishop said. 'I am doing everything I can to see that he pays for his crime. As you well know, the Earl of Arran is laying siege to the castle of St Andrews. And even as we speak, letters I have sent are on their way to Rome asking his Holiness to despatch a fleet to destroy these filthy assassins—including your precious Donald. So do not trouble me with your concern for his safety. While I have breath in my body, he will never be safe!' The Bishop struggled to compose himself. 'Now, go back to your mother and trouble me no more!'

Marie listened in silence. She was shocked at the change in her father. He had always been good to her in his own way—now she felt he was on the verge of hating her. The death of his friend the Cardinal had shaken him, but it had also made him a very dangerous man to cross. So she left without another word, filled with a terrible foreboding that she would never see Donald again.

VII

AT St Andrews, the siege dragged on. Winter came, and then spring. 'The Castilians', as those in the castle became known, were hopeful that the protestant English king—Henry VIII—would send a military force to relieve them. No such force came, but they did not despair, for they still held a number of hostages, among them the Earl of Arran's young son. Knowing this, Arran was unwilling to risk a full-scale assault on the castle, but chose instead to try to starve the Castilians out of their stronghold. Accordingly, he gave orders for his men to secure their positions and wait. There was on occasion a desultory exchange of fire, but casualties were surprisingly light for so serious a business.

Arran was not idle, though. He also set about digging a tunnel under the southern wall of the castle, into which his men would then pile gunpowder. The powder, when set alight, would blow a hole in the castle wall, and Arran's men would then charge through the gap, taking the defenders by surprise. Unfortunately for him, it proved impossible to keep his plan secret, because the Castilians could at times hear the hammering and scraping of the work in progress—the ground under the castle being solid rock. The only defence against this mining strategy was for those in the castle to dig their own counter-mine, another tunnel which would enable them to intercept the attackers underground. Donald McFarlane took charge of this most hazardous task.

Speed was of the essence, and Donald had no time to spare for making the counter-mine safe. In any case, wood was in short supply—the occupants of the castle had had to burn a considerable quantity in order to keep themselves warm through the long hard winter months. As a consequence, the roof of the mine was not strengthened, and there were frequent rock-falls. Inevitably, lives were lost.

Before long, their mine had progressed so far that they knew they must be getting close to their underground attackers. A new problem then emerged: it was vital that they broke into the besiegers' tunnel, but it was equally important that the besiegers should not break into theirs. That would be a catastrophe, as they would in effect be opening a way into the castle for the attackers. They had to stop at intervals, and listen for the sounds of the enemy.

So it was that Donald found himself crawling face down in total darkness, the dust from the hewn rock filling his lungs, the drip of water from the roof of the tunnel providing a steady rhythm to the scraping of his boots along the jagged floor. The sound of the water brought back memories of his childhood with Marie, of how they would play and fish together by clear streams, of his love for her. But there seemed no place for love in his life now—he had had to send her away, for her own safety, and they might never be together again. Crawling in this dark tomb brought home to him how cruel life could be. But he had no time for self-pity; he had a job to do. With an effort, he firmly pushed thoughts of his love aside.

As he neared the end of the tunnel, he could dimly see three men up ahead, digging steadily by the light of a single flickering candle. Large wicker baskets lay scattered about, some already filled with rubble, others waiting for their damp, dusty load.

'Is that yersel', Donald?' wheezed a voice.

'Greetings, Dougal, yes, it is I.' Already Donald's own voice was sounding hoarse, choked with the dust which formed a grey mist throughout the tunnel, and coated the workers so that they looked as though they had been fighting with bags of flour. One man took hold of a rope which was attached to one of the full baskets, tied it round his chest, and began to crawl back down the tunnel, dragging the basket after him.

Donald peered towards the end of the tunnel, and saw that they were making good progress. Dougal, to whom he had spoken, a veritable giant with an air of quiet determination, had turned back to the rock face and was once more hard at work with a small pick. There was not room for a man to stand, even an average-sized man, and no space at all for swinging the pick. Dougal had to lie on his side, and the work was painfully slow to watch. Donald shook his head.

'Stop, Dougal, we must listen. We cannot be far from them now.'

'Indeed not, Donald. Tam and I heard them afore, dingin' at that rock like demons. It'll no' be lang noo.'

'Quiet, then.'

Dougal put down his pick, and there was silence, broken only by the relentless dripping of water. Then another sound came to his ears, and Donald's heart leapt. It was unmistakably the sound of hammering, and could only be the attackers working in their tunnel.

'Which direction do you think it is coming from?' whispered Donald.

'Wha kens,' shrugged Dougal, 'the sound'll echo right through the rock.'

'But you can feel it as well as hear it. I could swear it was underneath us.' Donald put his ear to the floor of their tunnel, and held his breath. 'Yes! Both of you, put your ear to the ground and listen.'

They did so, and even in the semi-darkness, Donald could see fear enter their eyes.

'We must dig downwards. Now, while the sound of their own digging will make them deaf to our presence.'

With renewed vigour, Dougal grabbed his pick and began to tear at the floor. Donald found a similar tool and joined in, while the third man brought over a basket and started to clear away the broken rock as fast as he could.

They had gone down about a foot when Dougal gave a sudden cry.

'I can see a light! Doon there!'

Donald turned to the man with the basket.

'We need more men down here right away! And they must be armed. Have swords and knives brought for the two of us also. See to it, quickly!'

The man slithered off down the tunnel as fast as he could.

'Right Dougal, let us see if we can bring their roof down on their heads!'

'Aye, we'll teach them to go diggin' where they've nae right!'

Their efforts became frenzied, as they sought to break through as quickly as possible, before the enemy could bring sufficient armed men into their tunnel, which was the longer of the two.

It was not long before they had made a hole large enough for a man—even Dougal—to slip through. Peering through the hole, they could see a large chamber, dimly lit, and quite deserted. By this time they could hear the shouts of men coming along their own tunnel. When the first of these arrived, carrying weapons for the diggers, Donald told him to relay a message that each man was to proceed straight into the enemy tunnel. Then, taking a sword in one hand, he jumped through the hole and into the cavern beneath.

In a moment, Dougal and several others had joined him,

and he led them along the enemy tunnel. This was similar to their own, but much larger, so that they were able to walk upright.

Up ahead there was movement in the gloom. Suddenly, there was a deafening roar, and a man on Donald's left spun round and fell to the floor. Another shot rang out, but ricocheted harmlessly. Armed only with swords and daggers, Donald's men had no option but to charge.

'At them, lads!' he cried, and led them, running, towards the enemy.

The fight was bloody and confused. They had evidently taken those in the attackers' tunnel more or less by surprise, for the force they encountered now was ill-equipped, but there seemed to Donald to be hundreds of them. In the narrow passageway he and his fellow Castilians fought desperately for their lives, giving no quarter, and receiving none. Soon the floor of the tunnel was piled high with the dead and dying of both sides.

At last the enemy began to fall back, and soon Donald and his remaining men were left alone, exhausted, gasping for breath in the choking, stale atmosphere. But to linger here was dangerous, for another attack could be made on them at any time. He gave the order to fall back.

Getting back into their own tunnel was by no means easy, as the hole through which they had dropped was set quite high up, and in their weariness it required all their strength to help each other through.

Daylight blinded them when at last they emerged into the castle courtyard, caked with blood and dust, their clothes torn by both the sharp edges of the rock and the Earl of Arran's swordsmen. Donald made arrangements for their tunnel to be guarded at all times, for a route now existed through the castle's defences.

With his last remaining energy, he dragged himself away to his bed, where sleep almost instantly came upon him.

But he had done a good job, for the carnage left behind

in the Earl of Arran's tunnel was gruesome enough for the Earl to forbid any further forays under the walls of St Andrews Castle.

And so the stalemate continued.

* * *

'But you must have seen or heard something! Someone *must* know how he is!' Marie screamed as she shook poor Nellie roughly.

Nellie had just returned from a visit to her brother, who was a soldier in the Earl of Arran's army. Marie had pounced on her the instant she had walked through the door, and had plied her with desperate questions, hoping for news of those inside the castle, especially Donald.

'Please, miss, I've told ye all I ken! Naebody sees or hears much at all. They just sit aboot a lot and chuck a wheen insults ower the walls every now and then. All I can say for sure is that there's been nae real fightin' tae speak of. The only danger to yon Donald McFarlane is . . . is . . .' she hesitated, 'well . . . they say there's *plague* in the castle.'

'Plague! Oh Nellie, you have to help me. I must get word to him. It has been months since we left the castle, and I have heard nothing, nothing . . .' Her voice broke into a series of great sobs, as she thought of Donald, trapped, and in mortal danger.

'And that's exactly as it should be!' Effie, returning from the palace, where she had been entertaining the Bishop of Moray, had entered the room, and had overheard Marie's last words. 'It's high time you put thoughts of that man out of your foolish head. You have your whole life ahead of you, why waste it moping about like this?'

Marie buried her face in her hands and wept.

'Oh, this is intolerable!' cried her mother. 'Am I never to be free of these tearful outbursts? They distress me so, and

I wish to be happy. Your father and I have been having a wonderful time, and I will not have you spoiling my mood.'

At the mention of her father, Marie looked up at her mother.

'Does father say anything about the siege?' she asked.

'Now, why on earth should we talk about that dreary siege? We had plenty of other things to occupy ourselves with!' Effie giggled, running her hands over her dress, as if to straighten it.

'I shall die if I do not hear news of Donald. I must find a way of getting to him, I must!'

'You must do no such thing! Your father would not hear of it. And besides, I remember now, he mentioned something about plague in the castle. It is unthinkable that you should venture anywhere near the place.'

But Marie had made up her mind. The only problem was finding a way of getting into the castle. Perhaps Nellie's brother could help. She would speak to the maid alone, and persuade her to help. Nellie would not let her down.

Having made this decision, Marie's spirits suddenly lifted. Soon she would be in Donald's arms. She refused to believe that he could have succumbed to the plague. He would be there, and her place was at his side.

❖　　　❖　　　❖

The outbreak of the plague had been a bitter blow to the Castilians. Their mood had hitherto been one of hope. Now it became tinged with fear. There was an enemy within the walls, an enemy all the more deadly because it came unseen and unheard.

John Knox, fervent protestant and follower of Wishart, had arrived in the castle in April, and had been persuaded to preach to those within its walls. He had no hesitation in declaring, and repeating at every opportunity, 'that their corrupt life could not escape punishment of God', and that the plague was the instrument of God's judgement.

His was the voice of doom, prophesying their defeat by forces gathering outside the walls. He dismissed the Castilians' hope of rescue by the English: 'Ye shall not see them; but ye shall be delivered into your enemy's hands, and shall be carried to a strange country.'

Talk of this kind made Donald McFarlane's task extremely difficult. He and the other leaders of the Castilians had to maintain morale, and ensure that the occupants of the castle remained an alert and effective fighting force. Tireless in his encouragement of his followers was the Castilians' commander, Sir William Kirkcaldy, a powerful, fearless, hot-blooded swordsman. He frequently toured the walls of the castle, giving new hope to the defenders by sheer force of personality. He never shrank from giving his opinion, and there was no restraint whatsoever in his condemnation of the Earl of Arran and his men.

Donald, like everyone else, was perpetually weary. Food was in such short supply that the Castilians were reduced to catching rats, and they became adept at trapping sparrows and other birds that were foolish enough to land within the castle walls. Water was plentiful, for there was a deep well in the courtyard, but the situation was nevertheless becoming increasingly grave.

He trudged across the courtyard, having just left a meeting of the Castilian leaders. Morale was not good—John Knox's speeches were eroding what little optimism there was left among their community, and the plague was an ever-present threat. On top of everything, rumours had reached them that a French fleet was on its way, bringing with it a deadly cargo of powerful siege guns and expert Italian gunners. The Bishop of Moray's request to the Pope for assistance had been heeded, and the relatively easy time the Castilians had had at the hands of the Earl of Arran looked to be drawing to a close. Donald did not see how things could be worse.

'Donald! Oh, Donald!'

He turned, stunned. He knew that voice, yet it could not be . . .

'Marie! What in the name of God are you doing here!'

'I had to see you. I did not know if you were alive. There were such rumours about the plague and—'

'But how did you get into the castle?'

'I was escorted to the gate by one of the Earl's soldiers— my maid's brother. There I was recognised by Sir William Kirkcaldy, who let me in. . . . Oh Donald, I have missed you so much.'

She fell into his arms, and he clasped her to him. He could feel her heart beating wildly, as she sobbed gratefully at his breast.

After a moment she raised her head and gazed up at him.

'I thought I would never see you again. I thought we had held each other for the last time. Oh Donald, I shall never leave you again.'

'My darling Marie, I cannot tell you how pleased I am to see you. But there is nothing for you here but hardship and death. I cannot allow you to remain in this place.'

'I shall not leave you, my love.' Marie's voice was now firm. Donald knew better than to argue, and, besides, he had little energy for it.

But Donald had work to do. He had to make a tour of inspection, ensuring that all the lookouts were at their posts, and seeing to it that no-one stole any of the animals or birds from the traps that had been set, because it was the rule that all food was to be shared. He led Marie across the courtyard, and began to tell her of life in the castle. She looked around, her eyes missing nothing. Donald pointed out a huddle of shapes in one corner, explaining that that was where plague victims were herded.

'How bad is the plague?' asked Marie.

'It may well be our undoing. It has taken some of our finest men, and will no doubt take more. Our only consolation is that it keeps the Earl of Arran at a safe distance.' Donald laughed. 'At present, our most fearsome weapons are the dead bodies of plague victims—we cast them over the walls on to the heads of any of Arran's men who have not the sense to leave us in peace.'

Marie was surprised at the callousness in Donald's voice. Then she remembered his part in the murder of Cardinal Beaton, and the silencing of the castle guards. She had to accept that childhood had come to an end, for both of them. Life was now a deadly business.

As if to illustrate her thoughts, two men approached, carrying between them a stretcher. On it was the body of yet another plague victim. The men stopped as they reached Donald and Marie.

'Who have we here?' asked Donald.

One man replied by shaking his head sadly; the other was motionless.

Donald stepped up to the stretcher and looked at the bulky but emaciated form lying on it. The fetid stench of death made close examination unnecessary, as well as inadvisable, but Donald could not mistake the features of the man's face. It was Dougal, his staunch friend from their days in the tunnels.

⁂

Far out at sea, Leo Strozzi, Prior of Capua, Knight of St John and now commander of the French fleet bearing down on St Andrews, smiled as he caught his first glimpse of the Scottish coast. The sea was flat and calm as a millpond, and the sun reflected off the gleaming, gilded prow of Strozzi's massive galley as it surged forward. The only sounds that reached him were the rhythmic beat of the drum below the deck and the splash of the oars driving the galley through the waves.

Standing there on deck, Strozzi's thoughts went back to

51

the meeting at the Vatican with his Holiness only a few short months before. It was then that he had learned what his next command would be. As he had walked through the Pope's luxurious apartments, Strozzi could not help but congratulate himself on his spectacular rise. Who would have believed that an orphan from the slums of Naples could ascend to his present position? He had, of course, been truly fortunate to be taken into the local monastery and educated at the expense of the church, but how he had seized his opportunity! Perhaps his current status owed more to an assiduous study of all the latest techniques of siege warfare than to any real spiritual purity—but then, as the Pope was fond of saying,

'Saints? My dear Leo, I already have plenty of those! As for expert artillerymen like you, they are like gold-dust!'

And Leo Strozzi was truly an expert in the use of gunpowder and cannon. Many a time he had practised his art on the infidel Turk, and the very mention of his name was enough to strike fear into the hearts of his Holiness' enemies throughout the Mediterranean.

His Holiness, as ever, had been glad to see him.

'Ah, my very own dog of war! It is good to see you here again Leo.'

'Your Holiness is too kind. A humble man like myself is not fit to—'

'Enough, Leo, enough!' the Pope interrupted. 'We must get down to business.'

The Pope explained that Strozzi's next mission would be to sail to Scotland and put down a heretical uprising. Strozzi hardly knew where Scotland was, but he did not mention that to his Holiness. Anyway, what did he care where the heretics were? If his Holiness wanted them exterminated, then Leo Strozzi would not fail him. He would sail to the ends of the earth if necessary.

'I want them taught a lesson they will not soon forget, Leo. Show them no mercy, for those who reject the one true church deserve no mercy. You will have as many galleys and cannon as you require. And the next time we meet you will entertain me with tales of yet another glorious victory.'

And now, as the coast of Scotland drew ever closer, Leo Strozzi prepared himself for battle. He called his chief gunner to him.

'Is everything ready, Vincenzo? I have no love for these cold northern lands and I want this affair decided with all speed.'

'Fear not, my Lord, we will soon be back amongst the olive groves, drinking the good red wine of San Gimignano. My men have every gun primed and ready to blast the heretics from the face of the earth. A paltry fortress such as they inhabit will not stand long under the fire of our great cannons.'

Strozzi smiled. 'That is good, Vincenzo. For tomorrow at dawn, the heretics will wake to see us at anchor in St Andrews bay. And then, may God have mercy on their souls!'

❖   ❖   ❖

The early watch at the castle had had a quiet night. Nothing stirred, and as the sun rose, it looked as if it would be another fine summer's day. Suddenly, there was a shout from the sea tower.

'Ship ahoy!'

Donald had just risen, and heard the shout, as did half the castle.

'Damn!' he swore as he raced up to the battlements. The sight that met his eyes filled him with despair. He had been expecting an attack from the sea, but when he saw how many French galleys were at anchor in the bay, he knew in his heart that the castle was doomed. Even from this distance, Donald could clearly see the feverish activity on board the galleys, as every gun in the fleet was brought to bear on the castle walls. He had never seen so many cannon and he could all too readily imagine what the effect would be once they opened fire.

Donald spent the morning with Sir William Kirkcaldy trying to organise the castle defences with the men that were left, and his mind raced as he tried to think of a way to get Marie out of the castle. Arran's troops were more alert now than they had been for months. Where it had often been possible to find a way through Arran's lines in the past, now there would be none. Marie was trapped in the castle. The Earl and his newly-arrived allies would never let any of them escape.

Later Donald found time to speak with Marie.

'I *told* you this would happen, Marie,' he said, as he paced up and down her chamber, clearly agitated.

'I don't care about myself, Donald. I've told you that. It's you I'm worried about.'

'There's no need to worry about me, but we've got to get you out of here.'

'No, Donald, I'm not going anywhere, not now.'

'This time you will do as I say. I will get you out of here if it's the last thing I do!'

But despite his brave words, Donald had little hope that he would be able to fulfil his promise.

✤   ✤   ✤

Under cover of darkness, Leo Strozzi had come ashore and made his way to Arran's camp. As he passed through the Earl's forces, Strozzi was not impressed. Little effort seemed to have been made to press home the siege, and as he cast a professional eye over their few cannons, he was disgusted to see them lying unattended and rusty. They had clearly not been fired for weeks!

Barely able to conceal his contempt, Strozzi stormed into Arran's tent. Arran greeted him coldly.

'Good evening, my Lord Prior. I trust your voyage was an easy one.'

'It was. But I am afraid I have no time for pleasantries, my Lord,' Strozzi replied frostily. 'This so-called siege of yours has gone on too long already. His Holiness grows weary of your incompetence. He commands that the siege be brought to a successful conclusion immediately, and I expect nothing less than your full co-operation.'

Arran started to protest, but Strozzi ignored him.

'Tomorrow, we will bombard the castle from the sea. If our lesser cannons fail to breach the walls, we will bring our siege guns ashore and the walls of that little *fortezza* will be pounded to dust.' Strozzi paused for effect. 'If your men can summon the courage to walk into the ruins and despatch any heretics who may still be alive, then this whole sorry business will be at an end.'

❧   ❧   ❧

From the parapet of the sea-tower, Donald watched with grim fascination as the French galleys manoeuvred to bring their guns to bear on the castle. It would not be long now, he thought. But he had prepared his men well, and every gun in the castle had been brought to the north wall. At that very moment, a gunner stood at the ready behind each cannon, waiting for the word of command.

'We may well be doomed,' Donald had told Sir William, 'but by God we will sell our lives dearly!'

The Galleys were nearer now. Another few seconds and they would be within range of Donald's artillery.

'Wait for it, wait for it!' he told his men. 'Now!'

A deafening series of explosions shook the walls of the castle as the defenders loosed off their first volley at the French galleys. The effect was immediately obvious, as one galley veered away, holed at the waterline. The cries of wounded sailors and galley slaves drifted up through the dense smoke that now shrouded the walls.

'Again!' shouted Donald, and the gunners unleashed another shattering volley.

A few of the galleys had begun to return fire, but with

little accuracy, and only a few casualties were sustained inside the castle. After a third volley from the walls, the galleys turned away and made for the West Sands, where the first crippled vessel was already beached.

A loud cheer arose from the walls as the French broke away, but Donald did not join in. He knew they would be back.

✤   ✤   ✤

Strozzi, meanwhile was incandescent with fury. If word of this ever got back to his Holiness . . . ! Vincenzo suffered the full weight of his wrath.

'You have shamed me, Vincenzo. I expected better of you.'

'My Lord Prior, I . . . I . . .'

'No excuses, Vincenzo, after today's fiasco! Just do as I say. Take the siege guns ashore tonight. Mount them on the highest buildings in the town and demolish that damned castle.'

'Of course, my Lord, consider it done,' Vincenzo stammered, as he turned to go.

'And remember this, Vincenzo,' Strozzi continued, 'if you fail me again, you will spend the voyage home chained to an oar amongst those scum down below. Do you understand?'

'I will not fail you again,' Vincenzo told him.

'I hope not, my friend, for your sake.'

✤   ✤   ✤

After the initial jubilation, a bleak depression settled on the castle. They all knew it was not over, and their fears were confirmed when they saw the great siege guns being hauled ashore. Soon these fearsome weapons were in place on the Cathedral walls—perfectly placed to rain their fire directly down onto the castle.

Donald could do nothing but watch, with Marie standing silently by his side. He had not found a way to get her out of the castle and, as he watched the preparations for the final assault, he realised he had left it too late. Finally, he spoke.

'I am sorry.'

'For what?' Marie asked.

'I feel responsible for your being here.'

'It was my choice, Donald. You have nothing to reproach yourself for. Anyway, perhaps all is not lost. . . .' her voice trailed off.

'I am afraid we both know better than that,' said Donald.

They remained on the walls, but they did not have long to wait. With a tremendous roar, the first French siege gun opened fire, the shot crashing into the sea-tower with appalling violence. Screams rose up from the smoking ruins of the tower and within seconds the entire castle was a scene of panic and chaos. Shot after shot smashed into the walls, the courtyard, the towers. The air was filled with smoke and dust as tons of masonry came crashing down.

Donald tried to shield Marie as best he could, pushing her in front of him as they raced for the relative safety of one of the surviving towers. But they were soon separated in the smoke and confusion. Marie ran across the courtyard to the east wall of the castle, and hid behind the vast bulk of the East Blockhouse as another deafening volley hit the wall. Already it was breached in several places, and at this rate it would not be long before the whole wall collapsed. Running up the stairs to the battlements, Marie caught sight of Donald trying to rally his men and she called out to him. Donald turned and saw her, and started to shout something, but she never knew what he said. An instant later, the section of wall where he had been standing disappeared in a cloud of smoke and dust and he was gone. Marie could not believe her eyes. One moment he was there before her, living and breathing, and the next . . .

The force of the blast had thrown Donald from the battlements into the rubble of the courtyard below, where Marie could see his body lying motionless in the swirling smoke, half buried under tons of debris. She ran down the stairs, almost unable to see where she was going through her tears. She was intercepted before she got to him by a man with a grip of steel.

'It's too late lassie, there's nothing you can do for him now,' the voice boomed. 'He's deid.'

She turned to see the grim face of John Knox looking down at her. Looking past him to where Donald lay, she found herself transfixed by the staring, lifeless eyes of her lover. Her scream was lost amid the terrible noise of the guns.

As Marie turned away she stumbled against the pile of earth and rock that marked the entrance to the long-since abandoned mine. Numb with shock, all she could think of now was to get away from this hellish scene, the infernal noise, the smoke, the choking dust. She looked down at the gaping entrance to the mine and made her decision. Rushing down the rough wooden steps, she found herself in a dark, narrow passageway. The terrible sounds from above soon began to fade into the distance as she felt her way along in the darkness. Donald had often spoken about the mine, and she knew that it led in only one direction—out of the castle. If she could overcome her distress and fear and keep going, the way out could not be far away. She struggled on until, in the distance, she saw a dim flickering light. Dragging herself towards it, she found herself in a much bigger chamber, lit by one or two guttering candles. This was where Arran's guards were usually stationed—but, fortunately for Marie, they had been hurriedly called away to join in the final assault on the castle. Marie moved on and came to a flight of rough steps, hewn from the wall of the mine, which led upwards. Filled with relief, and with no thought for what might await her outside, Marie scrambled up the steps and emerged into bright sunlight.

Once her eyes had adjusted to the daylight, she looked around to be confronted by a scene of utter confusion. Everywhere, men at arms were rushing towards the breach in the castle wall, and the air was filled with shouted commands and oaths. The smoke from the guns and the dust from the collapsed wall made it difficult to see anything clearly, but it also meant that no-one had seen Marie emerge from the mine. After one last look back at the shattered castle, Marie turned and ran, desperate to escape the horrors of that place.

— VIII —

STROZZI'S glorious victory, the ending of the siege and the downfall of the heretics gave the Queen Mother great satisfaction, but there was little time for rejoicing. If only her good friend David Beaton were still alive, he would have known what to do for the best. She had always turned to him in times of crisis, and he had never let her down. But the Cardinal had been taken from her, and now there was no-one she could rely on. And there was still an English invasion to be dealt with. Although Henry VIII had died, the savagery of the English attacks on Scotland had increased, and the danger to the Queen of Scots was escalating day by day.

The fiery cross was sent to every district, and as a result the divided Scots united to the call to defend their nation. Thirty-six thousand ordinary citizens hastened from all over the country to fight the English, who were advancing on Edinburgh, and even members of the clergy rushed to battle against the invader. The army thus raised, under the command of Arran, assembled at Pinkie Cleugh behind the town of Musselburgh. Hearing that her forces were ready for battle, Mary of Guise awaited news of this fateful encounter with growing unease.

* * *

As dawn broke over Musselburgh, young Gavin McNaughton, only son of Machar McNaughton, Duke of Glasgow, was already up and about preparing himself for the battle ahead. Summer had come to an end, and the chill of the early September morning cut through even his heaviest clothing. But in his excitement, he hardly even noticed himself shiver. There was so much to be done.

He had been in Edinburgh with his father the previous day, when the main army had marched out to meet the English who were advancing towards Leith. News had come from Musselburgh that the English army had already intercepted the Scots vanguard. There had been some heavy losses, and Gavin McNaughton cursed his ill luck at missing his first chance to get to grips with the invaders. He immediately rode out to be with the army, but by the time he reached Musselburgh, all was quiet again. Now he was determined not to miss anything more.

As the sun rose higher over the Scots army, Gavin surveyed the scene and smiled to himself. He had been given command of a mixed company of swordsmen and pikemen, mostly men from Glasgow who were loyal to his father. Rough-looking and ill-equipped though they were, Gavin felt sure their spirit would make them more than a match for the enemy. Over to his left, he saw the massive figure of Guthrie Jamieson, Earl of Edinburgh, galloping towards him astride a magnificent black stallion.

'Good morning, my Lord,' he called out.

'A very good morning indeed, Gavin,' replied Jamieson. 'Are you ready for the day?'

'I am indeed,' replied Gavin. 'What plans are afoot?'

'You will stay close to me. I have spoken to your father

and he has charged me with your well-being. We will be moving within the hour, so make sure all your men are ready.'

'We await your orders.'

With this, the Earl of Edinburgh turned away, leaving Gavin to his preparations.

It was the longest hour that Gavin McNaughton could remember. The commotion around him was intense, with messengers coming and going, men laughing and shouting and the rasping of swords being sharpened, some for the last time. Eventually they received the signal to move forward and Gavin positioned his men beside the Earl's much larger company.

They marched out of the camp and on until they reached Inveresk, stopping just before the river. On the other side, swarming over the hill which faced them, were the massed ranks of the enemy. To Gavin's eyes, the English army looked enormous, and he felt a thrill of anticipation, or perhaps it was fear. Obviously the Earl had sensed it as well.

'Don't worry Gavin, it won't be long now. Just keep your horse steady, and your sword bloody.'

Gavin managed a glimmer of a smile, but his heart was now beating so fast that all other noise had receded.

The Earl gave the signal and the men in front started to wade across the shallow Water of Esk which flowed between the Scots and the English. Gavin couldn't understand why they didn't simply wait for the English to come down from the hill and attack—fighting uphill would put them at a disadvantage. When they had reformed at the other side, the main attack began.

Gavin watched as the first of the Scots soldiers advanced straight up the hill, but their attack was easily repulsed, and the English horsemen chased them back to where they had come from. Perhaps this had been the plan, though, because the horsemen immediately came face to face with the long Scottish spears. Riding so hard that they couldn't stop in time to save themselves, they broke like a wave against solid rock. Both horses and riders were impaled, and dozens met the same bloody fate. Eventually, those left alive managed to turn and flee, to a roar from the Scots.

This was the moment Gavin had been waiting for. As they advanced, he could hear the soldiers ahead shouting insults at the English:

'Away back home, ye English baistards!'

'Keep close to me, Gavin,' roared Jamieson over the din, as he raised his sword and spurred on his horse into the thick of the battle. Gavin did as he was bid, and kept tight to the flank of the Earl's horse. They met the English with a wild shout, and were soon in the thick of the fighting.

The English foot soldiers were no match for the mounted horsemen and Gavin soon felled his first Englishman, grimacing as he saw the blood on his sword. So this was war! Thereafter, all was a blur as the battle ebbed and flowed. But Gavin kept close to the Earl throughout it all.

But it was the roar of the cannon that brought him back to his senses, and as he looked around at the main battle on his left, he could not believe his eyes. The English artillery was now raking the Scottish lines. Everywhere was carnage, and the Scots were in full retreat—he could scarcely believe the battle had turned so suddenly. The grapeshot from the English cannon had ripped through the Scots and all around him men lay dead or dying. He and the Earl had stayed to one side of the battle, but they were now surrounded, and only one of the Glasgow men and a few of the Earl's mounted horsemen remained with them. Suddenly, a shattering blow felled his horse, and Gavin crashed to the ground. He lay there for a moment stunned, his leg trapped by the weight of the horse, and then he began to struggle desperately to free himself. At that moment, Guthrie Jamieson saw what had happened and leapt off his horse. He dragged Gavin clear and got him to his feet, for the moment protected by his horsemen.

It was then that Gavin looked down and saw the blood.

He could feel nothing, but that was definitely his own blood. There was a wound in his thigh which looked bad, maybe the horse had broken his leg, but there was also blood coursing from a wound to the side his head.

'Thank . . . you . . . Jamieson,' Gavin managed, before the world around him blurred and then dissolved into the blackness of unconsciousness.

'Help me get him on my horse,' the Earl roared to Gavin's last remaining man, a youth of about nineteen who Jamieson recognised as one of the Duke of Glasgow's servants. They struggled to get him up and the Earl mounted his horse behind Gavin's limp body. As the youth waited to be told what to do next he was seized by two of the Earl's horsemen. Bewildered, he looked towards Jamieson. 'Forgive me, my friend,' Jamieson said. 'I'm afraid I cannot afford any witnesses to what is about to happen, but be assured I will tell everyone you died a hero's death.' And with that he nodded to one of his men who, in one swift movement, drew his dirk and cut the astonished youth's throat.

Then the Earl turned to his men and shouted, 'Come on, we have a pretty prize here, but we had better hurry in case he dies before we can claim our reward.' With that, he spurred on his horse and made for the top of the hill. As the four horsemen rode on, they met little resistance. The battle was all but over now, and the English were too busy chasing the few Scots remaining on the field, cutting the throats of the wounded or looting the bodies where they lay.

As they crested the hill, the English camp came into view—rows and rows of field tents, some with flags fluttering in the afternoon breeze. The Earl recognised the pennant of his old friend Randolph, and made straight for it.

Luckily, Randolph was near at hand, and the Earl cried out, 'Randolph, my friend, I have what you wanted. Guthrie Jamieson always keeps his promises!'

'Jamieson, you never cease to amaze me,' Randolph replied. 'Is this Machar McNaughton's young pup?'

'It is indeed, though he is sorely wounded.'

'We must look after him well, then. He is worth a good deal to us, and, of course, to you.'

'A thousand gold pieces seems a small price for the trouble I have taken to get him here,' said Jamieson.

'There will be many more rewards if you continue to be useful, my friend,' Randolph replied. 'The money will be delivered in the usual way.'

'I thank you, and now we must take our leave and inform the Duke of Glasgow of the bad news!'

✦   ✦   ✦

When news reached the Queen Mother of this terrible defeat, it was clear to her that the time had now come to remove the young Queen of Scots from Stirling Castle. As a temporary refuge, she chose Inchmahome island on the Lake of Menteith, some twenty miles north of Glasgow. Accompanied by Lord Erskine and Lord Livingstone, two of the Queen's guardians, and Lady Fleming, the Dowager spirited the royal child away. Although she knew her daughter could not be safe there forever, it would provide a safe haven from her enemies for the time being. Here they could relax in the quiet of the priory, or walk amid pleasant trees. But it was only a temporary solution. It had become clear not only to the Dowager but to many Scots that a French alliance, at the price of marriage for their young Queen, was the only way out of the morass of defeat, disunity and suffering.

Between them, Mary of Guise and the Earl of Arran arranged for parliament to give its assent to the marriage of Mary and Francis, the French Dauphin, on the condition that the King of France would defend Scotland as he would his own realm. At the same time, he must respect Scotland's independence.

Only then could the Dowager breathe a sigh of relief. She knew that her child would be safe in France, the country of her own birth, where her mother, the Duchess Antoinette of Guise, and her powerful and ambitious Guise brothers, would make sure the Queen of Scots had not only every care, but every advantage.

But first there were preparations to be made for the journey. From Inchmahome, they would ride to Dumbarton. There a fleet of French galleys would meet the royal party, which would include the Queen's young companions—the four Marys—Beaton, Seton, Fleming and Livingstone; her governess, Lady Fleming; Lord Seton and Lord Livingstone. It was only once they reached Dumbarton that the Dowager began to realise what a personal tragedy the leave-taking would be for her. She loved her daughter dearly but she knew where her own royal duties lay. She had to remain in Scotland and carry on the fight to preserve her daughter's inheritance and the authority of the Crown.

To add to her anxieties, her daughter took ill at Dumbarton Castle and the journey to France had to be postponed. At first, it was thought to be smallpox, but to everyone's great relief, Queen Mary recovered with no marks to her face.

As their departure neared, the Queen Mother became fearful of the dangers of the sea journey. Even in summer the sea could be treacherous and stormy, and pirates could attack the royal ship at any time.

'Nonsense,' Lady Fleming laughed. 'What pirate would dare approach the royal galley when it is protected by such a vast fleet.'

Lady Fleming was the royal child's aunt, a pretty woman known more for her lively charm than her intelligence. She was the illegitimate half-sister of James V, the Dowager's late husband, and she had been given the post of governess only because of her charm and her royal connection.

Her confidence was of no comfort whatsoever to the Queen Mother. Indeed she had grave misgivings about Lady Fleming's competence in looking after the young Queen, far less teaching her. But, despite all her fears, the Queen Mother kept telling herself over and over again that she had no choice in sending the child to France.

'It is for the best,' she kept telling herself. 'It is for the best, both for the child, and for Scotland.'

— IX —

'I REFUSE to believe it, mother.' Marie Hepburn closed her eyes. 'I simply cannot believe that you are doing this to me.' But of course, knowing Effie Dalgliesh, it was all too believable. Marie was to be betrothed to the repulsive Duke of Glasgow, and her own feelings about this seemed to count for nothing when set against the burning ambition of her mother.

'My dear lassie, it's for your own good. Think of how lucky you'll be. Everyone says he's the life and soul of Glasgow.'

'Lucky? Lucky? Married to that slobbering fat mountain? You must be mad.'

'But Marie, think of it! A wealthy, influential man like that! He has a castle in Glasgow, another near Loch Lomond and vast tracts of land in between.'

'So you keep telling me. And I keep telling you, mother, I don't care how wealthy he is. Or how many castles, or how much land he has. I do not love the man. Indeed I loathe and detest the very sight of him.'

'Och, what's love got to do with it? You can have all the

love you want with lovers. The Duke of Glasgow wants you as his wife. He can give you comfort and security and position in the land. You can't refuse him. I forbid it. Anyway,' she said turning away and dismissing the subject, 'I've already agreed to deliver you to him. We're leaving for Glasgow within the week.'

Effie summoned Nellie and they began discussing what clothes she and her daughter should take to Naughton Castle.

'What dresses do you think we should include, Marie?'

Marie bit her lip. 'You have not listened to one word I have said. I do not wish to go to Naughton Castle. I will not go and discuss marriage or anything else with that great toad of a man.'

'I wish you'd learn to be respectful,' Effie said absent-mindedly. She was already intent on examining the heap of dresses the maid had dumped on the four-poster bed. 'Of course you're going.'

Marie left her mother's bedchamber in despair. Months had passed since she escaped from the castle and made her way back to Spynie, but she was only just beginning to come to terms with the loss of Donald and the other horrors she had witnessed during the siege. Effie had seemed almost completely disinterested in where Marie had been or what she had been doing—all she was interested in was marrying her daughter off as quickly as possible. Now Marie was faced with this awful prospect, and thoughts of intimacy with the Duke of Glasgow grew in her mind, making her feel violently ill. His appearance was gross. He had a flabby pockmarked face and his eating habits were coarse in the extreme. He literally shovelled food into his mouth and his beard and moustache were never other than wet and sticky with the remains of his last meal.

Marie had visited Glasgow before with her father's household and stayed at the Bishop of Glasgow's palace near the High Church of Glasgow. She would have been happy to live in Glasgow, had she been promised to almost any other man from that parish. Anyone but Machar McNaughton. Appalled at the prospect, she hurried out of the house and round to the stables. Her only hope was that her father would take pity on her and intervene on her behalf. Half an hour's ride would take her to the Bishop's palace.

Marie ordered the manservant to saddle up one of the horses, and without hesitation, she mounted the beast and galloped away towards the palace.

The Bishop was surprised to see her. Donald's death had quenched his thirst for vengeance, and he had long since resolved to put the whole dreadful business behind him. As a result, his attitude to Marie had softened. They now met each week to discuss the progress of her studies.

'What's all this? I wasn't expecting you until next week.'

'This can't wait, father. I must speak with you now.'

'Very well. Sit down. Tell me what ails you.'

'Mother has told me I'm to be promised in marriage to Machar McNaughton.'

'Ah yes, he's been widowed now for too many years. It's time he had a wife.'

'But father, what about me? I'm too young, and I have much studying to do.'

'You will soon have done enough studying. And age matters not. Our Queen was betrothed when she was but an infant.' He lowered his brows in disapproval.

'Very well, I accept that age does not matter. In truth, it does not matter a whit to me. I would gladly marry anyone else but him.'

'It is my duty to see you provided for. But both you and your mother are fast becoming too much of a drain on my purse. The Duke of Glasgow is a wealthy man.'

Marie's heart sank and she cried out,

'The mere thought of him as a husband fills me with horror.'

'You have no need to worry. Machar McNaughton will treat you kindly. Of that I am perfectly sure.'

70

'How can you be so sure?'

Anger flashed in the Bishop's eyes.

'I have known the Duke for many years. Please do not question my judgement.'

Marie was stunned. She could see the anger in his face and sensed the seriousness of her situation. The Bishop had clearly decided that this was his chance to unburden himself of Effie and herself, and their expensive upkeep. She remembered the last time her mother had warned her about such a calamity: 'We could quite easily be reduced to beggars if we're not careful. So watch your manners and your rash, impertinent tongue.'

Marie had laughed at the time and said,

'Mother, I swear you're the last person in Scotland who should be warning anyone to be careful, or watch their tongue!'

But she didn't think it so amusing now, as she searched for the right words.

'I'm sorry, father. I didn't mean to question your judgement. I'm sure the Duke must be a good man if you say so. It's just . . . it's just I don't feel ready for marriage.'

The Bishop shrugged.

'Well . . . I suppose we could suggest a compromise to the Duke. . . .'

'A compromise?'

'Yes. I shall accompany you and your mother to Naughton Castle and speak to Machar myself. You will be handfast to him for one year, and if, at the end of the year, either of you decide against marrying, then you can part honourably. Although how you and your mother will survive if you should decide on such a parting, I cannot imagine. Now, I must attend to my work, and you must return to your studies. I bid you good day.'

Thus dismissed, Marie left in a daze. She knew what handfasting meant. She would have to sleep with the revolting creature for a year.

She mounted her horse and slowly returned through the woods and across the fields.

Her mother pounced on her the moment she entered the house.

'Where have you been? I have been distracted with worry for your safety. You could have been murdered by robbers. Or kidnapped by—'

'Oh mother, be quiet. I'd rather die at the hands of robbers than have Machar McNaughton touch me, if you must know.'

'Where have you been?' Effie repeated.

'I went to appeal to my father.'

'Appeal? Appeal? What do you mean—appeal? What did you say? What did he say?'

'He is travelling with us. He is going to handfast me to the Duke for a year.'

'Oh mercy upon us!' Her mother fluttered over to the nearest chair, waving her hands in the air. 'I knew it. I knew it. You stupid lassie. I knew you'd spoil everything. After a year the Duke won't want to marry you. He'll have found out by then what a stupid, ungrateful, wicked lassie you are. . . .'

Marie was no longer listening. If Donald were still alive he would have found a way out. But he was gone, and she had no-one to turn to now. Already she could feel the Duke's fat, beringed hands upon her.

— X —

AS they prepared to leave for Glasgow, Effie was still in a state of fearful agitation.

'Now, you be nice to the Duke. Remember, do whatever he wants. Please him, for pity's sake. For my sake. For both our sakes,' she'd kept repeating to Marie before they set off.

The last time they had visited Glasgow, they had been en route for Dumbarton and the Bishop had remarked what a pleasure it was to survey Glasgow in all its splendour. Marie had agreed. But, on this occasion, the town's beauty brought her no pleasure. It nestled in a green valley with the River Clyde sparkling through it—the river that the Bishop said was famous for its wonderful salmon. Many of the dwelling places they passed were huts composed of turf, roofed with branches of trees and thatched with heath or straw. The inhabitants looked pleasant and friendly, chatting easily together. The men were wearing blue bonnets, and many were busy mending fishing nets. The women had white linen covering their heads which hung down the back as if a napkin were pinned about them. They sang as they washed clothes by the river.

The huts gave way to houses of wood and plaster which had a much more substantial appearance. Soon they reached the manor houses with their crow-stepped gables, but even these were dwarfed by the towering presence of the ancient Cathedral which had been dedicated to St Mungo, the patron saint of Glasgow.

Before long they had arrived at Naughton, and Marie was filled with panic at the sight of the Duke of Glasgow's castle. It was a traditional Scottish fortified house, with a sturdy square keep four storeys tall, and small crenellated turrets. The building had recently been extended to include a vast banqueting hall, and adjoining the hall stood Machar McNaughton's pride and joy—an ornate chapel he had built to house the elaborate family vault. Outside, a large geometric garden was laid out around a central fountain.

'Oh Marie, what a lucky lassie you are!' her mother declared. 'If you please the good Duke, and all goes well, all this could be yours.'

Marie glared at her and Effie shrank back. She was afraid of Marie's temper, and, as she had said only yesterday,

'Your temper will be the death of you yet. That and your impertinent tongue.'

'I'd rather be true to my feelings, whatever the consequences,' Marie had snapped at the time. Despite her brave words, she did not feel courageous now.

The drawbridge had been lowered in expectation of their arrival, and the whole party clattered noisily over it and into the courtyard. The Duke's servants met them, taking care of their horses and showing the guests to their bedchambers. A banquet was to be held that evening in the great hall, they were told, at which the Duke of Glasgow would formally welcome them.

It was the mention of the celebration banquet that really brought Effie back to bouncing, euphoric life.

'Isn't this wonderful, Marie? You must admit this is wonderful. What will we wear? I think my dress of shot red and yellow taffeta and my *vasquine* to hold out the skirt and my orange taffeta petticoat—the one lined with red serge.'

Marie refused to consider wearing anything so gaudy.

'When will you learn, mother, that your colours do not suit me.' As often as not they did not suit her mother either—but Marie managed to hold back the remark.

She chose a black gown stiffened with buckram, a white undergarment frilled high to her ears, and black shoes and stockings. She felt as if she was in mourning for herself. Her mother cried out in despair when she saw her.

'Och, you look like a spinster and far beyond your tender years. Why are you so stupid and thrawn? What have I ever done to deserve a lassie like you?'

❖   ❖   ❖

The banquet that evening was held in the great hall, a magnificent stone-vaulted room draped with vibrant Flemish tapestries depicting extravagant hunting scenes. Logs blazed and crackled on the stone flags of the huge fireplace. A long table groaned with the weight of several sheep, calves, capons, deer, geese and hare, and the other guests were already merrily indulging themselves in the Duke's wine from goblets being filled and refilled by an army of servants.

'Ah, my good Bishop!' Machar McNaughton came staggering towards them, arms outstretched in welcome. 'And the beautiful ladies Effie and Marie. Welcome to Glasgow!'

Effie bobbed a curtsy. Then she roughly nudged Marie, making her stumble off balance into a grudging curtsy.

'How was your journey?' Machar cried out in a voice like a bell in full clatter.

'Long, sir. Long,' Effie said.

'But without hazard, I hope.'

'Thankfully yes, my Lord, but we would have been happy to endure much in anticipation of your lavish hospitality.'

'And my beautiful Marie?' The Duke eyed her with happy

lasciviousness that made Marie lower her gaze and pray that God would remain by her side to protect her. Yet she prayed without hope and said nothing.

The Bishop broke the awkward silence. 'Is there any news of your son, Machar? I hear he was taken prisoner at Pinkie.'

'He was, yes. . . .' Machar was subdued for a moment. 'But have no fear, we shall secure his release before long. And he would not want this happy occasion spoiled by gloomy talk. Come, let us drink a toast!'

The Duke beckoned a servant and they all raised a glass.

'To my beautiful Marie—and my son Gavin, who, God willing, will be back with us soon.'

During the meal, no-one noticed Marie's lack of appetite or her pale, worried expression. She kept sipping at the wine that was poured into her goblet, grateful for the comfort it gave her. But soon her head began to swim, as lute players, singers, jugglers, and fools cavorted and tumbled around the table in their gaudy clothes and caps, the boisterous laughter of the company almost drowning out their exuberant and enthusiastic performances. The celebrations went rioting on until very late, and as darkness enshrouded the castle, many candles were lit, flaring and fluttering in the wind which whistled in through the deep slits in the walls.

There was a scream and a loud burst of laughter to one side, and Marie turned to see Effie being molested by a fat, bearded man whose doublet was stained with red wine. Effie was clearly enjoying every minute of it, but her mother's suitor reminded Marie of Machar McNaughton, and as she turned back she was surprised to see that Machar had staggered to his feet and was making for the far end of the vast banqueting hall. In the half-light of the flickering candles, she saw him disappear behind one of the stone pillars. She could just make out another figure, but he had his back turned towards her.

✤ ✤ ✤

When Machar got up, he felt distinctly unsteady, but it was not an unfamiliar or unpleasant feeling. He had got word that the Earl of Edinburgh had arrived, and he hastened to meet him in the murky shadows at the far end of the great hall.

'Good evening, Guthrie.'

'Machar, you look well. Perhaps a little too well.'

'My bride awaits me, so let us get down to business.'

'I can see why you are anxious to bed her, she's a pretty little thing, isn't she?'

'She is indeed,' said Machar. 'But enough of that. You have news for me?'

'I have. When Gavin disobeyed my orders and left my side, he was apparently wounded in the fight, but he is recovering slowly. Our English friends have no further use for him, but they are gravely displeased that you have not been as helpful to them as they had hoped. And they have paid you well for your 'services' and have had precious little return.'

'I have done all that was asked of me,' the Duke hissed, looking warily about, terrified that any of his guests should overhear. If anyone ever found out that he was in the pay of the English, God alone knew what would become of him. 'And now I want my son back.'

'That is easily done. Our friend Randolph does not think you will be of much further use to the English cause, and all he asks is two thousand gold pieces for your precious Gavin's safe return.'

'What!' cried Machar. 'That is an outrageous price!'

'Take it or leave it, Machar. It is, after all, a mere fraction of what you have already been paid by our English friends! And remember, if you fail to pay, your son will have nothing to look forward to except a long, slow death in an English dungeon.'

Machar thought for a moment. The conversation had sobered him up, and he realised that he had little option.

77

'Very well,' he said. 'I will make the arrangements to-morrow.'

'I think not!' Jamieson exclaimed. 'I leave tonight, Machar, and I must take the gold with me, wedding night or not.'

'All right, all right. Meet me in my private chambers in an hour. I will have the money waiting for you. No-one must know about this—you had better use the secret passage.'

Machar walked slowly back to his seat at the head of the table and poured himself a large glass of wine, and then another. The ransom payment would bankrupt him, and there would be no more English gold to replenish his coffers. God, how he hated that treacherous dog, Jamieson. As soon as Gavin was safely home, he would find a way to revenge himself upon the bold Earl.

As he took his place at table, the Earl of Edinburgh was delighted with his evening's work so far. He could not believe what a fool Machar was. He had not only taken English gold, he had passed on useless information about the Scots movements before the battle of Pinkie. And now, their English paymasters had decided that Machar had to pay the price for his double-dealing. He had to die. And Guthrie Jamieson was just the man to make it happen. Not only would he get a good price for murdering the Duke, he would also have the two thousand for the ransom and young Gavin could rot in an English dungeon for all he cared.

At the appointed time, Jamieson made his way along the secret passage to Machar's private chambers, and opened the door. Even with the door open, he was still concealed by a large tapestry hanging on the wall. He remained hidden, and waited. And waited. Twenty minutes passed. Then an hour. He was becoming furious now. Killing the Duke would be a pleasure.

✤   ✤   ✤

At the banquet, Marie was by now utterly exhausted. She kept widening her eyes in an effort to stay awake. Eventually, someone called over to the Duke.

'Machar, if you want tae have any sport wi' yer sweetheart tonight, I suggest ye bed her now.'

Having sought solace for his woes in an ocean of wine, the Duke was now much the worse for wear, and had to be helped to his feet. He had forgotten about his appointment with Jamieson.

'Aye, you're right, sir,' he slurred. 'Come on, lassie.'

He grabbed Marie's arm and linked it through his, jerking her from her seat and pulling her along. There was a noisy barrage of coarse and lewd comments as they made their way out of the hall. Then, as the long dimly-lit corridors engulfed them, the shouts and laughter faded away into the distance. Machar, muttering incoherently, led Marie up the narrow tower stairway and into his bedchamber, her fear and loathing of the Duke mounting dizzily with every step. Now, in a kind of drunken madness, she heard the animal-like noises as the Duke tore down his trouser flap and staggered towards her. She struggled to escape as his hands groped and tore at her clothing. Terror ballooned into panic as she felt his skin against the most private part of her body. The room seemed to spin around her: then suddenly she saw the dagger that glistened at his belt. She grabbed at it and, with a surge of manic strength, plunged it into the Duke. He gasped with shock and rolled off her. The sight of his blood on the starched white sheets and the awful realisation of what she had just done was too much for Marie to bear, and she collapsed in a dead faint beside him.

Watching all this from behind the tapestry, Guthrie Jamieson could hardly believe his luck. Nor could he believe that Machar had forgotten about their meeting. Drunken pig. Obviously his young bride was of more interest to him than his son. In an instant, Jamieson leapt out from behind the tapestry and ran to the bed at the far side of the room. Machar had not moved, but he was disappointed to see that the wound was in his shoulder and did not look too serious. But what a vixen Machar had chosen!

At that moment, Machar opened his eyes, looked around him and groaned pathetically, 'Help me, Guthrie.'

'Machar,' said Jamieson, picking up the Duke's own dagger, 'I don't think I can help you any more. But I will have the gold you promised me.' As he reached for the strongbox key from the Duke's belt, a fat hand caught him by the wrist.

'No-one . . . opens that box . . . but me,' the Duke gasped.

'You have no need of gold where you are going,' Jamieson replied steadily, and with a flash of cold steel he expertly finished the job Marie had started, plunging the dagger straight through the Duke's heart. Machar's inert body slid off the bed and onto the floor with a dull thud.

Jamieson quickly checked that Marie was still unconscious. It would be a shame to have to kill her as well—much better for her to live to take the blame.

Anyway, there was no time to waste on her. There was gold to be found. From a previous visit, Jamieson knew exactly where to find the Duke's strongbox, and immediately snatched the key from Machar's belt and opened it. There wasn't as much gold as he had expected. The old fool was obviously running out of money—no doubt he had wasted much of it on that ridiculous chapel. But he couldn't have carried much more anyway. Replacing the key, he made sure that Marie had not stirred. She lay still, the bloodstained dagger by her side. A sad end to a young life, he thought, laughing softly to himself, as he made his escape.

✤　　　✤　　　✤

Marie came to an instant later, and could not believe her eyes. The bloodstained corpse of the Duke lay beside the bed, his dead eyes staring blankly at the ceiling. Her own bloodstained clothing and the dagger lying beside her filled her with horror. It was then her eyes were diverted by a movement behind one of the tapestries. Grabbing a candle, she staggered across to the tapestry and jerked it aside. It revealed a half-open panel that led to a secret stairway, and she was just in time to catch a brief glimpse of a shadowy figure disappearing through another opening at the foot of the stairs.

Terror beyond all terror now. Marie had not only committed murder. Someone had witnessed it. Her first thought was to seek help and protection. But from whom? Running from the room, she hesitated in the corridor. In a blind panic, she opened the nearest door and hid behind it. After a few moments, she dared to look round the room, and recognised some garments belonging to her father. Otherwise the room, lit only by a few candles, was empty. She began pacing silently about, kneading her hands together and making little moans of distress. She longed to believe it was all just a dreadful nightmare but she knew it wasn't. The blood on her hands told her it was all too real. Suddenly, the door opened and both the Bishop and her mother entered.

'Marie!' her mother cried out. 'What are you doing here? What's wrong. Have you displeased the good Duke? Has he thrown you from his bed?'

Marie dug her nails into her hands, fighting back the tears. 'Please forgive me.'

'Forgive you for what?' the Bishop said coldly. 'Compose yourself and tell me what has happened.'

'He was so drunk. I think I must have been too. He was hurting me . . . I struggled and . . . his dagger . . . before I knew what had happened . . . I am so sorry.'

Her mother yelled out in disbelief.

'You stabbed him?'

'Be quiet, woman,' the Bishop commanded, and Effie collapsed onto a chair.

'I'm sorry,' Marie repeated.

'You're *sorry*?' the Bishop thundered. 'What good will that do?'

Marie closed her eyes.

'I didn't mean—'

'Be quiet. I'll have to think of something. Wait here.'

After he'd left the bedchamber, Effie began to wail.

'Dear God. Dear God. I always said you'd be burned at the stake one day but never in my worst nightmares . . . I can't bear it. As well as ruining your own life, you have ruined mine as well. It can't be happening. I'm dreaming all this. I must be. . . . Everything was going to be so wonderful.' She began to weep. 'Now what will become of us. Even the Bishop will be in danger. You have put his life in jeopardy. There is not a person in this castle who did not have some reason to be grateful to the good Duke.'

At that moment the Bishop returned and Effie quickly wiped her eyes.

'What's happening? Have you seen the Duke?'

'He's dead.'

'Dear God. Dear God,' Effie sobbed.

'Be quiet, woman. I need to think.'

Marie wanted to tell him of the figure hiding behind the tapestry in the Duke's room but she knew that would only make matters worse.

Silence held the room for what seemed an eternity. The candles were guttering low, and darkness was spreading from shadowy corners. Eventually the Bishop said,

'You must do exactly as I tell you. Both of you, do you hear? I'm not going to lose everything because of the stupidity of a bastard child.'

'What can we do?' Marie asked.

'Both of you stay in this room. Do not move from it until I tell you. No matter what happens, do nothing and say nothing. Do you understand?' With that he strode out of the room, slamming the heavy iron-studded door behind him.

'God help us!' Effie muttered, as she rocked herself backwards and forwards.

Marie was deathly pale but calm. She kept thinking of the shadowy figure who had been a witness to the murder. Why hadn't he confronted her right away or called the guards?

— XI —

THE Queen Mother knew her daughter's journey to France could not be delayed any longer. But she was pleased that another maid of honour to the Queen would be in the party. She had come with a letter from the Bishop of Moray. The poor girl had recently lost her husband-to-be, the Duke of Glasgow, in tragic circumstances, and to distance herself from her unhappy memories and dashed hopes, the Bishop had written, she needed a complete change. But she was a very mature, intelligent, indeed learned girl, and would be well able to assist the young Queen's governess in the tutoring of French, Latin and Greek.

Marie Hepburn had therefore been welcomed into Dumbarton Castle and now awaited the boarding of the French King's personal galley with the rest of Mary, Queen of Scots' party. The Queen Mother could see Marie now, standing alone, a little apart from everyone else, a tall, slim girl with red hair that flamed in the sun, in stark contrast to the pallor of her face. She could almost be taken for the child Queen's elder sister. Earlier the Dowager had inquired if she was well enough to make such a hazardous voyage, and her green eyes had immediately flashed into life.

'I am in perfect health, I can assure you, your Majesty.'

And so the time had come. Mary, Queen of Scots, who had been guarded by French soldiers in Dumbarton Castle, was now ready to embark. The French naval guns boomed out a salute. The goodbyes were said between mother and daughter in the presence of Arran and the many noble spectators, crowded together, a bright splash of colour on the stretch of green at the foot of the castle rock. The soft shade of the grass matched the dresses of the Queen's young companions—the four Marys—Beaton, Seton, Livingstone and Fleming. Alongside them, Marie Hepburn in yellow taffeta stood out from the crowd. The Queen, tiny beside her adult companion but even more vivid in her scarlet dress, had been well trained in the regal science of self-control, and even though her mother was unable to contain her tears, the young Queen remained perfectly composed. Others wept at the sight of the child and what might lie before her. Their anxiety overflowed despite or perhaps because of the child's innocent excitement.

What was to become of her once she left her native Scotland? Yet, her safety in Scotland was just an illusion. Danger and violence had swirled around her since the moment she had been born.

Now men bowed before her, women curtsied, but the little Queen, well-used to such acts of homage, had already turned her attention to the great galleys of France. They were hoisting their sails into the salt breeze, forming enormous white curves against the glowing sunset. It was an awesome sight that seemed to fill not only the Firth of Clyde but the entire sea, the horizon dominated by tall masts and billowing canvas.

The rhythmic chant of seamen as they laboured to hoist the sails was accompanied by the screeching of the blocks and the groaning and creaking of ropes under tension. The smell of wood, tar and mildewed canvas, mingled with the bracing odours of salt and seaweed, heightened the travellers' feelings of anticipation.

The weather had worried the Dowager. But she kept reminding herself that France meant safety and happiness for her daughter and a glorious future in the French Court. In France, the Guise family were the most powerful in the land. No-one there would dare to harm the Queen.

But even after the last goodbyes were said and everyone was safely on board, there was a further delay. The wind had changed, and the ships were unable to sail. As they waited impatiently, the fetid stench of unwashed galley slaves and human excrement hung like a pall across the midships of the galley. The light breeze, however, did a little to alleviate the appalling miasma which kept most of the elegant passengers confined to the poop deck. Finally the ships began to move out into the Clyde, although the galley slaves were not helped by the unfavourable wind. The rhythmic beat of the drum and the lash of the whip provided some encouragement, but the measured stroke of the oars seemed to have little effect in propelling the vessels through the wide expanse of water.

As they skirted along the coastline the sky grew darker by the minute. Sailors rushed to and fro clambering high into the rigging in response to seemingly incomprehensible directions from the bosun and officers. Soon the waves grew steadily heavier and heavier, but the ships raced on, bucking and jumping, driven hard even by the reduced sail. The bows punched into each successive wave and white and green water sluiced over the foredecks.

The Queen's governess, Lady Fleming, lay groaning in an agony of seasickness. Eventually, as they passed the coast of Cornwall, she cried out to the captain,

'Put me ashore, sir, I beg of you. I'd rather face the wicked English than go on in such misery.'

But the captain had more important things to concern him. The rudder of the ship had been damaged by the storm and he was acutely concerned about the safety of his precious royal cargo.

'You can either go to France or drown, *madame*, because I'm certainly not putting you or anyone else ashore!'

Marie hardly noticed the worsening weather. Her thoughts were elsewhere. Despite their differences, parting from her mother had been a distressing experience. Effie had been in a state of nervous collapse since the murder, and the Bishop had to accompany her home. But far worse than that, Marie did not even know what had happened in the aftermath of the murder. Her father told her that he would do whatever was necessary. First and foremost, he told her, she must get away from Glasgow. Dumbarton was the most obvious place.

'It's fortunate,' the Bishop had said, 'that a fleet waits there to take our Queen to France. A horse is being saddled for you. You must leave immediately.'

This was in the middle of the night, only minutes, it seemed, after the killing. But of course it must have been much later. The Bishop had written a letter to be delivered to the Queen Mother. He had allowed Marie to read it before he put his seal on it. Even in her anguish she could appreciate the irony of being described as such a grieving bride-to-be, with her wonderful suitor having been so cruelly snatched away from her. It was also from this letter that she learned of her fate. She was being banished to a foreign land. Reading this she felt sick at heart.

❖   ❖   ❖

The gales smacked and buffeted the ship from side to side, tossing it high and plunging it low. Marie clung tenaciously to the rail, her cloak tugging and swirling, her hair streaming out of control. As the icy water streamed down her face and neck, she felt perversely grateful for the pain of the wind whipping at her face and body, accepting it as punishment for what she had done. She wanted the elements to cleanse her of sin and guilt.

'Punish me, God,' she prayed silently, 'for I deserve it.'

Suddenly her prayer was interrupted by a firm hand on her arm.

'My dear young lady,' a man's voice addressed her, 'do you want to be washed overboard? Much as I admire your boldness in standing here defying the elements, I must insist that you return below deck.'

She turned to see an imposing figure in padded blue silk doublet and a darker velvet cloak, slashed to reveal a sumptuous fur lining.

'Who are you?' She had to shout the words to compete with the wind.

He managed a bow.

'Guthrie Jamieson, Earl of Edinburgh, at your service. I too am in the service of the Queen Mother.' His hand tightened painfully on her arm but his smile was charming and persuasive. 'Come now, have a glass of wine with me. If we can safely find the path to our mouths in this infernal rocking and plummeting! I swear my doublet has enjoyed more wine than I have since we embarked on this journey.'

She had to smile in return as she allowed herself to be led to safety. Once on the lower deck, he called for cloths with which she could wipe her face dry.

'Or would you prefer to go to your cabin and have your maid change your clothes?'

'It would be a waste of time. I'd only get soaked again.'

He helped her off with her cloak.

'You are a very brave young lady.'

'Why do you say that?'

He shrugged. 'Isn't it obvious? All your companions, even the men, cower down in the bowels of the ship while you venture on deck and sound as if you might venture there again. And you are not even seasick.'

'Nor are you.'

'Ah, but I have made this journey many times. My stomach is used to it.'

Now that Marie was not blinded by the gale, she could

regard Guthrie Jamieson in more detail. She noticed his well-groomed hair, his smooth, clean-shaven skin, his broad-boned face. The way he kept staring at her made her feel uncomfortable. She blushed and was angry at herself for betraying such weakness.

'Do you think the English fleet will try to capture us?'

'Not us.' His flinty eyes narrowed and glimmered. 'The Queen perhaps.'

'You know what I mean.'

'You are one of the Queen's tutors, I believe?'

'Yes, Marie Hepburn.'

He bowed over her hand.

'It is indeed an honour to meet you, Marie Hepburn.'

'You mock me, sir.'

'Not at all. I admire a lady with courage and spirit and you obviously have both.'

She withdrew her hand. For some reason, when his lips had lingered on her hand, she was reminded of Machar McNaughton. The Earl of Edinburgh was not by any means fat but there was a sturdiness about him that she could imagine might turn to Machar-like grossness with age.

To make up for her somewhat rude shrinking away from his courtly kiss, she smiled and asked pleasantly,

'Where exactly are we to land in France?'

'God willing and weather permitting, we will arrive at Roscoff in Brittany. After resting there we will proceed overland via Morlaix to our eventual destination—the castle of Saint-Germain-en-Laye.'

'I have never been to France before but at least I speak the language.'

He gave a short burst of knowing laughter.

'You will have plenty of experience, especially of the language. In the royal nurseries, there will be dozens of chattering children eagerly awaiting you and your royal pupil.'

'I look forward to meeting them,' she said. 'And to the journey across the country.'

He flung up his hands in a gesture of incredulity. And he raised a questioning eyebrow.

'Once more you reveal that brave spirit of adventure,' he told her. 'Most women would view such a journey with a sinking heart as not only long and exhausting, but perilous.'

'I'm sure with gentlemen like you to protect us,' Marie said, 'we will be perfectly safe.'

'That is true, of course.'

'And now, I'd better go and see if I can be of any help to the ladies and the children. They have been so miserably ill.'

'There is nothing you can do for them. Unless you can calm the storm and smooth the sea.'

She tossed him a dismissive look as she rose and made to leave the tiny low-roofed cabin. He raised his glass to her and smiled as, lurching from side to side with the roll of the ship and grabbing at whatever she could to steady herself, she hurried away.

— XII —

EVERYONE thanked God once they had safely reached the small fishing port of Roscoff. Odd-shaped rocks crowded the bay which was said to be a nest of pirates and smugglers. It was here that the young Queen first set foot on French soil. The royal party then entered the main street. The Queen was carried on a litter, her dress of sparkling gold, her red-gold hair, her luminous skin and almond-shaped eyes causing gasps of pleasure and admiration from the crowds.

'*La reinette! La reinette!*' was the cry that sped through the town and brought people running. The four Marys still felt somewhat unsteady but the relief of being safely on dry land soon made them feel better.

The house in which they first rested was an ancient building with gargoyles on the chimney stack. Along a passage the Queen and her Marys found a grey stone cloister. Behind it there was a cellar storeroom and from there a door led out to a small boat-shaped garden with a tall turret on its seaward angle. The Queen led the four Marys up this turret, racing in front of them with Marie hastening to try and catch

91

up. This caused much agitation to the Queen's guardian, Lord Erskine, who sent attendants after the Queen to plead with her to return to the house.

They left the next day on a journey that was to last two months before they reached the French Court. At Morlaix, the Queen was welcomed by the Lord of Rohan and the nobility of the country. The Queen and the Marys, Lady Fleming and Marie were lodged in a Dominican convent, then the Queen was taken to church where a *Te Deum* was sung in honour of her safe arrival.

During their time at Morlaix, and despite Marie's lack of encouragement, the Earl of Edinburgh seemed intent on forming some sort of relationship with her. He rode beside her at every opportunity, sat next to her at table, and continually sought her company. Jamieson was surprised to find himself drawn to her, but he was intrigued by her spirit and resourcefulness—especially in escaping the consequences of Machar McNaughton's death.

'Already Mary is being hailed as a brave little queen who has been forced to flee the barbaric Scots and the cruel English, for the safe arms and loving heart of France,' he said with one of the smiles that seemed to harden not soften his eyes.

'As long as they keep her safe,' Marie replied. 'That is all that matters.'

'Yes, of course.' He smiled again. 'But she is still the Queen of Scots.'

'Nobody is denying that,' Marie said. 'But she was not safe in Scotland.'

'Ah, the wicked English and their spies?' the Earl said, thinking all the while of the English gold he himself had taken so often. He was also beginning to think that as well as being a beauty, perhaps in years to come this Marie Hepburn could be a useful way into the Queen's confidence. Randolph, his paymaster at the English Court, would be greatly impressed to learn that he had a contact amongst the Queen's closest companions.

As Marie looked at him she could not determine whether he was being sincere or sarcastic, and she certainly had no inkling of the devious thoughts that were racing through his mind.

* * *

The second stage of the journey was supervised by the Queen's grandmother, Antoinette de Guise, a strong woman who had borne twelve children, of whom ten had survived to form the most powerful family in France.

'*Ma chère enfant*,' she remarked to Mary, 'I must see to your wardrobe as soon as possible. You need far more gowns and stomachers. And you haven't nearly enough bonnets and caps and shoes. The French Court demands a much higher standard of elegance than you have been used to. Nevertheless you are *très belle*, a credit to your name. Lady Fleming is pretty, and she too is tolerably well turned out. So is your other tutor. But . . .' She pursed her lips in disapproval. 'The rest of your train, with the exception of the dear Earl of Edinburgh, who is always most elegant, are thoroughly ill-looking and *farouche*. They are not even, in my opinion, properly washed.'

The four Marys, always in the Queen's company as they were duty-bound to be, overheard the criticism with bad grace.

But they soon forgot their resentment and became infected by the Queen's enthusiasm and enjoyment, as they continued with their journey overland to the Loire. There a beautifully decorated barge was waiting to carry them along the great river towards the castle of Saint-Germain-en-Laye, where the royal children were supposed to be waiting to meet them. On the journey Marie even became much better-tempered with Guthrie Jamieson. Or perhaps it was because she was enjoying herself that she no longer noticed the Earl so much.

During the long journey both Mary's guardians, Lord Erskine and Lord Livingstone, fell ill, but Duchess Antoinette's formidable presence overcame all difficulties. She was always well-prepared to cope with any misfortune. It was even rumoured that she kept her coffin at the entrance to her private chapel, and she was always dressed in black.

She told Lady Fleming and Marie, 'The King is away campaigning at present, but will return soon. But he has left orders about the precedence that Mary has to be given. Mary has to walk before his daughter, the Princess of France, firstly because she is going to marry the Dauphin, and secondly because she is already a crowned queen of an independent country.'

'And I'm also told,' the Duchess continued, 'that the King has sent written instructions for the thorough cleaning of the castle of Saint-Germain. Every corner, every nook and cranny, has to be absolutely spotless, in honour of the Queen's arrival.'

As it turned out, so detailed were the King's instructions and so thorough the cleaning operation, that the royal children were still waiting at the medieval fortress of Carrières when Queen Mary and her suite arrived there.

By that time Marie had coached the Queen diligently in French and she had proved so quick and eager to learn, she was already able to hold quite a reasonable conversation in the language. The Duchess of Guise had tutored the Queen in the ways of the French, and special attention was paid to preparing her for the important day when she would meet her future bridegroom.

Even more important still was her first meeting with the King. But that was still some time away. First there was the meeting with the French royal children. The result of all Marie's efforts was that the Queen could greet the royal children and converse with them quite happily in their own language, and the meeting went exceptionally well. But what delighted Marie more than anything was the meeting of the

Queen and the Dauphin, Francis. She knew that Mary was a kind-hearted child, generous in spirit and in practice. Her tenderness towards the frail little Dauphin, however, touched Marie's heart and gave an insight into the Queen's character that would always stay with her. It was obvious that, from the moment they met, the Dauphin liked Mary.

The meeting with the King of France was as successful as the meeting had been with his children. He came to the nursery once they'd eventually arrived and settled in the castle of Saint-Germain. Marie marvelled yet again at the royal child's grace and charm. The King of France was clearly impressed, describing Mary as 'the most perfect child I have ever seen.'

When the King visited the nursery he always brought with him a beautiful cultured lady that Marie assumed to be the Queen. She learned later that the woman, who took such an interest in the royal nursery—the children's education, ailments, food, their general upbringing—was Diane du Poitier, the King's mistress.

The true Queen was the sinister Italian, Catherine di' Medici. It was rumoured that Catherine had already caused the death of more than one person at the Court. It was even said that she dabbled in sorcery and the occult at the castle of Blois. Marie soon realised what a dangerous woman Catherine di' Medici was. However, they did not see too much of her and Marie's fears faded.

Often Marie thought how lucky she was. Fully occupied with the world of the royal child, Marie hardly saw the Earl of Edinburgh. The terrible events in Scotland had faded far into the distance, and only occasionally did the nightmare of the murder return to haunt her. Then one day when they were at the castle of Blois, an ambassador from Scotland came to pay court to the King and brought much news and gossip from the country of her birth. One piece of news that filtered down to the royal nursery was about a man being executed for the murder of the Duke of Glasgow.

Marie went cold with horror. A wave of guilt crushed her, as the terrible realisation dawned that some poor unfortunate had suffered in her place for the crime she had committed.

— XIII —

THE Bishop of Moray had felt no guilt at all. On the contrary, he thought he'd managed the unfortunate incident of the murder of the Duke of Glasgow with great skill and cunning. On that fateful night, Murdo McKeever had been waiting outside the door of the bed-chamber as usual to attend to him. Every evening, as far back as the Bishop could remember, long, long before he had become a Bishop, Murdo had attended him and pre-pared him for bed.

The servant was old and decrepit and should have been dispensed with years ago. However, the old man had young grandchildren to provide for since the death of their parents and Murdo's own wife from the plague, and he had pleaded so pathetically to be kept in his service that the Bishop had relented and allowed him to continue working. But the chances were that, despite the shadows of the passageway and the old man's short-sightedness, Murdo had seen Marie run from the Duke of Glasgow's bedchamber with the Duke's blood on her clothes. Just in case he'd seen anything, Murdo had to be dealt with. So much was at stake. The Bishop could not gamble on Murdo keeping quiet. He had to be silenced.

The Bishop had taken him by the arm and led him into the Duke's room. Murdo gasped in horror at the sight of the Duke's bloodstained corpse lying prostrate on the floor. He began to tremble so much that the Bishop lifted a jug of whisky from a nearby table and filled a goblet. He drank from it himself, then he held it to the servant's lips.

'This will give us both strength,' he said, encouraging the old man to quaff deeply. Spluttering and coughing, Murdo eventually managed to push the goblet aside. The Bishop took another drink.

'Go and look closer, Murdo. Tell me if he is dead.'

Violently shaking, Murdo crouched down beside the body.

'He's dead all right, maister.'

'Let me have the dagger.'

Murdo struggled to his feet, clutching the weapon.

'No, on second thoughts,' the Bishop raised his hand, 'just wait here. Watch over the poor man until I return.'

'Yes, maister.'

The old man looked helpless and confused, but as eager to please him as ever.

'You are a good and loyal servant,' the Bishop said in an unprecedented expression of praise. He even smiled at the old man although his eyes shifted from the crumpled face as it lit up with surprise and gratitude.

'Thank you, maister.'

'I won't be long,' the Bishop told him before leaving the room.

Downstairs in the great hall the revelry had become a mindless, drunken rabble. He raised a hand to quieten them. They fell silent.

'I have terrible news,' he called out. 'Our good friend and generous host has been attacked in his bedchamber as my poor child was saying goodnight to her mother. She has been denied her future, her home, her husband. The Duke was set upon and brutally murdered while she was with her mother and myself in the room next to his bedchamber.'

He had been heard in a drunken stupor by people who looked half asleep. He had meant to go on to say that they could rest assured that he would do his best, with God's help, to discover who had perpetrated the deed. But before he could say another word, the whole company had let out a sudden roar of grief as the meaning of his announcement had sunk in. As one man, they had stampeded from the hall, knocking candles over and plunging much of the place into darkness as they surged towards the passageway and up the stairs.

'Machar! Machar!' some of them were shouting as if they did not, or could not, believe that he was dead. They had to see for themselves.

The Bishop hurried after them and knew by the second roar, this time of rage, that they'd reached the Duke's bedchamber.

Shouting at the top of his voice—'In God's name, stand aside!'—he pushed his way into the room and forced himself between them and the terrified Murdo, who stood there dumbfounded, his mouth agape, still clutching the blood-stained dagger in his trembling hand.

'Gentlemen, I implore you, keep calm!'

Still there were shouts of 'Kill the murderer, burn him!' and 'Tear him limb from limb!'

'Listen to me! Justice will be done,' the Bishop shouted back, and held up the gold cross he wore round his neck. 'But in the name of Jesus Christ, I command you—calm yourselves. Tomorrow morning we will gather in the fore-court at first light. Then justice can be *seen* to be done.' They fell back from the cross, muttering, still unsure.

The Bishop continued, 'I shall personally see him locked in the dungeon tonight. You have my word as a man of God that he shall be secured until tomorrow.'

Deflated, they turned away and, silent now in their grief, they disappeared into the darkness of the corridor.

'Thank you, maister,' Murdo sobbed. 'God bless you. You are a guid man.'

'You understand I must take you down to the dungeon? But do not fear. I shall do my best for you. I will return before first light and speak to you again. Meantime, I must think what can be done for the best.'

The old man nodded.

❈ ❈ ❈

The Bishop awoke with a start to find daylight streaming in through the windows of his bedchamber. In a panic, he raced down the damp, evil-smelling stairs to the dungeons. He prayed that all was not lost, and he was relieved to find all was silent, except the turnkey snoring at his post.

He shook the man awake. The turnkey started to apologise but the Bishop ignored him and ordered him to open the door of Murdo's cell immediately. At first he could see nothing in the pitch blackness of the cell and he called for a candle. In the flickering light he could just make out a vague shape. Huddled in a corner, Murdo looked like a bundle of bones covered in rags. The Bishop heard the squeaking of rats and the candle reflected in rodent eyes, making them gleam wickedly as they scurried away through the blackness.

'Murdo?' The Bishop leaned over him.

The old man made an attempt to struggle up but was gasping for breath and obviously in pain. He was clutching at his chest. Suddenly, from above, came the noise of an angry rabble crashing down the stairs.

'My grandchildren.' Murdo put a hand out, caught at the Bishop's robe, and held on to it with desperate strength. 'What about my grandchildren?'

'I will take care of them,' the Bishop assured him. 'I will take them into my home and bring them up as if they were my own son and daughter. Have no fear.'

The old servant nodded and a look of gratitude and relief

filled his eyes before they closed, the Bishop hoped, for the last time. Outside, the crowd was screaming for vengeance.

'I think he's dead,' the Bishop announced as he emerged from the dungeon to face them.

'Justice must be done.' The cry echoed off the damp stone walls. 'McNaughton must be avenged.'

They pounced on Murdo's inert body, dragging it up the steps from the cell and out into the courtyard. There, although it was now obvious their victim was already dead, they tore the pathetic corpse apart and flung the pieces on to a dung heap. The Bishop looked on, horrified but relieved. It could all have been so much worse.

❖   ❖   ❖

Much later, after the Bishop and his party had returned to Spynie, he sent for Murdo's grandchildren. They lived in Murdo's cottage in the grounds of the palace. Joseph and Agnes McKeever had been devastated by the news of Murdo's fate. They were thirteen and twelve years old respectively, but neither of them shed a tear. Perhaps they believed that, at their age, it was too childish. For whatever reason, they just stared at him stony-faced.

'I did my best for your grandfather,' he assured them, 'but he took a seizure in the end. The people were angry and desperate for revenge. But he felt nothing. God in his infinite mercy had, by that time, taken his spirit.'

He then explained to them about the promise he had made to old Murdo.

It was true that God worked in mysterious ways. Everything had been resolved for the best. Marie was far away in France. He'd packed her mother off to live with an ancient aunt on Orkney. There she could be of no danger to anyone. He'd said it was for her own peace of mind, but it was very much more for his own. He had kept his word as a Christian and a gentleman and taken Joseph and Agnes McKeever into

101

his palace. He had even given them into the care of an excellent tutor, Mr Fraser—Marie's old dominie. It would be easier, he decided, to find Agnes a husband if she had the polish of some learning and sophistication. Although at twelve years she was already becoming a pretty young woman. Not as beautiful as his red-haired Marie, but with her dark eyes and black hair, there was a strange smouldering quality about her that was, to say the least, intriguing. Her brother had the same dark brooding look, and both of them were strangely quiet.

Of course, the Bishop didn't see them very often. They had their own quarters in the palace and their paths only crossed occasionally. The brother and sister answered any questions the Bishop put to them politely but briefly, and that was all. They gave no thanks, and showed no gratitude. The Bishop was disturbed by their strange behaviour but decided it was wiser not to pursue the matter. He wondered if they ever suspected anything. Yet how could they? They had not seen their grandfather alive since the Duke's murder and so had no opportunity to hear any protestation of innocence from the old man.

Everyone else, the clergy, the parishioners, the servants, all praised the Bishop for being so good to the family of Murdo McKeever. The man must have been overcome by the madness of senility to have committed such a crime, everyone said. Senility, combined with and probably accentuated by drink, because he'd reeked of whisky, it was said. Nevertheless, for the Bishop to have been so good and generous to the man's family after what he'd done . . .

'The family are innocent of any crime,' he'd pronounced. 'As a man of God, I cannot allow them to suffer. I feel it is my Christian duty to do what I can for them.'

Even the Archbishop of Glasgow had praised him for his saintliness. Yes, saintliness, they all said. Except for Joseph and Agnes McKeever, who said nothing.

Machar McNaughton had been extremely proud of his son, and had tried everything in his power to secure Gavin's release from captivity in England. But to no avail. On the night he was murdered, he was to hand over the ransom demanded, but the Earl of Edinburgh had had other plans.

And so Gavin McNaughton rotted away in an English dungeon, unaware that he was the new Duke of Glasgow. He thought that his captors would demand ransom money from his father, but as the months passed, he gradually began to realise that he had been abandoned. Why had no-one come? Surely the price demanded was not so high for a man of the Scottish nobility?

Then, at last, a message reached him from Scotland. It was from McNairn, his father's factor, who managed the Naughton estates, and it told him that his father was dead, murdered, and there was no money to pay the ransom. Apparently his father had large debts, and the English were demanding two thousand gold pieces. There was only one way of escape, the letter said, and that was to mortgage the estates and the castle itself.

Gavin sat in his cell, sunk in a deep depression. He could not believe what was happening to him. Finally he decided— if he had to mortgage the castle, so be it, he would do just that. It would be a damned hard struggle to pay back the ransom money, and it would mean risking everything his family had built over the years—but what else could he do? Only with his freedom could he discover who had murdered his father and take his revenge.

By the time the mortgages had been arranged with the English moneylenders, and he had finally been released, nearly a year had passed since Machar's death. When he arrived at Naughton Castle, he found it almost deserted, with only a few of the old retainers left. It was so different from the happy scenes he remembered from his childhood. He found the factor hard at work sorting through a pile of papers and accounts.

'Old Jock McNairn, as I live and breathe! It's good to see you!' Gavin shouted in welcome.

Jock turned around to see the young Duke standing before him. 'Maister Gavin! I thoucht ye were nivver comin' hame.'

'I'm here all right,' said Gavin, striding over to shake the old man vigorously by the hand. 'But I see the castle has changed nearly as much as I have.'

'Aye, ye're right enough. Ye're baith luikin' older!'

'Where is everyone? The castle is so quiet.'

'Well, it's been a sare fecht since the Maister was killt, a right sare fecht. I've had to let a'body go, there wis nae money tae pay them.'

'I'm sorry Jock, but I must know what happened to my father.'

'It wis terrible. Jist terrible. The Bishop of Moray wis here wi' his dochter. A beautiful young wumman. She and yer faither were to be handfasted that very night. They went upstairs efter the banquet, and we nivver saw him alive again. Appairently, one of the Bishop's men did it, a chiel by the name of Murdo McKeever. . . .'

'Murdo McKeever! Are you sure?' Gavin could not believe what he was hearing.

'Aye, Murdo McKeever. They tore him to bits like a rag doll when they heard.'

'But McKeever was an old man. I remember him well— the Bishop's own manservant. How? Why?'

'I dinna rightly ken. Efter it was a' over, the Bishop left wi' his dochter and his pairty. I dinna ken whaur they went. But naebody rightly kens.' A tear glistened in Jock's eye, as if it had only happened yesterday, but Gavin could not believe what he had been told. He made up his mind to travel to Spynie and hear the whole sorry tale from the Bishop of Moray himself.

'It was a terrible shock to us all. I don't think my daughter Marie will ever get over it,' said the Bishop. 'They hoped to marry, you know.'

'Yes, I have heard.'

'Oh yes. They were both very happy and looking forward to their future together. We had all journeyed down to Glasgow and were celebrating their betrothal. That was the night it happened. . . .'

'You think the old man was drunk and didn't know what he was doing?'

'That's what everyone said. But of course he was in his dotage. Half the time he didn't know what he was doing.'

Gavin McNaughton looked both sad and thoughtful. He was a tall handsome man of at least six feet, and broad shouldered. The paleness of his skin—no doubt a result of his incarceration—was in stark contrast to his piercing blue eyes.

'I hear that you have taken responsibility for McKeever's family,' Gavin said.

'They had nobody else. I felt I had to do something. Do you take exception to my action?'

'No. It is most generous of you.'

In the days that followed, the new Duke of Glasgow, as he was now, spoke at some length with Joseph and Agnes McKeever. The Bishop had watched them from his window walking together deep in conversation. Eventually the young Duke had said to him,

'The McKeevers are convinced their grandfather did not commit the crime and I have come to believe them.'

The Bishop smiled.

'They are naturally loyal to him.'

'It's not just that. They have convinced me that it was not possible. He was a frail old man who had no reason to commit murder. It seems completely out of character. All his long life, I'm told, he was a quiet-spoken, gentle person.'

'People have been known in their dotage to act out of character, quite differently than they would have done with all their senses about them. And he was smelling of drink, remember.'

'That was out of character too,' the Duke said thoughtfully.

'My dear boy,' the Bishop sighed, 'why do you keep worrying at this like a dog at a bone? The poor man is dead and gone, as is your dear father Machar. Nothing can bring either of them back.'

'But if Murdo McKeever did not murder my father, then someone else did. And that someone must not escape unpunished.'

'Gavin, it is all in the past now. Even if it is as you say, we shall never know who committed the crime.'

'Maybe not, but I will not rest until I know the truth.'

PART II

FRANCE
1558

— XIV —

'**M**Y dear Marie,' Mary said, 'you appear down-hearted. What ails you? Can I be of any comfort?'
Marie looked at her Queen with affection.

'My mind was in Scotland.'

The Queen looked surprised and a little distressed.

'You pine for Scotland? I thought you were happy here with me.'

'Oh yes, I am.'

'If you really wished to return, you know I would allow you to go, although with much sadness.'

'No, no. It's not that. It's just something in the past that I regret happening. No, I am truly happy here with you. I have never been happier in my life.'

The Queen embraced her and Marie felt a rush of love for the girl. She admired her too. Although only fifteen, the Queen had already shown a quick intelligent mind and was highly talented in music and the dance. She had also insisted on, and received, her own establishment. As a result they now had their own servants on the same lavish scale as the Court. Although Mary was still being trained in courtly accomplishments, she sang very sweetly and could play the lute, the harpsichord, the cittern and the harp. The wonderful agility of her tall, slim body gave way to a quiet grace when dancing and could suit any harmony of strings.

She could be equally happy to sit with Marie working at her embroidery. On other occasions Mary revelled in the hunt and could race a horse as well as any man. She often challenged Marie to a race and the two of them, dressed as boys, would gallop at speed through fields and woods until they were flushed and breathless.

But Marie was often worried about Mary. The Court was rife with rumours of plots against her, and many suspected that Catherine di' Medici was the driving force behind them. She was certainly a very dangerous woman—quiet, watchful, sinister—and she had never liked the Queen of Scots. One day, Marie mentioned her fears to Guthrie Jamieson.

'You're right to be fearful,' Jamieson agreed. 'That Medici woman has no scruples, but even she dare not harm the Queen. As for the Dauphin, however, now that is quite a different matter . . . his death might suit her purposes very well. She has never liked that pathetic weakling, and favours his brother, the handsome Charles.'

Jamieson's words did nothing to calm Marie's worries, and, still fearful of an attempt to poison the Queen, she kept keenly alert, often hovering around the kitchens at mealtimes.

Mary laughed at her but always added affectionately,

'But do not think I'm not grateful, dear Marie. I know that you love me and are anxious to do all in your power to protect me.'

Marie marvelled at her courage. Underneath, she knew, the girl suffered more anxiety than she would ever admit. Mary had begun to complain of sickness and a pain on her right side. Once she was ill with a fever. Another time she had a fainting fit. These ailments became more marked after Catherine di' Medici had banished Lady Fleming back to Scotland. In her place Catherine had put the sly Madame de

Paroy. Mary protested but Catherine wanted a spy to report everything that might be of interest or of use to her. She would not listen to any protests.

The loss of the merry, frivolous, flirtatious Lady Fleming and the acquisition of Catherine's spy had been a terrible blow to Mary and Marie. They wished with all their hearts that Lady Fleming had been more discreet. She had not only become involved with the King when his mistress was unwell, she had boasted about the result.

'God be thanked, I am pregnant by the King, for which I count myself both honoured and fortunate.'

Madame de Paroy asked many questions about Mary. And she also questioned Marie about herself, lingering over the tragedy in her past.

'No, we were not married. We were betrothed.'

'But still, such a tragedy. You came directly from Glasgow to join the Queen at Dumbarton?'

'Yes, I did.'

'How fortunate that you were so close at hand and your position of *maid d'honneur* could be arranged with such speed.'

'It wasn't a case of arranging anything with speed. We were many months on Dumbarton Rock. I do not know why you have taken such a particular interest in my life, *madame*. Or for that matter, the particular comings and goings of Mary, Queen of Scots. You are, I believe, to tutor the Queen, not to act as her jailor.'

Madame de Paroy flushed with anger and Marie realised that she had made an enemy.

*   *   *

The talk about the murder and Madame de Paroy's sly probing caused Marie's nightmares to return. At about this time, the Queen's ailments took a turn for the worse. A letter from Scotland from the Dowager had informed Mary that Madame de Paroy had written a long epistle, full of complaints about her. Mary's hands shook and she sobbed as she penned a reply. She could not bear to be thought ill of by her mother.

Marie also wrote to the Dowager saying she too was unhappy with Madame de Paroy. She was of the opinion, she wrote, that the woman was a bad influence on her daughter's health and happiness, and the Dowager was not the only person to whom Madame de Paroy had told lies about Mary. The Court was rife with evil rumours. In her distress, Marie confided in the Earl of Edinburgh about the problem of Madame de Paroy. Devious though he might be, she knew Jamieson was unswervingly loyal to the Queen of Scots. He advised that Mary should complain to her uncle, the Cardinal.

'I will also approach him in person,' Guthrie said, 'and put the case for Madame de Paroy's removal. No Medici spy will harm the Queen if I have anything to do with it!'

To the intense relief of Mary and Marie, the Earl eventually managed to have the woman removed. But it had taken considerable effort because Catherine di' Medici resented any opposition. The young Queen had always loved her grandmother, Antoinette de Guise, and her Guise uncles, especially Charles, the Cardinal of Lorraine. Now she adored the Cardinal for his help in freeing her of the evil shadow of Madame de Paroy. She was also profuse in her thanks and affection towards Guthrie Jamieson. Marie was grateful to him as well. In fact, she now regarded him as her close friend.

The four Marys had now rejoined them from the French convent where they had been educated in French language and French customs. They had been furious at first and consumed with jealousy of Marie because, right from the start, she had been allowed to stay at the Queen's side. It had been explained to them that the King wanted Mary to be as a French woman, and during her formative years, she had to be cut off from as many Scots influences and tongues as possible.

'But what about Marie Hepburn and Lady Fleming?' the girls had protested.

'They are the Queen's tutors and they will converse with her only in French. That is what you must learn to do.'

Mary enjoyed the company of all her *maids d'honneur* but she was always happiest when she was with the Dauphin. It was very touching to see the Queen and the Dauphin together. Mary was so sensitive and tender with him. He absolutely adored her, and despite the fact that he was sickly and, in Marie's view, unattractive in appearance, Mary showed every sign of loving him in return. Although Marie was sure she only loved him like a young brother, they seemed to enjoy nothing better than walking hand in hand, chatting easily together. But it was pathetic how the boy's passion for her made him strive in all sorts of energetic ways to impress the Queen and struggle to prove to her that he was neither weak nor sickly. Not that Mary demanded such behaviour. Time and time again, she assured him that her affection for him did not depend on how many stags he shot or wild boar he chased. All to no avail. The more the young Queen showed her affection for him, the more grateful he seemed, and the more feverishly he sought to perform deeds that he believed would make him truly deserving of her.

'The poor boy,' Marie confided in Jamieson, 'he has never received any love from his mother, that's the trouble. More than that, he is afraid of her, as all the other royal children are.'

'Maybe,' Jamieson replied, 'but our Queen deserves better than this puny French creature. She would have been much better served by Edward of England.'

Marie looked at him in surprise and alarm. 'You mustn't say things like that.'

He shrugged. 'It is the truth. You must see that.'

Despite everything Jamieson said, Marie still looked forward to the royal wedding. The prospect made her feel more secure, made her feel that she, like Mary, was being safely rooted in France. There would be no danger of the Scots Queen, particularly as French Dauphiness, leaving France with its magnificent palaces and chateaux and its fashionable Court, to return to the small and rugged country of Scotland. Especially now, when by all accounts that country was facing increasing trouble with the Protestants.

Mary was a devout Catholic and never missed hearing daily Mass. She glowed with pleasure when the Cardinal praised her devotion to the faith. Marie knew that the Cardinal's devotion had led him to persecute and put to death many French Protestants but she refrained from telling Mary this. Firstly because Mary's sensitive nature could not cope with violence, and secondly because she would never have believed the suave and handsome Cardinal with the neat pointed beard was capable of such cruelty. Marie sometimes worried about the influence the Queen's uncles had over her. This was one subject on which she was in agreement with the Earl of Edinburgh. Everyone, except Mary, could see that the Guise family were ruthlessly ambitious. She feared it was true what Jamieson whispered to her,

'They're using Mary as a stepping stone to ultimate power. Through their influence on her, and her marriage to the Dauphin, they'll have the chance, one day, of ruling France. You mark my words.'

But dear, loving, trusting Mary saw only the happy day ahead when she would marry her Dauphin. She was happy. For now, as far as Marie was concerned, that was all that mattered.

Although she did not see eye to eye with the Earl of Edinburgh on everything, Marie respected his opinion and she felt sure that he had the Queen's welfare at heart. When he was in attendance in the French Court she couldn't help noticing what a dominant figure he was. Not that she felt romantically attracted to him, she assured herself. She preferred lean men, not great hulks like Guthrie Jamieson. Nevertheless, it had to be said that his face was handsome enough. But there was something, however, that disturbed her, something she couldn't quite fathom about his eyes, and in the many meetings she had with the Earl, this strange frisson of—she knew not what—was always present.

— XV —

'THE wedding has got to be stopped,' the Earl of Edinburgh declared.

'The wedding?' Marie echoed. 'Don't be ridiculous.'

'You know as well as I do that it is not the best thing either for the Queen of Scots or for Scotland.'

'But she loves the Dauphin and her heart is set on it. Anyway, how could anyone stop it even if they wanted to?'

'If the sickly Dauphin were to die . . .'

'God forbid such a thing!' Marie cried out. But in her heart she often worried about the young man's state of health and feared that he might not be long for this world. But God forbid such a thing, she repeated to herself.

'Oh, I doubt if God would forbid it,' the Earl told her. 'But as for the wedding, however, you could have a few words in the young Queen's ear. You have great charm and influence, and you would do your country a great service by helping me put a stop to this nonsense.'

Marie was beginning to feel uneasy.

'Nothing I could say on the subject could possibly make

116

any difference. Especially at this late stage. Anyway, Mary's uncles have far more influence on the Queen than I could ever hope to have.'

'But if the Dauphin were to die—if not by natural causes, perhaps by poison say—then their influence would die with him. Their bid for power through Mary would be ruined.'

'Poison?' Marie was shocked. 'How can you even think of such a thing? I refuse to listen to any more of this treasonable talk.'

'Now, now,' Jamieson mocked. 'Don't pretend that you're shocked.'

'What do you mean—pretend?' She was angry now. 'I'm not pretending. I *am* shocked. You seem to be . . .' She could hardly form the words. Surely she must be mistaken. 'You seem to be suggesting that you . . . that we . . . might even bring about such a plot. . . .'

'There are no *mights* about it.'

'You mean you are actually . . .' Words failed her for a moment and then she said, 'I am going to warn both the Queen and the Dauphin. If you value your own life, sir, you had better make haste to disappear on one of your journeys.'

The Earl was unperturbed.

'No,' he said calmly, 'I have no journeys planned for the moment. And you will not repeat our conversation to anyone.'

'And who will stop me?'

Unexpectedly one of his big hands shot out and snatched her to him. She was surprised not only at his action but at the rock hardness of his body.

'How dare you!'

Before his mouth came down over hers, he whispered,

'I'd dare anything for you.'

At first, surprise immobilised her. Also she experienced a physical thrill of a kind she'd forgotten existed. In the long years since her intimacy with Donald, there had been no other man. Donald had told her that she was a passionate woman. Now she realised how true his words had been. If this man had not spoken of murder . . .

She began to struggle against him but punching at his chest only made him laugh. His laughter ignited her temper and made her, with all her strength and in one vicious move, bring her knee up between his legs.

'You . . . little . . . !' he groaned, staggering away from her, bending forward, nursing himself.

'Don't you dare touch me again.'

'What would you do?' he managed. 'Stab me? Do you always keep a dagger handy for killing your lovers?'

She froze.

'Oh yes, we have more in common than you could possibly imagine.'

Cold terror paralysed her brain.

'I . . . I don't know what you're talking about,' she managed to stammer.

'Come now, lady. Can you really be so stupid? Indeed, you are obviously exceptionally clever. To have begun as a poor bastard and end as a friend and confidante of a queen, not to mention getting away with murder en route, is no mean feat. I admire you. I will indeed be happy to pay court to you if you'll have me.'

'You keep talking about murder. . . .'

He smiled.

'You thought no-one knew. Well, I'm sorry to disappoint you, but I witnessed you despatching the old Duke. And a very thorough job you made of it!' The Earl laughed inwardly at the irony of his accusation.

'Why have you never said anything before?' she gasped.

'I've waited years for the right moment, and I'm pleased to say that you have not disappointed me.'

'I don't know what to say.'

'There's nothing to say. We'll talk again when I've decided how best you can help me despatch that pathetic weakling.'

Later in her room, one question would not go away. Why had Guthrie Jamieson been hiding behind the tapestry in the Duke of Glasgow's chamber? Why had he not rushed to the Duke's aid or called the guard? Surely that would have been the natural and instinctive reaction. Of course he was a devious man. She suspected that he might have something to hide and that was why he hadn't told anyone about her crime. Had he been saving his own skin, not hers?

The following day she sought him out and confronted him.

'Why were you hiding in the Duke's apartment?'

He laughed malevolently.

'I was about to kill him myself but you saved me the trouble,' he sneered.

'But why? Why would you want to kill him?'

'Let us just say he was taking English gold. He was about to betray many people. He had to be stopped.'

Was such a thing possible? She had become all too familiar with the treachery and double-dealing among the nobility. Perhaps it was true.

The Earl's face took on a more sinister aspect. 'So you have thought about my earlier proposition? After all, we wouldn't want anyone to find out what really happened all those years ago, would we?'

'You're not going to blackmail me,' Marie told Jamieson. 'If you try to drag me down, I'll take you with me. Believe me.'

The Earl studied her face for a few moments.

'Yes, I do believe you. You are indeed a woman after my own heart. But do not imagine for a moment that someone in your lowly position at Court could possibly do me any harm. Whether you like it or not, the Dauphin must die, and you must help me or suffer the consequences. It matters not to me if he dies before the wedding or after it. You will find I am a patient man.'

And with a flamboyant bow, he turned and left the room.

— XVI —

THE wedding day dawned bright and clear. The royal family and Mary's *maids d'honneur* had spent the night at the palace of the Archbishop of Paris. Marie had had to sleep in Mary's bedchamber and read to her well into the night to calm her.

In the morning, all the maids helped to dress the young Queen. As she stood before them in all her grandeur, they had to wipe tears from their eyes, so moved were they by the beauty of what they saw, a beauty touched by a certain fragility—the long swan-like neck, the small, well-turned head, the amber eyes.

Once ready, they proceeded from the palace to the Cathedral of Notre-Dame. To aid their progress, a walkway had been set up between the palace and the cathedral. The King of France himself led Mary by the right hand while her kinsman, the Duke of Lorraine, held her left. The Dauphin was led in by the King of Navarre and was followed by his younger brother, Charles.

The congregation made a magnificent sight in all their finery and sparkling jewels, but none was more splendid than the fifteen-year-old bride. Her garments were studded with so many priceless gems, however, that Mary's tall, slim frame could scarcely carry the weight of them. Her wedding dress of white damask was dazzling, the mantle and train a subtle mingling of blue and grey velvet decorated with pearls. To weigh her down even further, she wore a golden crown of diamonds, pearls, sapphires and rubies. In the centre was suspended a large luminous gem like a flame, worth in itself over five hundred thousand crowns.

✤ ✤ ✤

Amidst all this rejoicing, Marie was still reeling from the Earl of Edinburgh's revelations. He wanted her to help him kill the Dauphin. The poor sickly Dauphin . . . it was too dreadful even to think about. But she had suffered agonies over committing one murder, and had no intention of going through all that again. She'd rather die herself, and had made that perfectly plain to Guthrie Jamieson. He had just shrugged and said,

'We shall see.'

The events of the last few days had changed her view of Guthrie Jamieson completely. Yet she was still fascinated by him. He could be most elegant and courtly in his behaviour, yet there was a sexual coarseness about him at times. She sensed it, saw it in his eyes. When he looked at her with those hard, suggestive eyes, she experienced an answering sensuality. At the same time, she hated herself for it. A part of her nature responded to the wickedness of him. She hated him too. She hated the arrogant swagger of him. What would he do if she refused to help him? She now knew he was capable of anything.

Yet the Earl of Edinburgh was not her only concern. Marie feared that somebody from Scotland might be at the wedding who remembered her, and who also had suspicions about the real reasons for her flight from Glasgow. And they,

121

unlike the Earl of Edinburgh, would have no reason for keeping quiet.

❖   ❖   ❖

The first group to arrive outside the cathedral was the Swiss guards resplendent in their liveries. They arrived to the sound of tambourines and fifes. Then came the Duke of Guise; then there was the Bishop of Paris. Then a procession appeared headed by a series of musicians, all clad in yellow and red, with trumpets, sackbuts, flageolets, violins and other musical instruments filling the air with their cacophony of rejoicing. Following the musicians came a hundred gentlemen-in-waiting of the King. After them strutted the princes of the blood so gorgeously dressed that the onlookers gasped in wonder. Next came the *abbés* and bishops bearing rich crosses and jewelled mitres, and after them, the princes of the church, even more magnificently dressed. They included the cardinals of Bourbon and Lorraine.

Behind them came the Dauphin, Francis, and finally Mary with two young girls bearing her immensely long train. The young Queen was followed by Catherine di' Medici, then princesses and ladies including Marie and the four Marys, all dressed in spectacular grandeur.

Once the ceremony was over, there was a banquet and a ball. Later in the afternoon, the entire Court proceeded to the palace of parliament, the Dauphin and his gentlemen on horseback, their horses adorned with crimson velvet trappings.

Mary was on a golden litter. Her red-gold hair vied in brightness with that of Marie. Except that Marie's was more fiery. In other circumstances, they would have been taken for sisters with their similar colouring and the fact that both were unusually tall for females. The young Queen could not only stand shoulder to shoulder with Marie, she could also stand shoulder to shoulder with her Guise uncles.

Mary confided to Marie afterwards that although she had enjoyed the proceedings she felt utterly exhausted, and the young bridegroom was also wearied. The King Dauphin, as he was now to be called, had always been delicate and since Mary, now the Queen Dauphiness, had reached her adolescence, she too had ceased to be robust.

And so, after the wedding celebrations, they were very glad to leave for the Chateau of Villers-Cotterets where they could be alone.

✤   ✤   ✤

Then, in November, Mary Tudor, Queen of England, died. As far as the Guises were concerned, Mary should now be Queen of England. The King of France declared that Elizabeth, who now claimed the crown, was a bastard but Mary, on the other hand, was in direct line of descent from Henry VII and therefore the rightful heir. The Duke of Guise wanted to raise an army and invade England to wrest the crown from Elizabeth, but the King would not go so far as to declare war over such an issue. However, he did have Mary proclaimed Dauphiness of France, Queen of England, Scotland and the Isles.

Yet all these intrigues hardly touched Mary, Queen of Scots. As far as she was concerned, England and Elizabeth were far away. They had nothing to do with her. She was happy with her Dauphin, and content in her beloved France.

But her new-found contentment was shattered when tragedy struck, one day in July. Crowds had gathered in the rue Saint-Antoine, near the Bastille, to watch the royal jousting tournament. The King and the Dauphin had been practising every day at the tilt. Henry was well known for his love of combat, and on this occasion, looking magnificent in black and white, the colours of Diane du Poitiers, he mounted his horse to the resounding cheers of the onlookers. As was his usual habit, the King broke three lances with three princes.

123

All was going perfectly, the King and the princes having acquitted themselves gallantly, when, as the afternoon light was declining and the tournament was drawing to a close, the King suddenly decided that he wished to break one more lance. This time he challenged the Comte de Montgomery.

Montgomery was a colonel of the archers of the guard and famous for his courage. He quickly saw that the King looked fatigued. He was also aware of Queen Catherine di' Medici's unease, and he begged to be excused from the encounter. Finally, Henry commanded him to obey as his sovereign. Queen Catherine tried to persuade her husband not to take part in the joust, telling him she had a premonition that something evil was about to happen. The King did not share the Queen's interest in the occult, nor did he give much credence to her talk of signs and premonitions, and this occasion was no exception. In the end there was no way out for Montgomery—he could not disobey the King's order and so the joust began.

Montgomery heaved himself into the large jousting saddle, leather creaking and groaning. As his horse pranced and skittered sideways, men at arms held its head still. Settling himself deep in the saddle, legs pushed forward, heels tensed, he lifted a heavy mailed fist and pulled his visor down over his face. His page handed up his shield and lance. Then he looked down the long tourney field to see the King's impressive black and white draped horse rearing and pawing the air.

The marshal dropped his brightly coloured flag, Montgomery kicked his heels savagely backwards into the horse's flanks, and his mount sprang forward.

Hooves thundered, and as the King charged towards him, Montgomery instinctively levelled his lance, tucking his chin down and bracing his shoulder. The impact rocked him back in the saddle as his lance snapped and jagged splinters of wood flew upwards, ripping into the King's right eye and throat. The King's horse came to a standstill with the inert figure of its rider slumped in the saddle. He was hastily lifted down, and carried into the palace of Tournelles as a shocked silence descended onto the field.

Nine days later, the King was dead.

❧　　　❧　　　❧

The Dauphin was now King Francis II at the age of fifteen and a half. Mary Stewart was Queen at the age of sixteen. Later the whisper went round the Court that now there would be three kings of France—Francis, who would wear the crown, while the Duke of Guise and his brother, the Cardinal of Lorraine, would be the true rulers.

— XVII —

IN the Great Hall of Naughton Castle, the Duke of Glasgow was entertaining his friends, Joseph McKeever and Magnus Hepburn, with tales of the recent adventures of the notorious James Hepburn, Earl of Bothwell. As the son and heir of the 'Fair Earl', Bothwell had inherited the offices of Sheriff of Berwick, Haddington and Edinburgh, of Baillie of Lauderdale, with the castles of Hailes and Crichton, and of Lord High Admiral of Scotland. Now the Queen Dowager had made him Lord Lieutenant of the Borders.

The friends were gathered at Naughton awaiting Bothwell's imminent arrival from France, a messenger having reported that his ship had docked a few days previously.

McKeever said, 'I suspect his adventures in France will have been amorous ones.'

'I doubt it,' McNaughton said. 'What about his beloved Janet?'

'I heard,' McKeever persisted, 'that he had moved on from that little affair some time ago.'

The footsteps of servants echoed along the bare boards of the hall. More logs were thrown on the fire, candles were lit, and the goblets refilled.

'I don't know about any other ladies, but he's certainly gained the Dowager's trust,' Magnus remarked. 'Now that she has given him Hermitage Castle, she's made him the most powerful man in the country.'

'Let's face it.' McNaughton stretched his tall form back in his chair and enjoyed another deep swig of wine. 'The reason she trusts him is obvious—he's just about the only one of the Protestant nobility who is not in the pay of the English. And that's despite the fact that he's desperate for money. No wonder the English loathe and detest him.'

Magnus Hepburn shifted uncomfortably.

'I confess I don't understand him. Not about refusing English gold,' he added hastily, 'but the fact that as a Protestant he is willing to risk his life for a Catholic queen.'

'Oh, Magnus, who can tell what motivates people?' McNaughton said thoughtfully. 'Look at Guthrie Jamieson. He is one of the Dowager's most trusted envoys—and he is not only a Protestant, but I've often heard it said that he favours an English alliance.'

'You think the Earl of Edinburgh is in the pay of the English?'

McNaughton shook his head.

'I am certain he is not. After all, he fought with me against them at Pinkie, did he not? But I know there are many who suspect him.'

McKeever shook his head.

'I for one cannot believe it. Guthrie is such a gallant gentleman.'

McNaughton nodded in agreement. He had never forgotten how Jamieson had saved his life, even if he hadn't been able to prevent his being captured. But Hepburn just laughed, and said,

'You are too trusting. The Earl is an intelligent, charming and courageous man, no doubt, but he's as devious and cunning as a fox as well.'

McNaughton pointedly changed the subject. 'Bothwell is

one of the few men left in the country who still has faith in chivalry. I fear it is a peculiarity that will cause his downfall. Nevertheless I admire him for it.'

'Nonsense!' McKeever said. 'You admire him for the same reason as the rest of us. He's more daring and courageous than any of us, including Jamieson.'

'Anyway, enough of politics, my friends,' Hepburn interrupted. 'I for one will be most interested to hear what Bothwell thought of the Dowager's daughter. Can she really be as beautiful as everyone says?'

'And surrounded by beauties as well,' McNaughton winked. 'Of the four Marys, I've heard Fleming is the most voluptuous. But I like the sound of Livingstone—'The Lusty', as she's known.'

'Do you remember my half-sister, Marie?' Hepburn asked. 'She was often at Spynie when she was a girl. I just wondered if your visits had ever coincided.'

McNaughton looked grim. 'The daughter of the Bishop of Moray?' He paused for a moment. 'I never met her, but she was betrothed to my father just before his death.'

Magnus Hepburn looked embarrassed. 'Of course. I had forgotten. Forgive me, Gavin, I did not mean to rake up old, bitter memories. . . .'

McNaughton sighed,

'That's all right Magnus. I wish I *had* known her. By all accounts, she and my father were very happy together. But, as you know I was imprisoned by the damned English at that time, and when I returned, my poor father had been long buried and your kinswoman gone over to France.'

'As tutor and *maid d'honneur* to the Queen of Scots, no less,' Hepburn said, unable to conceal a note of bitterness in his voice.

'Is there not much love lost between you?' McKeever asked.

Hepburn shrugged.

'I've neither seen nor heard from her for years, and—

pardon me for speaking my mind Gavin—I could never understand what my father saw in her or her stupid mother, Effie Dalgliesh.'

'Effie Dalgliesh went to live on Orkney and as far as I know, she's still there,' McKeever added.

McNaughton looked surprised.

'I wonder why she didn't accompany her daughter to France? One would think a chance of being part of the French Court, even as just the mother of a tutor . . .'

'Marie probably regarded going to France as a God-given opportunity to escape from her mother. If she'd married your father and become Duchess of Glasgow, I'll wager she wouldn't have had Effie come here to Naughton very often either. They didn't get on well as far as I remember,' Hepburn told him.

'Just think, Gavin,' McKeever said, 'she might have been your stepmother and lady of the castle if things had turned out differently.'

'I wonder what she's like,' McNaughton said. 'We must ask Bothwell what he thought of her.'

*　　*　　*

But when Lord Bothwell eventually arrived, he had more important news to discuss. He was not the 'Fair Earl' his father had been. But he had presence. When he entered a room, he dominated it, as he did now, with his scarlet lined cloak tossed back from his broad chest. He had lean, saturnine features, dark hair and jet black eyes. His enemies described him as ape-like because of his broad shoulders and long muscular arms. His dark eyes could fix one with such a disturbing stare that some people, enemies and friends alike, believed he had magical powers.

Once he had settled himself in front of the roaring fire, Bothwell began to recount his adventures. 'I had barely left the French Court,' he told his friends in his deep husky voice, 'when I received word that King Henry had died.'

The others were shocked.

Bothwell described the jousting accident. 'This means of course,' he went on, 'that Mary, Queen of Scots is now Queen of France. Yet she seemed hardly more than a child to me. Beautiful, certainly, but too delicate and virgin-like for my taste.'

'She's obviously no virgin if she's married,' McKeever remarked.

'You haven't met the Dauphin. I have. A puny, sickly fellow. Rumour has it his privates are deformed and he can't act like a man to his wife or anyone else.'

'She'll never have an heir then.'

'She's about as sickly as he is,' Bothwell added. 'But I must give them some credit. There's nothing wrong with their spirit. For taking part in any sport, at least.'

'And what of the beautiful Diane du Poitiers then?' McNaughton asked.

Bothwell gave a mirthless laugh. 'At the mercy of Catherine di' Medici, I'd say. That ugly old bitch will have been biding her time. Now she'll have her revenge.'

'And how will the young Queen fare?'

'I think that Mary could be in grave danger. Catherine di' Medici favours the new King's young brother, Charles. God alone knows what she's capable of!'

'By the way,' Hepburn suddenly remembered the conversation they'd been having earlier, 'did you meet my half-sister, Marie Hepburn, the Queen's tutor?'

'The one with the fiery red hair?' Bothwell gave one of his deep throaty laughs. 'I was introduced to her. But I first met her many years ago, don't you remember? At Spynie when we were both children. She is certainly a great beauty. But as you know my heart is elsewhere.'

They all knew he meant Janet, the niece of the murdered Cardinal Beaton. At the age of forty-three and with seven children, she had become the object of twenty-four-year-old Bothwell's unchaste affections.

'So, Marie has not yet found a husband?' Magnus Hepburn said, his mind still on his sister.

Bothwell shrugged.

'She seems devoted to the Queen.' He hesitated. 'But as far as men are concerned, I thought she showed a marked reserve. Yet I imagine your sister could be a passionate woman. Perhaps with her friend, the Earl of Edinburgh—I suspect he wants more than just friendship. But, even with him, she retains a measure of reticence.'

'She's been ill-treated by fate,' McNaughton said. 'She was the one who was to marry my father.'

'That was over ten years ago,' Bothwell scoffed. 'Surely she can't still be affected by that.'

'I am,' McNaughton said. 'Every time I look at that portrait of my father,' he paused, looking toward the painting that hung over the fireplace, 'I am consumed with hatred for the person who took his life.'

McKeever looked concerned at this rekindling of tragic memories.

'Gavin, I hope you never entertained the slightest doubt about my grandfather. . . .'

'No, no, Joseph. I never believed old Murdo had anything to do with the crime. Indeed the thought that your grandfather died so unjustly makes me even more angry. The murderer killed your grandfather too, McKeever, as sure as he killed my father. And he's still free. Never a day passes that I don't look up at that portrait and vow vengeance. Surely you feel the same?'

'I used to. It nearly destroyed me. But life goes on. One cannot live with such hatred forever.'

'I can,' McNaughton said coldly.

Bothwell shook his head.

'Och Gavin, the past is past. Concentrate on today.'

'It is not in my nature to forgive or forget, Bothwell. I tell you, as God is my witness, one day I will have my revenge.'

131

— XVIII —

MARIE watched in silence as the young Francis was solemnly crowned King of France at Rheims. As Queen of Scotland, Mary had no need of further coronation. Outside, rain lashed against the roof and windows and the wind howled as if in mourning. There was no great display of pageantry owing to the recent tragic death of Henry II, and Francis wore a coat of black velvet, while Mary alone of all the ladies present was not dressed in dark colours.

Soon after the coronation, the Court of France, with Francis, Mary and Catherine di' Medici at its head, resumed its endless travelling. To Marie's dismay, however, Guthrie Jamieson accompanied them wherever they went. He had become almost a permanent presence at Court since he had won the young Queen's admiration by ridding her of the detested Madame de Paroy. Every time Marie saw him now, her heart sank. She knew what he was planning, she knew the terrible threat he posed to the Dauphin, and yet there seemed to be no way she could warn Mary without implicating herself. Marie decided there was nothing for it but to confront Jamieson and plead with him to abandon his plan.

Her opportunity came while the Court was in residence at Amboise Chateau on the Loire. One evening, after dinner, Marie sought out Jamieson. She found him alone in the formal garden.

'Ah, what a very pleasant surprise!' he remarked. 'I had thought you were avoiding me.'

'Enough of your flattery, my Lord! I have to speak with you.'

'Of course. I presume you have come to tell me that you have seen sense and are ready to help me with my *endeavours*,' He said, a wicked smile flashing across his handsome face.

'No!' Marie gasped. 'How could you think that? I have come to beg you to stop this madness and leave the Queen and her husband in peace.'

'An admirable thought, my dear. Your concern for the Queen does you credit, but you are meddling in matters you do not fully understand. I am afraid that things have already gone too far, wheels have been set in motion that cannot be stopped. Even if I wanted to, there is nothing I can do now. The Dauphin is already doomed.'

For a moment Marie was unable to speak, shocked at what she had just heard.

'Oh Guthrie, what have you done?' she whispered.

'All I have done is try to do what is best for my country and for my Queen.'

'Liar!' Marie hissed. 'You care for nothing but the English gold that will doubtless reward your treachery.'

'You may believe what you like,' Jamieson replied, 'so long as you keep your mouth shut. At any rate, it is too late to save Francis now, and I would, of course, deny everything. Who do you think your precious Mary would believe? Her devoted protector the gallant Earl of Edinburgh, or the Bishop of Moray's bastard daughter? I think we both know the answer. . . .'

As she watched Jamieson turn away and walk back

towards the Chateau, Marie knew he was right. She knew she could say nothing, but how was she going to face Mary knowing what she did?

✤ ✤ ✤

One evening over their embroidery, the Queen mentioned to Marie the names Lord and Lady Cairncross. This had meant nothing to Marie until the Queen said,

'Of course Lady Agnes's family has been touched by tragedy.'

The Queen's ladies were all ears, their needles poised in mid-air, waiting.

'Her grandfather was executed for murder.' Mary turned to Marie. 'It was only later, my dear Marie, that I was shocked to discover the victim had been your betrothed.'

'Why have Lord and Lady Cairncross come to France, I wonder?' Marie managed.

The Queen shrugged and continued with her embroidery.

Later Mary suddenly said,

'It is time you were married, Marie. Why have you no young gallant courting you? Or does our good Earl of Edinburgh come into this category. You often seem to be flirting with him when he is at Court.'

If only she knew the truth, Marie thought bitterly.

'No, no. Definitely not. I mean, he is a friend,' she lied, 'but I feel nothing else for him.'

'Well,' Mary said, 'I have heard him give you some pretty compliments.'

'I care nothing for his compliments or those of any other man. I am perfectly content to continue serving your Majesty.'

'Nonsense. It is not natural. You must find some worthy gentleman before you are too old.'

Marie smiled.

'I'm not yet thirty.'

134

'I was married when I was barely fifteen,' replied the Queen.

'Royal marriages are different.'

'Love is love. I have the love of my husband. I want you, my dear Marie, to be loved as well. You have my love, of course, but the tender love of a husband is your right, as well as mine. Are you sure you have no warmer feelings than friendship for the Earl of Edinburgh?'

Marie avoided her eyes. 'Maybe . . . my original misfortune means that I am fated to be on my own.'

'Quite the reverse, I'd say. You were unfortunate, I agree, in losing your first love. But that is all the more reason now for you to seek happiness elsewhere.' She tapped one of her long white fingers against her chin.

'Very well. If you will not have the gallant Earl of Edinburgh, we must arrange festivities and balls to which I will invite other noblemen of the highest quality. Nothing less will do for my dear Marie. And who knows, if all goes well, I will also pay for a magnificent wedding for you. That is a promise.'

Marie smiled.

'You are too generous for your own good, your Majesty. But, honestly I have no inclination.'

This was not true. Often she felt strong impulses and passionate desires which she struggled to control. But how could she even think about romance now, weighed down as she was by guilt. By not telling the Queen everything, Marie felt she too had become a traitor. It was all Guthrie Jamieson's fault, and how she hated him for it.

✤   ✤   ✤

At the French Court masques and banquets were noisy, colourful affairs enjoyed by all the ladies, young and old. Even the preparations were a great excitement and pleasure.

The Queen and her companions loved to dress up in male

135

attire, while the men painted their faces and dressed as women in silks and satins and furs sugared with jewels. Outrageous flirting and hilarity were the order of the day. The Queen insisted that Marie join in the merrymaking, although Marie studiously avoided the Earl of Edinburgh and made a point of flirting with a masked man, even allowing him to steal a few kisses. At one point in the evening, however, the Earl caught up with her and, before she could protest, he had whirled her into a dance. Once again, she was surprised at the iron hardness of his body and the almost painful strength of his grip on her.

'Take your hands off me, you filthy traitor.'

'What can you possibly mean?' he laughed. 'This is neither the time nor the place to speak of politics. I for one have other things in mind on this merry occasion,' he said mockingly.

She tried unsuccessfully to break away from his embrace.

'We are two of a kind, you and I, admit it.'

'No,' she replied.

'Oh yes! And one way or another, I'm going to bed you.'

'Your conceit appals me.'

'Conceit has nothing to do with it. I'm just stating a fact.'

'It is not a fact, sir. It is only a figment of your lurid imagination. It is nothing more than wishful thinking.'

'I think we both know it's more than that!'

'No, we do not!'

Finally, she broke away from him and returned to her previous partner. Later, as the *maids d'honneur* prepared the Queen for bed, they all laughingly exchanged stories of their adventures of the evening.

'Ah, there is hope for you yet, my dear Marie.' The Queen clapped her hands enthusiastically when she heard about the stolen kisses. 'My plans are bearing fruit.'

✤   ✤   ✤

Then, a few days later, word came from Scotland that the Dowager's health was failing fast.

The subsequent news of the agonising death of the Queen Mother from dropsy was kept from Mary for ten days. When the Cardinal of Lorraine eventually broke the news, Mary collapsed. Marie and the Marys were acutely distressed for her and fluttered over her, doing their best to nurse and support her. But she refused any sort of comfort or consolation from anyone.

Heartbroken, Mary retired to bed and stayed there. Only gradually did she return to the routine of Court life.

And now she had something else to worry about. Francis's health had worsened since his accession to the throne. His skin now had a greyish pallor and was blotched with red patches. Different diagnoses were made. It was claimed he suffered from a number of dreadful ailments. A wasting disease, possibly leprosy, was hinted at. Worst of all were the rumours that he was being slowly poisoned.

Marie guessed the truth, yet did nothing. How could she say anything now? It was too late. Several times, she almost broke down and told the Queen, but at the last moment her resolve always failed her and, racked with guilt, she remained a helpless onlooker as the Dauphin's condition deteriorated.

As his condition grew worse, everyone at Court shrank back from Francis in distaste. There was only one person he could turn to and that was Mary. She never shrank from him. She, the great beauty of the Court, the most desirable woman in the country, never failed to show patience, tenderness and loyal friendship to her husband.

As she sat one day with Marie, her embroidery lying untouched beside her, Mary broke down and wept, saying,

'I fear the end is near for my poor husband.'

Marie looked away to avoid meeting the Queen's gaze. 'Can't the physicians do more to help him?' she asked.

'So far none of their potions seem to be doing any good.

They want to keep him in bed but Francis was always happiest when he was active. Now he can hardly move.'

They fell silent. Although she said nothing, Marie was consumed with guilt. She had betrayed her friend. The Dauphin was dying and there was absolutely nothing she could do about it.

✤   ✤   ✤

Within days, Francis was seized by a fainting fit followed by a fever. A large swelling had appeared behind his left ear. He was violently sick and in agony with head pains. Mary never left his side, nursing him and trying to comfort him.

Rumours flew around the Court. A Huguenot valet had put a poisonous powder in the King's nightcap. An English spy had poisoned him while he slept. An Orleans barber had poured poison in his ear while cutting his hair. Catherine di' Medici publicly sought answers in the occult, although many pointed the finger at her. But nothing helped Francis— not Mary's patient and devoted nursing in his darkened chamber, not the manifold remedies tried, not the rages of the Guises.

All Mary could do was try to alleviate her husband's suffering, and to that end she sent for Ambroise Pané, a Huguenot who was the best surgeon in France. But it was to no avail.

Finally, a month before his seventeenth birthday, the King's ordeal came to an end.

Marie later went to attend to Mary in her darkened mourning chamber lit only by tapers. Mary was the only person in the Court who had abandoned herself to passionate grief.

'Dear Marie,' she whispered, 'I am desolate. I have not only lost my loving husband, but a friend and dear companion of my childhood and youth. He was always part of my life, as far back as I can remember.'

138

Although full of remorse about the Dauphin, Marie was ashamed to admit to herself that she was relieved it was all over. Perhaps now she could put this dreadful episode behind her and make a fresh start.

*　　　*　　　*

But the harsh realities of royal life were all too soon brought home to her. Only one day after her son's death, Catherine di' Medici made an inventory of the crown jewels and asked Mary to return them to her.

Marie realised exactly what this signified—that their time in France was coming to an end.

— XIX —

ALTHOUGH they hardly met now, their shared secrets bound Marie and Jamieson together. She could see it in his eyes. He had seen her commit bloody murder, and he had involved her in the death of the Dauphin. Fear of what he would do next kept her mind forever focused on him, even when he was not there. Yet on the surface, as far as anyone else could see, they were still friends.

She despised herself, but she also felt murderously angry at him for what he had turned her into, a traitor and an accomplice to murder. More and more often she wished that somehow he would just disappear, go away and never come back. Sometimes she was horrified to find herself imagining what it would be like to kill him.

But the plain fact was that Guthrie Jamieson had never revealed her secrets to anyone. Why should she be so apprehensive about him ruining her now? Even if he wanted to, he couldn't without risking bringing about his own downfall.

Still she worried. And each time he returned to the Court, she experienced yet another kind of agitation. A physical need had been awakened and was growing into a torment of desire. She felt deeply ashamed.

140

She didn't even *like* the Earl of Edinburgh, she hated him. But that did not seem to matter to him. One day as she sat alone, engrossed in her embroidery, the door suddenly flew open and Jamieson strode into the room. Marie immediately stood up, surprised, and he grabbed her and pinioned her against his massive rock of a body. In a panic, she struggled and stamped on his feet and was about to knee him in the groin when he jerked up his own knee to prevent her.

'No,' he said, 'I have a better use for that part of my anatomy.'

Despite her struggles and the way she jerked her face from side to side, his mouth found hers.

After a long kiss, she surfaced to tell him breathlessly,

'For God's sake, leave me alone! I hate you, you pig!'

He just laughed and kissed her again. Then he carried her through to the bedchamber. She still blushed with shame when she thought of how they had behaved like animals. The grunts and growls, all the animal noises, had echoed and re-echoed in her head, firing her senses long after he had left her bed.

That had been the first of many couplings between them. Soon the Earl began to insist that she marry him.

'No, I cannot,' she told him. 'I don't love you and that's the truth of the matter.'

'Is that so important?' he asked.

'It is for me,' she said.

'But we enjoy each other so much. You are far more passionate than any other woman I've ever known. Indeed, you have spoiled me for any other woman.'

'I will never marry you, sir.'

'We shall see,' he said.

He was corrupting her, changing her character. She had always vowed that she would never end up like her mother. She would never be in any way dependent on a man's whims, particularly not a man as dangerous and deceitful as Guthrie Jamieson.

One day Marie might marry, but it had to be for love, not for money or power or position. However, she had never reckoned on this overwhelming physical passion. It was something different, separate, totally self-indulgent and selfish. It had nothing to do with love.

XX

THE death of Francis had left Mary, Queen of Scots in a precarious position. She was no longer Queen of France and she was surrounded by enemies. A return to Scotland seemed her only option, and by the summer of 1561 the decision had been made. Mary and her chosen courtiers, servants, and ladies-in-waiting, accompanied by the Earl of Edinburgh, were to leave for Scotland.

Marie felt that a net was closing in around her. For her, returning to Scotland was like stepping back into a nightmare. She had hoped the murder of the Duke of Glasgow was buried in the past, a dreadful episode that had long been forgotten, but the prospect of the journey and the thought of setting foot once more on Scottish soil brought all her fears flooding back. She tried a thousand times to tell herself she was being ridiculous. After all, even at the time of the murder, no-one had suspected her. As far as everyone else was concerned, the guilty person had been found, revenge had been taken and that was an end to it. In fact, it was the thought of being responsible for not one death but two, and worse still for the death of an innocent man, that disturbed Marie most.

But even so, she told herself, there was nothing she could do about any of it now.

Then, to make things worse, Effie Dalgliesh wrote from Orkney. It was a long, rambling letter in which Effie upbraided Marie for her lack of correspondence.

'You could be dead for all I knew. Or I could be long dead for all you cared. As it is I haven't been well for some time and only now, knowing (from every other source but you!) that at long last you are returning to Scotland, I feel able to make the effort to join you and hope and pray that you will remember your filial duties and take care of me in my feeble old age. . . .'

In her late forties, Marie thought derisively, her mother was surely not as yet in her 'feeble old age'. Above all, on no account could Effie be allowed to join Mary's Court. No doubt the young Queen would be generous enough to allow her to do exactly that, but remembering Effie's empty-headed foolishness and her dangerously loose tongue, Marie knew she could never trust her.

✤ ✤ ✤

When all the preparations had been completed, the Queen sent for the Earl of Bothwell, to act as Admiral of the fleet which would take her back to Scotland. The Earl of Edinburgh was to have the honour of commanding one of the leading galleys, which would be on the lookout for English men-o-war, but would also carry the Queen's horses to Scotland. These magnificent beasts, powerfully-built white stallions, were to be the centrepiece of Mary's magnificent procession through the streets of Edinburgh. It was only natural that the Queen should entrust this precious cargo into the safe keeping of Guthrie Jamieson, one of her most trusted courtiers.

On hearing that he had been chosen for this task, Jamieson

could hardly believe his luck. Randolph had been insisting for some time that he find a way of delivering the Queen of Scots into the hands of the English, promising a reward beyond even Jamieson's wildest dreams if he was successful. Now, he had the perfect opportunity, and he quickly despatched letters to Randolph informing him of the exact route the Queen's fleet would take. Soon after, he received word that an English fleet would be ready and waiting to ambush the French galleys. All Jamieson had to do was to make sure the Queen sailed straight into the trap.

✤   ✤   ✤

A few days later the journey began. A brilliant cavalcade accompanied Queen Mary, daughter of the house of Guise, and her companions to the coast. In gilded carriages bearing the arms of Guise and Lorraine, rode the brothers, the Duke and the Cardinal, who were to see Mary safely on board her ship. They sat, hair and pointed beards well groomed, gold earrings glittering, white satin robes vivid with large red crosses. Mary's equally splendid carriage followed theirs. Then came the rest of the company including the Earl of Edinburgh, Marie and the four Marys.

Mary was wearing a traditional French gown of cloth of silver, with a headdress shaped like a scallop shell and decorated with pearls. A wide necklace, like a collar studded with pearls, framed her lovely oval face.

Marie was filled with apprehension but struggling, for the Queen's sake, to appear composed. The Queen herself looked pale and acutely distressed. Nothing augured well—even the weather was hazy and dull despite the fact that it was high summer.

Finally, as the great galleys of France pulled away from the shore, the tragic figure of the Queen could be seen weeping at the poop of the leading ship. She wasn't afraid of the six hundred mile journey to her kingdom, even though she knew that she would be in danger of being captured by the English, whose ships patrolled these seas. Up until that morning, she had displayed admirable courage in keeping to her decision to risk everything by going to Scotland. Now, the reality of leaving her beloved France struck her. She realised that she was bidding goodbye to all she had known, and loved, and held dear, for what seemed her whole life. As the galleys surged into the unknown, Mary clung to the part of the ship which was still nearest to the French shore and sobbed.

'*Adieu* France, *adieu*. Will I ever see you again?'

— XXI —

MEANWHILE, the Earl of Edinburgh stood at the prow of the galley that was conveying the Queen's splendid white horses to Scotland. But his thoughts did not dwell on the Queen's arrival in her native country. Instead he saw this journey as the culmination of one of his greatest ambitions—the union of the Crowns of England and Scotland. And, of course, if all went well, such an outcome would also make him a very wealthy man indeed. His musings were rudely interrupted by the ship's Captain, Lefevre—a stocky, piratical figure who always wore a wicked-looking cutlass at his side.

'*Bonjour*, my Lord of Edinburgh. I trust all is well.'

'Very well indeed, Captain,' Jamieson replied. 'And how stands the wind for England?'

'Not so good,' Lefevre frowned. 'And I like not the look of the sky ahead. Maybe we will have fog before we reach land.'

'Damnation!' thought Jamieson. One thing he had not allowed for was the weather. In a thick sea fog it would be only too easy to sail straight past the waiting English without ever being seen. If that happened, all his plans would come to nothing.

He looked back towards the shore. Already the land had disappeared in the haze which clung to the horizon, so that their fleet seemed entirely alone on an endless sea.

But Guthrie Jamieson was not one to worry over the future. He took a deep breath of sea air, the salt-laden spray giving him renewed vigour. He turned and took in the sights and sounds around him on the ship, the creak of timbers, the groaning of the many ropes, as taut as sinews, the sharp smell of tar, the bronzed sailors hurrying like rats up and down the rigging as harsh orders were bellowed from the deck. The captain had given strict orders as to how the sails should be set to take best advantage of the unfavourable wind. Jamieson had been pleased to see the eagerness with which his officers leapt to obey their glowering leader. Certainly he seemed a tough, ruthless figure, one who would stand neither argument nor incompetence. An important ally, but a dangerous enemy, Jamieson decided. He would make it his business to befriend the captain.

Later, down in his cabin, Jamieson felt quite at ease, as he poured himself a glass of wine from his personal, and plentiful, supply. They were on course and making reasonable speed, helped greatly by the efforts of the oarsmen on the lower deck. Echoing through the ship Jamieson could hear the rhythmic beat of the drum, the splash of the oars, and the frequent lash of the whip. It mattered nothing to him that the galley slaves were being cruelly abused so that the fleet need spend as little time as possible in English waters.

There was a knock at his door. It was the captain.

'Ah, captain, you have come at just the right time. You will join me?' Jamieson held up his wine glass.

The captain's glower lingered for a moment, but the prospect of wine had a powerful effect. His weather-beaten face cracked into a devilish smile as he advanced towards the table.

'Yes, I thank you,' he said, sitting opposite the Earl and

peering greedily into the recently opened wine crate from which Jamieson extracted a bottle.

'You provide well for your comfort, I see,' said the captain, running a leathery tongue over his lips.

'And you for yours, captain—you have your wife aboard, I see.'

'Wife? Ah, you mean Lolita. She is very beautiful, yes? She is one of the many treasures I have captured on my travels.' Lefevre leered across at the Earl.

Jamieson had caught glimpses of the captain's woman. She had the dark complexion, jet-black hair and fine bones of a gypsy, and her eyes burned with fiery passion. She behaved like a wildcat, but Lefevre had evidently tamed her, for towards him she behaved like a devoted slave.

For Jamieson, however, she had had nothing but a smouldering hatred, from the instant she set eyes on him. She was a creature of primitive, animal instincts, and some strange intuition seemed to warn her that here was a man not to be trusted. To Jamieson this was a novelty, but she did not figure in his plans, so he quickly dismissed her from his mind.

The captain tasted his wine. 'And this wine is most excellent.' He raised his glass, already half empty, then finished the contents in a single gulp.

'What about the weather? Is there any sign of the fog you predicted?' A trace of anxiety belied Jamieson's calm demeanour, but the captain did not notice, being more interested in the bottle, which had been returned to its crate.

'Fog? Pah! Yes, it is in the air, but this does not matter. If we are quick, we will be beyond the reach of the English sea-dogs before they can mount an attack on so large a fleet as ours. But if fog comes, no-one can reach us. Then there will be nothing to disturb our comfort, yes?' The captain laughed and nodded at the crate beside them.

Jamieson forced himself to smile. His mind, however, was working furiously as he tried to think of some way to make sure that not only this ship, but also the Queen's, reached the appointed rendezvous.

'We cannot take chances with the Queen of Scotland, captain. What you say is right—we must be quick, and make certain that we are not intercepted. Can the ship be made to go any faster?'

'Of course, but there will be a cost. Already we are working the oarsmen below harder than is wise. It may be that one or two will die—these things happen—but if you want more speed than this . . .'

'Whatever it takes, captain, you must get us safely to Scotland.'

'It shall be done.'

When the captain had gone, Jamieson sat for a long time, desperately seeking a plan which would ensure that, whatever the outcome of their voyage, it would be to his advantage. His position was not strong, as his treachery was no light undertaking. It had not been easy to persuade his English associates that his plan was foolproof. They had been unwilling to put their reputations at stake by ordering the despatch of an English fleet, at great expense. But Randolph had finally arranged everything, and Jamieson did not intend to let his old friend down.

At least, not while the Englishman could still be of use to him.

✤   ✤   ✤

The following morning, after a large but uninspiring breakfast served in his cabin, the Earl of Edinburgh stepped wearily into the passageway.

He had managed only a few snatches of sleep, and even these had been punctuated by the incessant thump of the drum down below, where the slaves toiled ceaselessly to keep up with the quickened rhythm, the racing pulse-beat, which Jamieson himself had demanded.

His tiredness, the throbbing noise in his head, and perhaps the effects of the large quantity of wine that had accompanied his meditations of the previous evening, combined to disorientate him. He staggered onwards, unsure for the moment where he was, wanting only to escape the fetid stench which assailed his nostrils—the foul odour of unwashed bodies and human excrement.

As he lurched along the passageway, the smell became stronger, and soon he discovered its source.

A hatch in the floor of the passage stood open, and as he approached, the sound of the drum became louder until he could feel as well as hear it. He looked down through the opening, and the vision he saw was to haunt him for the rest of his days. It became for him a vision of hell.

At first, the deck below appeared to be packed with gigantic worms, writhing and straining in a surging mass of ordure. Gradually the scene resolved into human limbs pulling relentlessly on long oars, but the noise and smell were too much for Jamieson's stomach. Retching violently, he staggered towards the light.

Once on deck, he hurried over to the side of the ship and leaned over the rail, gasping gratefully in the clean air.

After a time, he started to feel better, and began to take in his surroundings.

Out on the water, he could see two other ships, one quite close by, which he recognised as the Queen's galley. The other was almost lost in the morning haze, but it looked like the Admiral's own ship.

He moved to the other side of the ship and looked around for the rest of the fleet. The sea was smooth, calm and quite deserted. He looked again, scanning the horizon, but could see nothing at all. In fact, the horizon itself was hard to locate, as both the sea and the sky were grey and flat. Jamieson did not like the look of this. He went in search of the captain.

He found Lefevre overseeing the plotting of their position on a huge chart. The two others with him were listening intently to his stream of commands. Then they hurried off to carry out his orders.

'Good day, captain.'

'Ah, my Lord, I see that you are awake at last.'

'Where is the rest of the fleet? I see only two ships.'

'The fog, it comes now. Already there are patches. Soon it may be complete. It is necessary that we do not sail too close together, or we may collide. We have just received the Admiral's orders. We are to maintain our course. Your Queen will go further to the south, away from the English coast. Soon we will be on our own.'

Jamieson was momentarily dumbfounded. This was terrible. He must think of something.

'Surely, captain, someone must stay close to the Queen's ship—she cannot be left alone in these hostile waters. Her captain must be ordered to follow us.'

'But this is madness. Once the fog descends, we have no way of seeing, and the sound of our oars will prevent us from hearing. There must be distance between us.'

'No, captain, I insist. The Queen's ship must be kept in sight for as long as possible. I will not desert my sovereign. Have her captain follow us. Our route will be the shorter.'

'Pah! You would have us all killed. But not on my ship, my Lord, do you hear? On this ship it is *I* who give the orders.'

Jamieson's voice softened, and a note of menace entered it.

'As you wish, captain,' he said, 'but if any harm should befall her Majesty as a result of your cowardice, whose head do you think it will be that swings from the yard-arm?'

'Do you call me a coward, my Lord?' Lefevre's voice also had become quiet, but the lowering of his black brows, and the movement of his right hand to the cutlass at his side, spoke eloquently of the immediate danger Jamieson faced.

'Not at all, captain,' he smiled. 'I have every confidence that you will do everything in your power to safeguard the

152

Queen of Scotland. Your French masters would, I am sure, share that confidence.'

Lefevre was motionless for a moment. Then he seemed to relax. Turning to his men, he barked more instructions. Then he fixed his gaze on the Earl.

'Very good, my Lord, we will do this thing your way. But'—he glowered darkly—'the responsibility is now yours. It is perhaps fortunate for you that, should we collide with and sink your Queen in the fog, you will not live long enough to pay the price of your folly.'

Jamieson's calm had been restored now that he was back in control. His smile at Lefevre was arrogant and mirthless.

'Trust me, captain. I accept full responsibility for the Queen's safety.'

❖ ❖ ❖

The Queen, accompanied by Marie, paced the deck of her ship. From the moment France had disappeared from view the previous day, she had been anxious to be in Scotland as soon as possible. Each pace she took represented for her another step nearer to her destination, although a mounting sense of the difficulties that lay before her made her feel as though she were wading through this sea, instead of skimming swiftly over it.

She forced her thoughts away from her impending responsibilities—for the moment she was being well taken care of by those she trusted. Looking over one side of the ship she saw one of her escort ships. In the breeze she could see the many brightly-coloured flags and pennants streaming out majestically from its masts.

'Oh, look Marie! Those red and green flags flying from the main mast. That must be the Earl of Bothwell.'

She led Marie over to the other side, and pointed out Guthrie Jamieson's ship, identifiable by the blue and white of its flags.

'And there is the Earl of Edinburgh! It is so reassuring to be in such capable hands. We are sure to reach Scotland unharmed with so loyal and brave an escort. Do you not agree that your fears for our safety are unnecessary?'

Marie sensed that the Queen was trying to sound more at ease than she really was, but could find no words of re-assurance. The sight of Jamieson's ship troubled her. Was she never to be rid of that man? Apart from his and Bothwell's ships, they appeared to be alone on the sea. A mist was gradu-ally descending on them. She shivered involuntarily.

The captain of their ship approached deferentially. He stood crisply to attention, before bowing deeply to the Queen.

'Your Majesty, please excuse this interruption. As you can see, there is fog coming upon us. The Admiral is signal-ling that we are to sail on alone, a little to the south. That way we shall avoid any chance of a collision. But you are not to be alarmed, for in a fog we are invisible, and thus per-fectly safe. I guarantee it!' He smiled, revealing a dazzling set of white teeth against the deep tan of his face and the navy blue of his immaculate doublet. Again he bowed.

'Thank you captain. I am sure that under your protection we need have nothing to fear.' She looked at Marie, who was lost in thought, and still staring out towards Jamieson's ship.

The captain turned as one of his officers approached. They seemed to argue for a moment, then the captain turned to the ladies, with a concerned expression.

'Your Majesty, *mademoiselle*,' he bowed to each of them in turn, 'there is another signal. The Earl of Edinburgh wishes to escort us personally through the fog. He asks that we fol-low him for as long as it is possible to see. But this is most *dangereux*, I think.'

The Queen gazed over at the Earl of Edinburgh's ship, carving its way purposefully through the hostile grey water.

'Ah, captain, it is indeed heartening to have so many loyal friends about me. Let us stay near to my courageous Earl, as he requests, for as long as is possible.'

Marie's hands had gripped the ship's rail tightly when she heard of Jamieson's keenness to have them near him. She prayed for the fog to come down quickly and hide them.

Her prayer was soon answered. Bothwell's ship veered away, while Jamieson's came closer, so that they could even make out the figure of the Earl himself as he stood calmly watching them. Then it was as though a veil had been drawn between them, uneven at first, before becoming a heavy blanket that quickly blotted out the image of the Earl, after which his whole ship simply dissolved before their eyes.

Marie relaxed her grip and breathed a deep sigh of relief.

⚜　　⚜　　⚜

'Curse this thrice-damned fog!' snarled Jamieson, as he surveyed the grey pall which still hung over them on the afternoon of their third day at sea.

He had just consulted with Captain Lefevre, and had been told their approximate position. Of course, in the fog it was not possible to be sure, but they must be approaching the area where the English fleet would be lying in wait.

Since the previous morning, when Mary's galley had faded from his view, he had frequently scanned the horizon. Lefevre had sent lookouts up the masts to keep a constant watch, for the Queen's ship might well still be near, and in any case the Straits of Dover, which they had to pass through, would be littered with all manner of vessels. Their speed had slackened a little, but they knew that best use could be made of the fog by travelling as far towards safe waters as was possible before it lifted.

They had come through the Straits without incident, and were now on their way past the mouth of the Thames—the area fixed for the rendezvous. Lefevre had been a persistent visitor to Jamieson's cabin, clearly torn between the lure of the wine and the charms of Lolita. The roguish captain had become quite talkative once the wine had loosened his tongue, and Jamieson had listened to numerous stories of desperate courage and adventure on the high seas. The Earl even found himself being drawn into the spirit of comradeship, and had recounted a couple of heart-stopping tales from his own past.

As Jamieson leaned against the ship's rail, the sky suddenly lightened. He instantly looked up, and almost cried out as he caught sight of the sun, just discernible through the thinning fog.

In a moment the sea around them came into focus, and suddenly they were in clear water. Looking back, Jamieson saw the thick bank of fog from which they had emerged. Ahead were similar patches of grey mist, but for the moment they could see around them.

'A sail! A sail to starboard!' The shout came from one of the lookouts, perched high up in the rigging. All eyes turned to scan the sea on their right side.

Jamieson hurried to the poop, where the captain was standing. Lefevre had a powerful telescope, which he was looking through as Jamieson approached.

'What ship is that?' demanded the Earl.

'It is far off, but it is the Queen's ship, almost certainly,' replied Lefevre.

'Quick, man, steer towards her then!'

Lefevre regarded him closely. He could not understand why this Scottish nobleman should need to be so near to his Queen. Perhaps she was more to him than his Queen, perhaps they were . . . Lefevre grinned wickedly at the thought.

'So, you wish to be able to wave to your Mary, *hein*?'

'How dare—' Jamieson stopped himself. It might serve his purpose better if Lefevre thought he was in love with the Queen. He laughed.

'Take me close enough, captain, and I'll show you.'

Lefevre gave the order, and they turned slightly, so as to intercept the distant galley. They increased speed, and could soon easily identify the flags of Mary's galley.

'A sail, a sail!' came the cry again from one of the lookouts.

Jamieson looked up into the rigging and saw an out-stretched arm. It was pointing a little to the left, the side away from Mary's ship. He turned to the captain, who had swung his telescope into action again.

'*Mon Dieu!* It is an English warship,' said Lefevre with relish. 'Now we shall have some sport, *n'est-ce pas?*'

'Remember, captain, our first duty is to stay close to the Queen and protect her.'

'Yes indeed, my Lord, and we shall protect her best by sinking these filthy English scum! Ramming speed, I think!'

'No!' Sinking the English ship did not fit in with Jamieson's plans at all. With fog patches all around, they might not chance upon another, and his plan to hand Mary over to his friends would fail. He had to act now. As calmly as he could, he continued,

'We must place ourselves between them and the Queen, and then shield her galley as we go around them.' Jamieson was aware that their galleys would be faster in a straight line than the English sailing ship, but were less manoeuvrable. Since the English ship was across their path, they would have to circle around it, and this would give the English time to attack them. With luck, both galleys would be forced to sur-render. As long as Lefevre could be made to co-operate . . .

'*Diable!* Are you insane? We must attack!'

'You have your orders, captain. The Queen's ship must be closely protected, at all costs.' Jamieson turned away and stared across at Mary's galley, not far off now to their right, as it carved its way through the water.

Both galleys began a slow turn to the right, so that the Earl of Edinburgh was, as he intended, placed between his Queen and her enemies.

A faint rumble came across the water to Jamieson's ears, and then a sudden scream pierced the air overhead as a sailor fell from the rigging and crashed to the deck with a sickening thud. The English had opened fire, and great cannon balls began to tear through the sails of the galley, ripping canvas, snapping ropes, and smashing through flesh and bones as if through soft fruit. The Queen's horses, sheltering as best they could in the hold in the fore-part of the ship, began neighing in terror as they sensed the approaching danger. They were tethered tightly, and had no way of escaping the brutal onslaught from the English cannon, which tore into the galley with increasing rapidity.

As the English ship closed in, its fire became more accurate. Jamieson watched as, all around him, the wood of the galley splintered and flew into the air, as though a giant hand were wielding an invisible hammer indiscriminately, and with great wrath, intent on turning the ship into matchwood.

A terrible rending of timber sounded behind Jamieson, and he turned just in time to see a heavy wooden beam swinging towards him. One of the ship's officers was beside him, and was caught in the face, the force of the blow hurling him into Jamieson, who was thus spared the full force of the impact. Even so, the breath was knocked out of him and he was flung headlong onto the deck, his head thumping cruelly against the planks. As he picked himself up, he saw blood on his hands and chest. In his dazed state, he was not sure if it was his own or, more likely, that of the officer, who was now lying groaning at his feet, one side of his face literally torn off and nowhere to be seen. Jamieson turned away and was sick.

He picked the officer up, trying not to look at him, and struggled below to where the wounded were being laid out. The ship's doctor, in fact more of a ship's butcher, was there, but in many cases was unable to do anything other than chop off shattered limbs, and apply unclean rags to staunch the flow of blood from gaping wounds. Men were then left alone, in unimaginable pain, to live or die as they would. The stench of blood and death was more sickening than the chaos on deck, and Jamieson was almost relieved to return to the open air.

Lefevre had ordered their own guns to open fire, so that soon a cloud of smoke rose over the ships, and it became difficult to see what was happening. It was like a new kind of fog, a black, evil-smelling, clinging mist. Jamieson's throat became choked with the acrid fumes of gunpowder, and his whole head throbbed with the noise of the guns. Everywhere men were running and shouting, some issuing orders, but many staggering blindly, with terrible wounds, screaming and writhing in agony, desperate to escape the slaughter that was sweeping over the deck and turning its shattered planking into a field of death.

The captain, his forehead grazed by a splinter and oozing blood, emerged from the smoke, shouting new orders in a hoarse voice. Jamieson went to his side, and heard instructions being given to turn and ram the English ship. A moment later Jamieson felt the wind on his face as they changed course.

Lefevre turned to him.

'We cannot go on like this! We are—how you say?—sitting ducks. Now we do it my way. Your sword-arm will be busy in a few moments, my Lord. Prepare for boarding!'

Lefevre, a demonic look in his eye, drew his wicked-looking cutlass and swung it above his head. A cheer rose from those near him, and a motley array of swords, pikes and boat-hooks rose and whirled in anticipation of imminent action.

'Prepare for boarding! Prepare for boarding!' the cry resounded around the ship as the contingent of French soldiers, who were stationed on board for just this purpose, prepared to earn their pay.

Jamieson, smiling darkly at the captain, drew his sword.

The captain grinned at him. 'It is good, my Lord, yes? We defend your beloved Queen now in the best way possible. Cold steel and hot blood, *hein*?' He laughed devilishly.

'Yes, captain, it is good,' Jamieson, still smiling, agreed. The stress of impending combat had focused his mind, and he was ready now to do what had to be done. He had calmly resigned himself to the fact that his plan had failed. The Queen's galley would not come to their assistance—it was unthinkable that Mary should be placed in such a dangerous position—but would make off towards Scotland and home as fast as possible. He, the Earl of Edinburgh, would be hailed as her saviour, nobly sacrificing himself for her. He could not help laughing at the irony of his position.

But, he calculated, all was not yet lost. This galley would make a valuable prize, and some of the Queen's horses would surely have survived. If he could deliver the ship to the English, perhaps he could still emerge from this episode with his reputation, both with the Scots and the English, intact.

There was little time for further thought. The English were almost upon them. Jamieson decided that his best policy would be to keep close to the captain, and await his opportunity to betray the Frenchman and ensure the surrender of the ship.

Out of the smoke of battle, the English ship emerged alongside them. A loud shout went up all around him, and to his horror Jamieson found himself being crushed and propelled violently forward, near the head of a seething torrent of French soldiers, towards a solid wall of English swords and muskets. Desperately he tried to melt back into the crowd, but it was too dense. The hideous noise and the smell of sweat were overpowering, and he was unable to move his arms, so tightly packed was the mass of bodies.

Completely trapped, he looked ahead again, to where the English waited, and knew that his end had come.

✤   ✤   ✤

A ghostly grey mist kept the Queen's galley hidden as it neared Scotland. Then, on the morning of their arrival at Leith, yet another thick fog descended. Thick fogs were not unusual along the Scottish coast but, especially in view of the ill-fortune that had dogged them on their voyage, the royal party took this as another bad omen.

At long last, the galleys dropped anchor in the safety of

160

Leith harbour, and Mary, Queen of Scots once more set foot on Scottish soil. Despite the loss of her magnificent horses, not to mention her friend the Earl of Edinburgh, she held her head high and Marie was filled with admiration at the sight of the Queen's tall, commanding appearance. But for herself, Marie felt nothing but foreboding. For her, Scotland seemed an alien country full of danger. Yet she could not help feeling an overwhelming sense of relief that she was free at last from the threats and demands of Guthrie Jamieson.

PART III

SCOTLAND
1561

— XXII —

FAR out at sea, Jamieson shivered in his cabin, greedily quenching his thirst with a long draught of wine. His wounds still ached, but at least he was alive.

'That was quite a close run thing, my Lord,' laughed Randolph as he settled back in his chair and poured himself some wine.

'Too close,' agreed Jamieson. He took another drink. The heat of battle had left him, but the memory of his desperate fight for survival was as vivid in his mind as if he were still on the deck of the galley, with hatred and death still pressing tightly around him.

Never before had he stared death so clearly in the face as he had then, so near to his English allies and yet so far.

He could see, as in a dream, his advance towards the English line, could hear the crack of their muskets, could smell the stench of fear, sweat and gunpowder.

It was, incredibly, the musket fire that had saved his life—it caused the French ranks to break, as men threw themselves aside to avoid the leaden death it carried. Jamieson himself was pushed, still part of the charging horde of men, away to one side, from where he was finally able to break free of those near him.

Gasping for air, he had allowed the French advance to continue without him. He looked back to where Lefevre had been standing.

The captain had waded into the thick of the fighting, and his cutlass could clearly be seen whirling in the air and then plunging into the English ranks, to rise again dripping with fresh English blood.

All around the Earl similar battles were raging. The general impression was one of mad confusion, but there was to each individual conflict a demonic purpose, a primitive will to survive. Jamieson, keeping a careful watch all around him, made his way towards the captain.

His way was blocked by a giant of a man, English undoubtedly, who without hesitation lunged at him with a mighty sword already stained bright red. Of course the English soldiers knew nothing of Jamieson's identity or his treacherous purpose. He therefore had no option but to fight.

He darted to the right, the great sword grazing his left arm slightly, and then he advanced swiftly with his own weapon aimed at the giant's throat. For a man of such weight, the Englishman was surprisingly agile. He stepped back and brought his sword to bear again, swiping powerfully at Jamieson, who almost tripped as he retreated hastily.

The Englishman lunged again, and caught Jamieson's sword near the hilt, wrenching it from the Earl's grasp. The giant grinned hungrily as he stepped in for the kill. Jamieson took one pace back and felt solid timbers behind him. He looked about wildly for a weapon.

The Englishman stood motionless for a second, his expression changing from one of triumph to one of shock. Then his eyes closed, and he pitched forward onto his face, landing right at Jamieson's feet. The Earl looked up in surprise, and met the gaze of Lefevre, who with a lascivious grin was withdrawing the cutlass which he had plunged deep into the Englishman's back.

'I see you were having a small difficulty, my Lord. There is no difficulty now, yes? Come, this way.'

He led Jamieson to the stern-castle of the galley, where his men were grouping. The fight was going badly for them, as the English had come aboard in great numbers. If the French were not to be slaughtered *en masse*, thought Jamieson, they must surrender now. But Lefevre was again slashing madly at the English with his cutlass, determined, it seemed, to fight to the death.

So be it, thought Jamieson. If the captain wished to die, then he, the Earl of Edinburgh, would see to it that he did. The fact that Lefevre had saved his life a few moments before did not cross his mind. He moved towards the Frenchman, unsheathing his dagger as he went.

The English were advancing steadily now, and most of the French were lying dead or dying on the deck. Jamieson had to pick his way carefully to avoid tripping. He reached the captain's side, and shouted,

'Captain, this is futile, we must surrender at once!'

'Pah! I shall die before I lose my ship to these pigs!'

'As you wish, captain.' Without hesitation, Jamieson plunged his dagger into the Frenchman's back.

Lefevre spun round, staring at him in wide-eyed astonishment. As blood began to trickle from his open mouth, a single word escaped from his lips—'*Merde!*' The cutlass dropped from his hand, and he clutched desperately at Jamieson, before his legs gave way beneath him and he slithered down on to the deck, to join the other corpses, French and English, who had given their lives as part of the treacherous plan masterminded by the Earl of Edinburgh.

Lefevre's death marked the end of the battle. As if a signal had been given, men drew apart. After the noise of battle the silence was intense, eerie, broken only by the scraping of timber as the two ships moved against one another.

The English commander marched up to Jamieson.

'Good day, my Lord. You are unhurt?' He surveyed the carnage around them. 'Most regrettable. We had hoped to avoid all this. . . . And the Queen?'

Jamieson shook his head. He suddenly felt dreadfully tired. It was all he could manage to remain standing.

The commander grunted. Then he turned and issued orders for the rounding up of prisoners.

A piercing scream rent the air.

'You dog! You have killed him, you have killed him!' Lolita appeared and ran to where Lefevre had fallen, dropping at his side and taking his head despairingly in her arms. She stroked her lover's hair, sobbing uncontrollably.

After a moment she fell silent, and looked up at Jamieson.

'You did this! You . . .' She rose and stalked towards him, like a lion about to leap on its prey. Her eyes burned with a terrible hatred. Jamieson saw a flash of metal, then suddenly felt a searing pain in his shoulder. He staggered back, clutching his arm, as English soldiers took hold of Lolita and dragged her away, her screams and oaths echoing in Jamieson's head.

The Earl looked at the small jewelled dagger which she had planted in his shoulder. He found he was having difficulty focusing on it. He looked up. As if in a dream, the deck began to swim before his eyes, and his legs felt as though they were disappearing from under him.

With a long sigh, Jamieson slipped gratefully into unconsciousness.

When he came to, he was lying in his cabin, and his old friend Randolph was standing over him, holding a glass of wine.

'Here, my Lord, this will put new life into you.'

Jamieson pulled himself up into a sitting position, and took the proffered glass. He drank deeply, and instantly felt refreshed.

'Ah, nectar, pure nectar,' he sighed.

'Welcome back to the land of the living,' said Randolph. 'I presume, though, that your Scottish friends will at this very moment be mourning your untimely demise.'

'Yes, indeed, my noble sacrifice!' Jamieson smiled.

'How fortunate that you will be able to spend your after-life at the English Court, instead of at the bottom of the sea.'

'Would that I could, my friend. But if I am dead, it might be better if I remain dead—for a time at least.'

Randolph frowned.

'I do not understand.'

'Am I not my Queen's most devoted servant? Have I not shown my willingness to lay down my life for her? Imagine, Randolph, how dear I must now be to her heart. And just think what a joyous welcome would be accorded me if I were to return to Scotland, having escaped from some foul English prison.'

'You would go back?'

'Of course. It would be the crowning irony! And besides, my mission today failed, and I do not like failure. Yes, I shall go back. But not just yet.'

He smiled at Randolph, and continued,

'I must lie low for a time. Somewhere discreet but comfortable.'

'I have an excellent hunting lodge on my estate at Oxford. You are most welcome to stay there. What say you?'

'It would be an honour.'

'Good. The thing is settled. All that remains is for us to make port somewhere where we can avoid sharp eyes and loose tongues. I shall go at once and see to it.'

When Randolph had gone, Jamieson sipped his wine thoughtfully. He was imagining the reception he would receive one day in Edinburgh, the glory, the adulation, the gratitude of the Queen.

He laughed long and loud.

— XXIII —

'*GARDYLOO!*' came the cry from a tenement window.

Gavin McNaughton, Duke of Glasgow, was making his way down the Canongate, his mind on meeting once more with his good friends Bothwell and Magnus Hepburn over a tankard of ale in one of Edinburgh's finest taverns. He only just heard the cry in time to take evasive action. The foul smelling fulzie splashed down onto the street a few feet away from him, and he looked up to see a face disappearing back through the window. He cursed under his breath and continued more carefully on his way.

Gavin was relieved to reach his destination a few yards further on. Pushing open the heavy tavern door, he peered into the gloom. In a corner, at a table heavy with foaming pewter tankards, sat the two noblemen.

'Greetings, my friends! It is good to see you again, Bothwell, after all this time. I trust you are well?' he said.

'Fighting fit as ever,' said Bothwell heartily. 'Sit and pour yourself a drink.'

'Have you recovered from your voyage home with the Queen—I hear it was not without hazard?'

'Indeed,' Bothwell replied ruefully. 'And I think the Queen found the journey more arduous than the rest of us. We were just talking about her ill-health.'

'What ails her?' the Duke of Glasgow asked.

Bothwell shrugged his powerful shoulders. 'No physician can discover the truth. She has been back in Scotland for weeks now, and she has hardly been seen outside Holyrood. I hear there have been fainting fits, and she has spent much of her time in bed of late.'

'Whatever it is that ails her, it cannot be too serious,' said Magnus, stroking his moustache. 'I visited Holyrood today, and I'm told she will be attending the ball tomorrow as planned.'

To welcome the Queen back to Scotland, a masqued ball had been organised and was due to be held the next evening. McNaughton, Bothwell and Magnus Hepburn had all been invited, along with the most of the Scottish nobility. It would be the biggest celebration to be held in Scotland for some time.

'I hope the Queen has recovered enough to reward you for your part in her safe arrival at Leith,' said Gavin.

'Hardly! She's more taken with that scoundrel the Earl of Edinburgh than me. I'm sick of hearing about it. All he did was lose one of the finest ships in my fleet! He could easily have outrun the English, but he chose to turn and fight, against my express instructions. I told the Queen this, but she takes no heed. She thinks he's a hero!'

'Is there any news of him?' said Gavin.

'None,' Bothwell replied. 'And I doubt we will see him again! Anyway, at least the Queen has included me in her list of Privy Councillors. So perhaps I should not be too un-happy.'

Gavin McNaughton's thoughts strayed back to the ball, and he turned to Magnus.

'I take it your sister Marie will be attending?' he asked.

'Of course . . . but she's become more the Queen's sister than mine. She never leaves her side.'

'I look forward to meeting her,' said Gavin. 'And I'm sure you will now have time to catch up with your other *affaires*, eh, Bothwell?' The Duke's tanned features broke into a broad smile.

His companions well knew Bothwell's notorious reputation for affairs of the heart, and they all laughed together at the prospect of the evening ahead in the company of the splendid James Hepburn, Earl of Bothwell.

⚜ ⚜ ⚜

The next day, the three of them sat down along with hundreds of other guests for the banquet at Holyrood. The long tables groaned under the weight of an endless procession of dishes. Beef, mutton, and poultry, game and wildfowl, were followed by venison, boar, hares and rabbits. These dishes were served alongside pigeons, pheasants, curlews and capercailzies.

The Queen's French chefs had introduced new ways of preparing and presenting food. Whole deer, boars' heads, huge savoury jellies and pastry castles were the magnificent set pieces of the feast.

'At the German Court,' Magnus Hepburn said, 'I have heard they serve roast horse and cat in jelly.'

But the Duke of Glasgow was not interested in food.

'Is that your sister in the green satin?' he asked.

'It is.'

'The colour becomes her well.'

The meal ended with candied fruit and nuts, sugar cakes and marzipan, and the Duke of Glasgow and his companions washed it all down with a glass of Athole whisky. Wine was also served with 'confits' in the French fashion, and Magnus remarked,

'They say the Queen is creating a little France here and I'm beginning to think they are right.'

The dances confirmed it. The ball was opened with a slow

and stately pavanne. This gave courtiers a chance to display their finery and the Duke of Glasgow made a splendid show in dramatic black velvet, with a high white lace-edged ruff. He sought out Marie Hepburn and she rose smiling to take his hand. His father, he thought, had good taste. This girl was breathtakingly beautiful. It was amazing she had not found a husband long ago. Her loyalty to the young Queen was admirable but still . . .

Now, however, he could see what Bothwell had meant when he'd described her attitude to men. There seemed to be an invisible wall around her keeping men at bay. She danced with grace and dignity, but there was something strange about her . . . especially after he'd introduced himself. Of course he could understand how his sudden appearance in her life could bring back memories, but she looked startled, almost shocked, when she heard his name.

After the dance, he led her from the floor saying,

'I never realised my father's chosen lady was so beautiful. What a tragedy he never lived to know the happiness that I'm sure you would have given him.'

'A tragedy indeed, sir.'

'Marie . . . may I call you Marie?'

She nodded, avoiding his eyes, and then attempted to take her leave of him, but his firm hand detained her.

'Marie, you are promised to me for this galliard. Come.'

'I don't think—' She began to protest but before she could finish speaking, he had dragged her back onto the dance-floor. He had begun to whirl her into the complicated and lively sequences of hops and jumps that made up the galliard. Such was the energy and skill needed for the dance she had neither the breath nor the concentration for anything else.

As the music came to an end, the Queen came towards them, clapping her hands in delight.

'What splendid dancing partners you make, dear Marie, and . . . ?'

The Duke of Glasgow bowed over the Queen's hand.

'Gavin McNaughton, Duke of Glasgow, your Majesty.'

'Ah yes, Glasgow. A very pretty place. That name? Yes, of course, I remember. My dear Marie was betrothed to your father. I have told her many times that she has been mourning far too long. My poor Marie has been living like a nun for years.'

Marie flushed. 'Not so!'

'You dare to contradict your sovereign?' the Queen said in mock anger. 'Marie Hepburn, I sentence you to dance with the Duke of Glasgow and keep his company for the rest of the evening.' And with that she swept away.

Despite herself, Marie couldn't help enjoying the company of the handsome young gallant with eyes like blue diamonds. Here was a man whose appearance at least was more to her liking. He was slim and elegant, but not flamboyantly turned out. She concluded that he must have inherited his good looks and good taste from his mother. He certainly bore not the slightest resemblance to his father. They quaffed wine together and danced until she was dizzy and had to plead with him to stop. He flirted with her quite outrageously. She was glad that the Earl of Edinburgh was out of her life. Although, strangely, at the same time she missed him.

Never before had she drunk so much wine. Her head was swimming with it. It also heated her blood until her whole body throbbed with passionate need. Willingly, if somewhat drunkenly, she allowed the Duke to lead her away from the ballroom. She was so dazed and in such heat she was not even aware of how she reached her bedchamber. She had a vague memory of being carried, of floating along through shadowy corridors, of being undressed, then caressed. Then, with closed eyes, she relaxed to intoxicating and unadulterated pleasure. Eventually, she fell into a deep sleep. In the morning she awoke feeling refreshed and with a wonderful, sweet, soothing contentment in every part of her body. Then, gradually, her brain sharpened into awareness. Everything that had happened the night before pained her. The Duke of

Glasgow was the last man on earth she should have been intimate with. She felt sick with disgust at herself.

'How could I?' As if her life was not complicated enough.

✦   ✦   ✦

The Queen and the Marys were delighted. Mischievously, they tormented her by plying her with sly questions. Marie tried to appear cool and casual.

'I don't know what you are hinting at. The Duke is very handsome but we are used to seeing many handsome men at Court, are we not?'

'Indeed we are,' the Queen laughed, 'but we do not immediately fall in love with them.'

'Or dance so often with them or allow so many stolen kisses,' Livingstone teased.

Marie flushed. Livingstone was a fine one to talk.

'I am deeply embarrassed. I fear I must have indulged overmuch in wine.'

'More than wine,' Livingstone said, making them all giggle behind their palms.

Marie tried to smile and at least give some appearance of good humour but her mind and her emotions were in disarray.

The next time Marie and Gavin McNaughton met was at the wedding of Bothwell's sister, Lady Janet, at Crichton Castle, in the rolling hills to the south of Edinburgh. The Queen was to attend the wedding celebrations and stay the night at the castle.

Despite his finances being at a low ebb, Bothwell was determined to give his sister a wedding worthy of a queen's presence, and so, after the ceremony, there was a splendid banquet. There were countless wild does and roes, rabbits, partridges, plovers and moor fowl, wild geese, wild ducks and other kinds of exotic wild beasts. Afterwards, the bracken-clad haugh below the castle was the scene of great revelry.

The Duke of Glasgow, however, was finding it surprisingly difficult to renew his attachment to Marie Hepburn. Her coolness towards him, her constant avoidance of his company, pained him after their last meeting. On the way to the wedding she had kept away from him, riding as near as she could to the Queen. At the ceremony she had sat with her head bowed as if in constant prayer, and during the banquet she had made a point of sitting between Seton and Beaton and ignoring him completely.

He was determined to get an explanation, yet it was very late before he managed to waylay her amid the shadows of the ornate Italian cloister that enclosed the courtyard.

'You startled me,' she cried out, then shrank back from him as he made to embrace her.

'What is the matter? Surely I'm entitled to know what I have done to offend you?'

She hesitated, then shook her head.

'It is nothing you have done.'

'What then?'

She hesitated again and avoided his gaze.

'It's . . . it's just who you are.'

'You mean because I am my father's son?'

'Yes.'

'Sweetest girl, I loved my father greatly and I can appreciate, indeed applaud, your loyalty and sensitivity. But many years have passed and life has to go on. One thing I'm sure of is my dear father would give me, give both of us, his blessing. In life he denied me nothing. Death would not change him.'

Marie gazed up at his handsome face, and when he took her into his arms his gentleness enfolded her. She could have wept. She had such a grateful tenderness for him. She felt she couldn't deceive him. Yet she could not hurt him either. She wept and he kissed her tears away and told her everything would be all right.

And she longed to believe him.

— XXIV —

THE old town of Edinburgh was buzzing with the news. The gallant Earl of Edinburgh was alive! The sole surviving member of his ship's gallant company, he had been captured by the English, but had managed to escape and would soon be returning to the capital. Marie heard the news with a mixture of dread and—though the realisation shamed her—relief. And so it was with mixed feelings that, on the day of his triumphant return, she found herself amongst the crowds who lined the ancient High Street to welcome the hero home. The whole town had heard how the Earl had saved his Queen from the English.

They did not have long to wait. Mounted on a magnificent black stallion, Guthrie Jamieson surveyed the scene around him. He could not help thinking how amusing it all was, and remembered the words of his friend Randolph before they parted, words of gratitude and thanks for all he had done for the English cause.

The time he had spent in England had been pleasant enough, although, as he was supposed to be a prisoner, he could not enjoy life at Court. Instead he had visited some of his close friends, who entertained him royally at their own expense. Although he had failed in his mission to hand over the Queen to the English, there would be other opportunities.

And then there was Marie. He had spent much of his time in England thinking of her, and wishing that she was there with him. He had never had such power over a woman before, but he was starting to believe that it was more than that.

But this was *his* day. His triumphant return to Edinburgh. As he passed the Tolbooth, he lifted his hand from the bridle and saluted the crowd, who roared back in approval. He was enjoying this mightily. Especially the irony of it all. If only they knew what he had done, and what he was planning to do. And he smiled to himself at his own audacity and cunning.

As she watched him pass through the Canongate, Marie couldn't help thinking how handsome he looked in his finery, sitting astride the huge stallion, waving and smiling at the crowds. She had not wanted him to see her, but as he surveyed the crowd he caught her eye and bowed his head towards her. She could feel her face turn red, and turned and hurried off in the opposite direction. Guthrie Jamieson smiled as he watched her go.

Later, as he dressed for his audience with the Queen, he caught up with all the Court gossip. He had been away for some time, and his first concern was Marie. As he listened to the news of the ball and Marie's blossoming relationship with Gavin McNaughton, his face became thunderous.

'How long has this been going on?' he demanded.

'Many months now, my Lord,' came the reply.

'We shall see about that,' he bellowed as he stormed off in search of her.

When he found her in her chambers, she gave him a frosty welcome.

'Do not pretend that you are coy or shy, my lady. I know you are neither,' he sneered.

'I'm not pretending anything. But I am no longer the plaything of your ravenous appetites, my lord.'

'Ravenous, yes,' he grinned, 'for I have sorely missed you.'

'Well, I have not missed you.'

'Liar.'

'What conceit!' She stamped her foot in annoyance and frustration for indeed she had been perfectly happy and content in the company of the Duke of Glasgow. He was such a considerate and tender lover.

'Am I not entitled to some conceit when a beautiful creature like yourself has such an appetite for me?'

She flushed deeply at the memory his words brought to mind. She had literally crawled all over him, biting, licking, sucking. It had been a kind of madness.

'I'm ashamed of myself. I admit it.'

'No, no,' he protested, 'you mustn't feel like that. There is no need.'

'But I *do* feel like that.'

His eyes glimmered.

'I'm sure it would help if I made an honest woman of you.'

'You don't understand. Things have changed while you have been away.'

'Yes, I know. I know all about you and the Duke of Glasgow. I admit I am surprised at you, especially after what happened to his father Machar.'

She looked away, her face pale and strained.

'But I don't care about that,' he continued. 'We've been friends for a long time, have we not?'

'Were we ever really friends, Guthrie?' she asked. 'I certainly never loved you.'

'Ah, love—what is that?'

She was shocked.

'What a question to ask. Have you never known love?'

He shrugged.

'I have had many woman but you are the first that suited me so well.'

'Oh!' Frustration welled up again. 'Well, you don't suit me any more.'

'How can you say that when our couplings were so wonderful?'

'Couplings? We are not animals, sir. Nor shall we allow ourselves to behave like them. There is more to love than physical excitement.'

'Is there?'

She began to suspect he was teasing her. It made anger flare up and fire her cheeks.

'You know perfectly well there is.'

'My lady of the fiery passions,' he said.

'You're not paying attention to what I'm saying.'

'To the devil with talking. Let's go to bed. You've kept me waiting long enough.'

'No!' she gasped, and turned away. 'I refuse to have anything more to do with you.'

'Come here.' He made a rough grab for her. 'If you won't walk with me to your bedchamber, then I'll carry you there.'

She began to run frantically calling back at him,

'For pity's sake, stop this. I don't want you. Why won't you believe me?'

He caught her and threw her on to the bed, tearing off her clothes. As she sobbed, he passionately kissed every inch of her body. Eventually she began to respond, mindlessly but with equal passion.

'That's why I don't believe you,' he said afterwards, as they lay on the bed.

'Get out,' she whispered, looking away from him.

'As my lady pleases . . .' he laughed. The bed creaked and bounced as he left it, and he sang as he dressed. His loud and bawdy song infuriated and offended her.

'I hate you,' she said.

180

'Yes, so you keep telling me. I wonder why I don't believe you.'

The door banged shut as he left. Marie sank into the mattress, physically and emotionally drained, the bawdy song still reverberating in her head. And to think he could be so elegant and courteous in the presence of the Queen. Devious, two-faced swine! She drifted helplessly into an exhausted fitful sleep, punctuated by a terrible nightmare, in which she was frenziedly stabbing the Duke of Glasgow. The son, not the father. She sat up, sweat coursing down her face. Yet she was shivering.

Suddenly, she knew what she had to do. There was only one way she could free herself from the malign influence of Guthrie Jamieson. She had to marry the Duke of Glasgow. Without hesitating, she dressed hurriedly and rushed to tell the Queen of her decision.

'Of course,' she was suddenly subdued, 'he may not want to marry me.'

'Nonsense,' Mary assured her. 'He has been paying court to you and has professed his love for you. There *will* be a proposal or I shall want to know the reason why.'

They both laughed and Mary added,

'I am so pleased to see you happy at last, my dear Marie.'

But Marie was already beginning to dread telling Guthrie Jamieson. What would he say? And what would he do? He could ruin everything for her.

✣   ✣   ✣

It was difficult to find a few minutes alone with him however. He was always deep in conversation with one person or another. Finally she cornered him.

'I must speak with you,' she said.

'You cannot wait to bed me again?' the Earl said. 'Your appetite for love never ceases to astonish and delight me.'

'It is about love I wish to speak. I'm going to marry Gavin McNaughton,' she said with cruel bluntness.

'McNaughton?' the Earl sneered. 'You cannot be serious!'

'And why not? He has professed his love for me.'

'I will tell you why not.' Jamieson's face darkened with anger. 'You are only doing it to assuage your guilt. The very idea is ridiculous.'

'Why is it ridiculous? He is charming, handsome, with every material advantage to offer me.'

The Earl could not help smiling to himself. The poor fool, he thought, clearly knew nothing of the Duke's debts. Jamieson knew from his English contacts that McNaughton was being bled dry by the moneylenders who had paid off his ransom. But Jamieson kept this knowledge to himself, preferring to try a more subtle approach. . . .

'Marie, you are so transparent. You have been carrying a burden of guilt for years. Now you foolishly imagine that by giving yourself, tying yourself for life to this man, you will lose that burden.'

'I intend to devote my life to fulfilling his every need and comfort as any good wife should. But I will do that because of love, not because of guilt.'

'Liar.'

'I have always been honest with you. I have made it only too plain how I feel about you.'

'Yes, you have indeed, on many pleasant occasions!'

'You have misconstrued my physical weakness for love. I have told you this before but you always refuse to listen.'

'You realise of course that I could soon put paid to this nonsense? Without even lifting a finger.'

Her face drained of colour.

'You wouldn't!'

'Why not?'

'Guthrie, I'm sorry. But for all these years you have not betrayed me and you can't now. Not if you have any feelings for me at all. You realise he would kill me.'

'Yes, I don't think there's any doubt about that.'

'Please.'

He shrugged.

'We shall see.'

Later, when he was alone, Jamieson realised that if he was to have Marie, he would have to destroy Gavin McNaughton first. To that end, he would contact Randolph and have him acquire the deeds to Naughton Castle and all the Duke of Glasgow's lands from the English moneylenders. They had been holding them as security ever since Gavin had been forced to mortgage everything to pay his own ransom after the battle of Pinkie. No doubt Jamieson would have to pay Randolph more than their real value, but it would be worth it. With the deeds to Naughton in his possession it would be easy to ruin Gavin McNaughton. Marie would hardly want to marry a penniless beggar—and that was exactly what Gavin would be once Guthrie Jamieson had finished with him.

— XXV —

JUST when Marie needed him most, the Duke of Glasgow
disappeared. His good friend the Earl of Bothwell had
fallen foul of the interminable feuding that was tearing
the Scottish nobility apart at this time. As a result, his enemies
had engineered his imprisonment in Edinburgh Castle. The
resourceful Bothwell, however, had managed to get word of
his predicament to Gavin McNaughton. The young Duke
was his only hope, and he had immediately rushed to his
friend's aid, without telling anyone what he was doing or
where he was going.

Gavin's unexplained absence from Court left Marie
feeling shamed. She had obviously been no more than a bit
of sport to him after all. The Queen soon noticed her pale
countenance.

'Dear Marie, you are distressed at not seeing the Duke of
Glasgow again.'

'Not at all.' Marie made an effort to look cheerful. 'I
have a headache, that is all.'

'Then you will have no interest in knowing that he is unable to attend Court because he is mixed up in the troubles
of Lord Bothwell.'

'What does that mean? Is he imprisoned?'

'No, but only because he proved more slippery than Lord Bothwell. However, I have a mind to forgive him. He, after all, has committed no crime that I know of. Except, of course, that of being a friend of Bothwell's.'

Marie's relief was to be short-lived, however, as the news spread around the town concerning Lord James Stewart's persecution of Bothwell's friends. Lord James, desperate for power, would stop at nothing to destroy anyone who came between him and the Queen. He was furiously jealous of Bothwell—who was a favourite of Mary's—and he had managed to trump up some spurious charge, so that he could have Bothwell arrested. Not content with this, he had had more than fifty of Bothwell's closest associates arrested at Hawick. Many had been summarily executed.

Marie was in an agony of suspense and distress, not knowing if Gavin had been among those who had died. She had to find out, even pleading with Guthrie Jamieson to help her. But no-one knew exactly who had met their fate at the hands of Lord James. Only that there had been many. All Marie could discover was that the Duke was not in residence at Naughton Castle and had not been seen there for some time. Neither was he among the prisoners confined in Edinburgh Castle. But before she could discover the truth, the Queen and the royal party set off for the Highlands, and Marie had no choice but to go with them.

❈   ❈   ❈

After many weeks of tiring travel, Mary and the royal party arrived at the palace of Spynie, home of Bothwell's uncle and Marie's father, the Bishop of Moray. It was the first time Marie had seen her father for many years, but he hardly even acknowledged her presence. After she had rested, Marie went to find the Bishop, who was working in his study.

'Ah, Marie,' he said, looking up. 'Come and sit down. I want to talk to you.'

'Father, it is good to see you after all these years. How are you?'

'Tolerably well, thank you. And I am glad to see that the Queen regards you with such favour. It is a blessing she knows so little of your past.'

Marie was silent, and looked into the fire, a tear welling up in her eye.

'I cannot pretend I have forgotten that night, Marie. Nor can I pretend that time has healed the wounds. I have often wondered if I did the right thing. But seeing you again has brought it all back to me, and I think it would be best if we see as little of each other as possible while you are here.'

Marie was shocked. 'Since that night, I have had to live with what I did. I came to tell you that I now have a chance to put right the wrong. It will not please you to hear this, but Gavin McNaughton has proposed marriage to me, and I have accepted him.'

'What?' the Bishop gasped. 'This cannot be. You must not!'

He slumped back into his chair, and quite suddenly Marie saw what her father had become—a bitter old man, scared of what might happen to him and intent on self-preservation at all costs. The youthful vigour had gone, and his face looked waxen as parchment.

'You know that Gavin came to see me when he was released by the English,' he continued quietly. 'He never believed that old Murdo killed his father. He knows there was more to it. And if he finds out? What then?'

'He will never find out from me,' Marie replied.

'Perhaps not, but he is no fool. And it would be wrong for you to marry him.'

'I have made up my mind, father. It is the only way I can ever put things right.'

'Then I can only pray that for both our sakes he never finds out the truth.'

While still at Spynie, Marie received a letter from her mother. She was surprised to learn that Effie was now in Edinburgh, awaiting the return of her daughter. Marie told her father about this and he left her in no doubt that he intended to take no responsibility whatsoever for Effie's welfare or up-keep. He had not spoken to her for years, and another much younger concubine than Effie was now comfortably settled in the house beside the woods that had once been her mother's home.

Marie worried about what was to become of Effie. She had not seen her mother for many years. But in her late forties, she would surely have lost much of her attractive-ness. Could she find another lover to support her? Marie prayed that at least her mother had saved enough money from the times when she had been comfortably placed. Marie had mixed feelings about seeing her again. But Effie was, after all, her mother, and in a way she would be glad to see her, and to help her if she could. If only she could trust her. The Bishop certainly had not trusted her, otherwise he would not have packed her off to far-away Orkney.

He had always been a cruel, selfish and ambitious man who did not truly care for anyone or anything except himself and his own worldly pleasures. His only reason for helping her all those years ago had been to save himself, she thought bitterly. But the Bishop's callous disregard for Effie only brought out in Marie a stubborn resolve to do whatever she could to see that her mother survived.

And so, when the Court moved back to Edinburgh, Marie set out to find Effie. She began her search in the heart of the town—the two main streets, the High Street and the Cowgate, which stretched down the steep spine of rock that joined the castle to the Abbey of Holyrood. On these busy thorough-fares, the horses' hooves clanged noisily on the square boulder stones that paved the road, and wayfarers walked down the middle of the street avoiding the horses as best they could. On either side, at right angles to the two main streets pitching steeply down off the ridge, ran the wynds. No attempt was made to keep them clean. Low arches spanned crooked, shadowy passages blocked by middens, tar barrels, stacks of heather, broom or peat.

Marie did not venture down into any of these dangerous places and felt certain her mother would never have dreamt of doing so either. Instead, she enquired in respectable places in the High Street and was very soon directed to where a 'merry lady' from Orkney was lodging.

'Marie, my dear lassie!' Her mother greeted her with bouncing enthusiasm. They embraced and Marie said with a laugh and a shake of her head,

'Mother, you have not changed one whit—either in looks or character.' The heart-shaped face had admittedly become a little loose. Her rosebud mouth and wide, childish eyes, however, were just as Marie remembered them. Even her shapely figure had not been spoiled by the passing years.

'Change? Change? Why should I change?' Effie cried out.

'Well, you're a few years older than when we last met, and I'm sure life must have been much quieter on Orkney.'

'Nonsense! You have no idea what island life can be like. My dear lassie, their social gatherings are wild, really wild, and the men—big, rough fellows who can be very merry indeed. Oh no, if the truth be told, I was getting too much attention from one laird in particular.' She giggled like a girl. 'A very wild fellow indeed. He wishes to wed me as well as bed me but he has a large family of equally wild children. One child has been more than enough for me, I told him. No, no, I said, I could not cope with such a responsibility.'

Marie began to feel the usual anger and frustration that her mother had such a talent for arousing in her.

'So that is what you meant by needing to be looked after in your feeble old age.'

Effie gave a flap of her dainty hands and enjoyed another giggle.

'Oh that? Laud's sake, it will come soon enough, no doubt. But I do not mean to succumb to it for many a long year yet.'

Marie flopped down on to the nearest chair. 'What am I to do with you?'

'You could have me comfortably installed in Holyrood. I have heard that there are many handsome and wealthy men at Court.'

'It is not in my power.'

'Surely you have influence with the Queen. After all these years of faithful service? I'm sure she will be delighted to grant you any favour.'

'Don't be ridiculous, mother. Sit down and compose yourself, please do. We must talk seriously. I must try to make you understand the dangers of your being here.'

'Dangers? How can there be any dangers to me? I have done nothing.'

'Danger to me, mother. You talk too much.'

'Talk too much?' Effie looked both wounded and puzzled. Then suddenly a light dawned.

'You mean the *murder*? Och, that was years ago. I'd forgotten all about it.'

'Just banish it from your mind again. That's all I ask.'

Her mother put a finger to her pretty painted lips.

'I'll never breathe a word to a soul. Not a living soul. As God's my witness, no word of the dreadful crime you committed will ever—'

'Yes, all right, mother. That's enough. I believe you.'

Yet still Marie could not rid herself of a desperate sense of foreboding.

XXVI

BOTHWELL watched the rain fall outside the bars of his cell. It had not stopped for days—dousing the daylight and making each gloomy hour darker than the last. It seemed so long since he had returned from France, his days full of vigour and hope, his nights a riot of joyous carousing with his friends on the streets of Edinburgh. And now he found himself incarcerated in the grim dungeons of Edinburgh Castle, only a few hundred yards from the scenes of his former, carefree life.

Desperate to regain that freedom, he had managed to send the Queen a message, and a reply was successfully smuggled back, but it gave him little comfort, saying that she was unable, for the time being, to give him any help. The message left him with the distinct impression that he was on his own.

Bothwell realised that he would have to rely on his true friends, like the Duke of Glasgow. By devious means, he managed to contact Gavin McNaughton with details of a plan, informing him that he intended to escape—by breaking one of the bars of his cell, and climbing down the face of the castle rock.

The message ended with the words 'Have a horse waiting for me, and, God willing, before the night is over we will enjoy many a tankard of ale together.'

Knowing his friend, Gavin believed that if anyone could succeed in such a daring and dangerous feat, Bothwell could.

At considerable risk, the Duke did as he was asked, and at the appointed time he was waiting in the darkness at the foot of the castle rock. As he strained his eyes towards the sheer rock face, he struggled to see by the faint light of the moon any sign of movement. But the moon kept slipping behind clouds, leaving only blackness.

This same blackness engulfed Bothwell as he managed to force his body through the gap in the bars. Once out, he clung to the window ledge, his feet scrabbling along the rock face below. Even though he couldn't see, he could sense, with terrifying clarity, the height at which he was so precariously perched. He loosened one hand from the window and searched for a lower hold. Finding a rough protuberance at the same time as his feet, strong as a gorilla's, clamped on to a sharp ridge, he slid his other hand down, his nails digging and breaking against the icy rock. Now that he had left the comparative safety of the ledge, he was conscious of his total vulnerability, the slightest gust of the wind could now toss him into eternity. His saturnine features hardened in defiance. He would not be destroyed by either wind or rock. He had always thrived on danger and he grimly accepted the challenge now before him.

*   *   *

'Bothwell!' McNaughton cried out in astonishment at the apparition before him. 'I can hardly credit it. You have my undying admiration, sir.'

Bothwell shrugged aside the compliment and mounted the horse McNaughton had brought him.

'And you have mine. It takes more courage to be a friend

191

of Bothwell than it takes to scale a rock face! I swear, McNaughton, I will never forget your part in this adventure. And now let us be gone from this place, for my thirst is great and that tankard of ale awaits us!'

Later, in a tavern in one of the wynds, Bothwell looked very much at ease and in no hurry to take his leave of Edinburgh. When Gavin remarked on this, Bothwell replied,

'I doubt if there will be any great zeal to renew my confinement. Anyway, I have business to do here. My troubles have emptied my purse.'

'I have business too,' McNaughton said, 'but of a more pleasant nature. If, that is, I succeed in getting past the guard at Holyrood—Lord James is there, and any friend of yours would doubtless receive a more than warm welcome at the hands of his men.'

Bothwell's dark, weather-beaten features relaxed into a grin.

'Ah, you are going to see the beautiful Marie Hepburn! She's worth a risk or two, I'll wager.'

'I'd risk my life for her.'

'That is perhaps what you will do, my friend, if you venture near Holyrood.'

'You advise me against it?' McNaughton laughed. 'After the risks you have taken yourself this very night?'

'Not at all.' Bothwell raised his tankard. 'Here's to success in all our ventures.'

They arranged where next to meet, planning to go first to Crichton Castle and then to the Hermitage. Bothwell had a powerful force stationed there.

After they parted, Gavin gave some thought to how he could get into the palace of Holyrood. He was prepared to do anything that was necessary, no matter how dangerous. But the obvious thing to try first was to bribe the guard.

He was surprised at how easily his ploy succeeded, and he proceeded swiftly on his way to Marie's bedchamber. It was very late and she was already in bed. The curtains of the four-poster were closed against the cold nocturnal draughts.

'Marie,' he whispered, not wanting to startle her. 'I had to see you. I am forced to leave the town to escape the wrath of Lord James. . . .'

The curtain was drawn aside by a shapely white hand. Emerald eyes widened when she saw him.

'I know all about your troubles, Gavin. But I had begun to think that you had only been toying with me and did not truly care. . . .'

'My love,' he came over to her, pulling the bedclothes back so that he could lie beside her, 'how could you think so after I told you of the depth of—' He stopped when he noticed the changed shape of her body. 'You are with child?'

She nodded.

'I hope you are pleased.'

'Of course! I am delighted and proud. When I return, we will be married and I will take you to Glasgow. In the meantime, you must try to obtain the Queen's permission.'

'The Queen is already softening towards you.'

'Good. Then we have nothing to worry about. Naughton Castle will have its Duchess, and I will have not only my heart's desire, but a son and heir.'

She gazed up at him and he cupped her face in his hands.

'Smile! As your future husband, I command it.'

He was rewarded by a quiver of her lips which he immediately stilled with a kiss. He made love to her gently, tenderly. Then he left, assuring her that he would return as soon as possible.

'I will speak to Bothwell. I have promised to accompany him as far as the Hermitage. Once there, my services will no longer be needed, and I will return to you with all haste. I give you my word.'

⚜   ⚜   ⚜

The fugitives rode through the night, and by morning they had passed Hawick on the road to the south. Away from

Edinburgh and his enemies, Bothwell now seemed more relaxed, as the massive hills of Cauldcleuch and Greatmoor towered above them, and their horses' hooves splashed through the clear waters of mountain streams. As they cantered on, Gavin began to whistle a familiar tune.

'You are in happy mood today,' Bothwell remarked.

'I have good reason to be happy, my friend. Although you have no good reason that I can see to be at ease with the world.'

Bothwell smiled knowingly.

'Do I take it that the meeting with your lady was successful?'

'We plan to wed. She is with child.'

'I see! If you wish, I can release you from your word now. I can go on alone from here.'

'No, my word is my bond. I'll not break it. I could not live with myself if you perished for the want of another sword-arm. And while I'm away, Marie will put in a good word with the Queen—for both of us, Bothwell. She is close to the Queen. Let us hope she has influence enough.'

✤   ✤   ✤

The Hermitage was a huge and gloomy fortress, dominating its windswept moorland vantage point. It could hold more than six hundred men, horse and foot, within its towering walls, and almost fifteen hundred moss troopers could be raised from the surrounding countryside. Its reputation, however, was dark and unsavoury. It had been built over two hundred and fifty years before by the family of Nicholas de Soulis. It was said that De Soulis dabbled in sorcery and kept a familiar spirit in one of the dungeons. Finally the King had become weary of his notorious and bizarre behaviour, and cried out in exasperation, 'Oh *boil* him. But let me be plagued with him no more.' His courtiers had taken the King literally and, in the words of a song Bothwell was fond of singing,

> *'They rolled him in a sheet of lead,*
> *A sheet of lead for a funeral pall;*
> *They plunged him in the cauldron red*
> *And melted him—lead, bones and all!'*

The dungeons were still said to be haunted, but this did not appear to concern anyone unduly. Certainly not the sentries or any of the occupants, and now that Bothwell had returned, the castle buzzed with military activity.

'I know only too well,' Bothwell said, as Gavin prepared to take his leave, 'that my chances of a full pardon depend greatly on the Queen's good-will. Without it, I am at the mercy of my deadly enemy, Lord James Stewart. But enough of my troubles, my friend. You have business of your own to attend to.'

Gavin set off for the return journey to Edinburgh with a happy heart. For the moment all his troubles—all his debts and the ever-present threat of ruin—were forgotten. If all went well, he would soon be married to one of the most beautiful ladies of the Court.

— XXVII —

'WONDERFUL! Wonderful!' Effie clapped her hands in delight. 'You will be the Duchess of Glasgow and mistress of Naughton Castle after all!'

'That depends on one thing and one thing alone,' Marie said.

'And he is such a handsome young laddie. Such fair hair and blue eyes I have never witnessed in my whole life—'

'Mother, will you listen to me,' Marie broke in, her voice loud and harsh. 'Everything can very easily be ruined. My life, my happiness . . .'

'Foolish lassie, what could possibly go wrong. He has asked you to be his wife.'

'You could ruin everything, mother. I have nightmares about it. Do you understand what I'm saying?'

'Oh tuts. Do you mean that unfortunate business again? It was an age ago. Everybody has forgotten about it long since.'

'He was Gavin's father. Gavin McNaughton hasn't forgotten.'

196

'Well, that may be so, but what does it matter now?'

'What does it matter?' Marie echoed incredulously. 'Mother, are you mad? Of course it matters. This is exactly what worries me. Your carelessness in what you say and do. You must never, *ever*, breathe one word about what happened that night, to anyone, not to a living soul, do you hear?'

'My dear lassie, have I said one word to anyone in all these years?'

'Maybe not . . .' Marie admitted, in a worried and uncertain tone.

'I may be a little foolish at times, Marie, but I'm not mad. I will not do or say anything, I promise you, that will injure our standing at Court. Especially with our dear Queen who has taken such a liking to me.'

It was true that the Queen was thoroughly enjoying Effie's cheerful company. Not so much for her good cheer and capacity for merrymaking, Marie suspected, as her mother's expert knowledge of all forms of gambling. Gambling was an obsession with the Scottish nobility.

'Do you swear to me . . . will you swear on the Bible . . . ?'

'Of course, of course, but why such a fuss? Now let us try to forget all this nonsense and talk about your marriage. There is so much to prepare. The Queen and I will have a wonderful time planning the wedding. She is such a dear, generous girl, and no expense will be spared. She is sure to dig very deeply into the royal purse for her Marie. Do you know what she told me the other day? . . .'

Marie allowed her mother to chatter on about dresses, and all sorts of other nonsense. Meanwhile, her mind turned to more important matters. She was glad that the child she carried would have its chance of legitimacy, as the legal heir of Naughton Castle. In due course, he would inherit the dukedom and all the lands that went with it. Secure in that knowledge, she eagerly anticipated welcoming Gavin back to Edinburgh. Yet she still feared what the Earl of Edinburgh might do or say. She had avoided him as much as possible since his return, but she had not forgotten his threats. She prayed that her pregnancy would cause him to show mercy towards her. And it seemed her prayers were answered.

✤   ✤   ✤

As soon as the Duke of Glasgow returned, he sought an audience with the Queen. Marie stood at his side, while the Earl of Edinburgh looked on in stony silence. He was as usual flamboyantly and fashionably dressed in a massive blue and gold doublet and slashed satin and fur cape. Gavin was dressed in elegant black and white. Marie, wearing a floating gown appropriate to her pregnancy, made a formal curtsy to the Queen. The Duke gave a deep bow, and thanked her for allowing him to return to Holyrood once more.

Later, Gavin and the Queen spoke of Bothwell, whose fortunes had once more taken a turn for the worse. He had been shipwrecked while en route to France, and taken prisoner by the English.

'He has now been confined in the castle of Tynemouth, until the Privy Council decide what to do with him. I fear for his life, your Majesty. If only something could be done to help him. Despite your differences, he has served you well in the past.'

The Queen nodded.

'I will give the matter serious thought, and in due course, I will discuss it with my advisors. But I think it will be difficult to offer him any help.'

As he listened to all this, Guthrie Jamieson wished it had been Gavin McNaughton who was languishing in an English dungeon once more. What had once been a mild dislike for the Duke had now turned to burning hatred. But just then an idea struck him. Perhaps McNaughton's loyalty to Bothwell could provide Jamieson with the means of bringing about the downfall of the gallant Duke of Glasgow.

A plan began to take shape in his head, and he consoled himself with the thought that soon enough he would be rid of Gavin McNaughton for good. Then he would finally claim Marie for himself.

⚜ ⚜ ⚜

In no time at all, the day of Marie's wedding to the Duke of Glasgow had arrived. A most excellent musician called David Rizzio had recently joined the Court, and he and the other Court musicians were to provide the entertainment. Rizzio could both sing and play the lute and although he was an ugly man, small and hunched, his Latin love of fine clothing made him stand out in a crowd. Few could have guessed then what tragedy lay in store for the Queen and her new musician.

Among Marie's wedding gifts from the Queen was a sparkling diamond necklace to wear with the bridal dress. To the bridegroom the Queen had given a jewelled sword and an outfit glistening with gold buckles and silk embroidery.

Not to be outdone at the wedding, Effie wore her hair dyed chestnut and spangled with jewels. She had painted her face and plucked her eyebrows. Her dress was a nest of gauze over scarlet taffeta pinned at the neck and breast with a plethora of different coloured brooches. A pair of long earrings waggled continuously as she spoke. At the wedding feast she sat next to the Earl of Edinburgh and it was he who had to listen to her frivolous chatter. As they drank many toasts, the Earl managed to retain his look of polite interest, a feat that gained him much praise and sympathy from the other guests. For their part, they would have long since strangled the awful woman if they had been trapped in his unfortunate position.

Marie had seen Effie behave in this way so often it did not unduly surprise or trouble her, and she was grateful to Jamieson for containing Effie's behaviour rather than allowing it to encompass the whole table. Before long, two of Effie's maids had to be called to help her from the table and lead her, none too steadily, away to her bedchamber.

She was very annoyed to have missed the dancing but as Marie told her next day, she had hardly been able to walk from the banquet hall.

Effie had just laughed at this revelation. She had no memory of it and would not have cared even if she had.

'The difference between you and me,' she told Marie, 'is that I know how to enjoy life and you don't.'

'We certainly have different ideas of what is enjoyable,' Marie said.

As the dancing continued, Marie tried her best to keep away from Guthrie Jamieson. But he was determined to dance with her. As they danced he said,

'This marriage will never last, Marie.'

'You don't know what you are talking about, Guthrie. You are jealous of Gavin,' she retorted.

'You know it's me you really want. Perhaps I should ask your husband if he is sure the child you carry is his? Or maybe I could tell him one of our other little secrets?'

'You wouldn't dare! It would finish you as well.'

'Maybe the price would be worth paying, just to see his face when he discovered the truth about his precious Marie.'

'Guthrie!' she pleaded, 'this has to stop! I do not love you. Maybe once . . . but not any more. It's Gavin I love, and I only want to be a good wife to him.'

'You must do as you see fit. But consider this: perhaps you don't know him as well as you think you do. . . .'

'What do you mean?'

'One day you will see. And when you do, you will beg me to have you back.'

'Never!' Marie said bitterly, with tears in her eyes, as she turned and walked quickly away before the music had stopped.

— XXVIII —

HUDDLED in the corner of his dank, freezing cell, Bothwell was being slowly driven mad by the howling gale that lashed against the castle walls. His new prison was situated on a headland lashed by the North Sea. From morning till night, his ears were assailed by the ceaseless din of the elements. His despair was only relieved by the occasional visits from his few loyal friends, most notably the Duke of Glasgow.

It was during one of these visits that Gavin brought Bothwell the news he had been waiting for. Gavin had long since abandoned all hope that the Queen would intervene on Bothwell's behalf, and so he had decided to mount a rescue attempt. But it had been the unexpected intervention of the Earl of Edinburgh that had finally convinced him to take such drastic action. As he told Bothwell,

'I had not thought Guthrie Jamieson was a friend of yours, but there seems no doubt about it now. He came to me a few weeks after my wedding with a plan to free you, and a most excellent scheme it is too.'

Bothwell looked uneasy.

'Guthrie Jamieson, you say? Well, well. I wonder what that sly fox is up to? If I were you, Gavin, I would not place my trust in him. We never were friends before, so why should he help me now?'

'Frankly my friend,' Gavin replied, 'I don't care *why* he wants to help, so long as he does and we get you out of this hell-hole with all speed.'

'Perhaps you're right,' Bothwell relented. 'But take care, Gavin, take great care.'

Later, to relieve the oppressive atmosphere of the cell, they talked of other, more pleasant matters—not least Gavin's new family.

'We have twins, a little son and daughter. The Queen keeps my wife and I at Court in order to have the infants near her. She showers them with gifts, and as often as not I am forced to leave Marie and Kate and Machar at Court while I attend to the running of my estates.'

'You called your son after your father?'

'Yes. Marie was very much opposed to the name but I insisted. At least my father's memory will live on in my son.'

He hesitated.

'The matter of my father is the only discord that ever arises between me and my wife. It is a worrying obsession with her. She even ordered the servants to remove my father's portrait from its position of honour above the fireplace. It dominates the room, she said. And why not, I said. I confess I was very angry and ordered its immediate return.'

'One would think,' Bothwell said thoughtfully, 'after all this time . . .'

'Yes indeed. It is most peculiar to say the least. Yet in every other way my beautiful wife is perfectly reasonable and normal.'

Bothwell shrugged.

'Women! Will we ever understand them!'

✦   ✦   ✦

On Gavin's return to Naughton Castle, McNairn the factor informed him that Marie was with the Queen at Holyrood. Two letters also awaited him. To his dismay, Gavin noted that the first was from the moneylenders. Their demands were becoming more and more outrageous. How much longer would he be able to keep these dogs at bay, he wondered, as he flung the parchment down in disgust. Picking up the other letter, he was cheered to see that it bore the seal of the Earl of Edinburgh. Guthrie Jamieson wanted to meet him that very day to discuss their joint endeavour. He would be at Naughton that afternoon. Gavin was impressed. Once Jamieson decided to do something, there was no stopping him.

But when the Earl arrived, he brought unexpected news.

'My contacts tell me that my Lord Bothwell is soon to be handed over to Sir Henry Percy at Norham Castle on the Border. He will be held there under a much reduced guard.'

'Excellent news!' said Gavin. 'That will make things much easier for us, will it not?'

'Indeed it will, Gavin, indeed,' Jamieson nodded; but perhaps not in quite the way you mean, he thought to himself. 'Anyway, here is the plan,' he continued. 'I will assemble a raiding party of hand-picked men and then you and I will lead them in a dash across the Border. I have managed to bribe certain members of Sir Henry's household, and they will smooth our way into the castle. Once we're in, it will be a simple matter to find Bothwell and spirit him away.'

Once more, Gavin was impressed.

'An admirable scheme, Guthrie,' he said. 'But should I not bring some of my own men-at-arms with me?'

'There is no need, my force will be more than sufficient— they will all be battle-hardened veterans, have no fear! One more thing,' Jamieson added. 'If word of what we are planning gets out, then Bothwell will undoubtedly be moved far beyond our reach. So no-one must hear of our adventure, do you understand? No-one. Not even your wife—and especially not her mother!'

Gavin could see the sense in that.

'Nobody will hear a word of this from me, I can promise you that.'

'So that's decided then,' said Jamieson. 'One week from today, we cross the Border and free the bold Earl of Bothwell!'

'I'll drink to that,' said Gavin, and they lifted their glasses to toast the success of their venture.

✤   ✤   ✤

Around this time all the gossip at Court was about Mary, Queen of Scots' romantic attachment to the utterly unsuitable and shallow Lord Darnley. Although Marie was concerned for the Queen, she was preoccupied with her own problems. At the moment it seemed as though her own happiness at Naughton lurched from one extreme to the other, and sometimes she felt almost suicidal.

Gavin never seemed to be at home for long—he was always away, mostly in the service of his friend the Earl of Bothwell. During these absences the Earl of Edinburgh would often visit.

'I would not neglect you, if you were *my* wife,' he told her. 'I always said that marrying Gavin McNaughton was the worst mistake you ever made.'

Marie protested, but she couldn't help thinking that perhaps there was a grain of truth in what he said.

Mostly though, Marie felt like killing her mother. Effie had been living with them ever since the wedding, and Marie often lost her temper with her, actually attacking her once, after being driven to distraction by her reckless drinking. Effie had fought back as best she could but was no match for the maniacal strength of Marie's fury. After much struggling and tearing of clothes and hair, the older woman had been sent reeling and screaming to the ground. With an effort, Marie fought to regain control. A servant, hearing the commotion,

204

burst into the room, helped the dishevelled Effie to a chair, and poured her a goblet of wine.

'No!' Marie commanded, 'take the wine away.'

Effie's screams had withered into sobs.

'You have shocked me beyond measure,' she told her daughter. 'Beyond all measure. It is no wonder to me now that you behaved so violently to poor, dear Machar McNaughton.'

Marie's fists clenched again.

'I warned you. And I warn you again. You are to put that night out of your mind. You must never divulge to a living soul—'

'But I never have,' Effie sobbed. 'I have behaved on each and every occasion in the most circumspect fashion.'

'No, you have not! You have been indulging in so much drink you do not know what you are saying or how you are behaving. Do you wish to continue living here, mother?'

'Of course I do. It is my home now. Where else could I go?'

'You could go back to Orkney and your eager suitor there.'

'To such a rough, coarse fellow with all those wild children. No, I will never do that.'

'If you are not careful, you will be forced to take that course, mother. If you don't drink yourself into an early grave first!'

Later, she had told Gavin what had happened.

'I know she has a problem with drink,' Gavin said, 'but that is no excuse for what you did to her. I confess I am disappointed in you.'

'I'm sorry.'

'It is to Effie you should be apologising.'

For an insane moment Marie was tempted to confess to her husband the real source of all her fears and anxieties. But the terrible confession stuck in her throat. How could she have said, 'I killed your father'? It was absolutely impossible.

The mere idea filled her with horror. And she prayed to God that Effie would never reveal her secret. She didn't believe her mother would betray her on purpose, but if she was drunk . . .

Afterwards, Marie was shocked at her own behaviour. Although she knew she had a hot temper, she was not normally violent. At the same time, she realised there was nothing she would not do in order to protect her children and her life at Naughton Castle.

— XXIX —

AS Guthrie Jamieson waited patiently in the darkness of the woods just above the castle, he had time to reflect on how well things were going. Like the young fool he was, McNaughton had put his life in Jamieson's hands. Very soon he would come to regret that.

Close by, Gavin McNaughton was feeling uneasy. As he looked around him in the silence of the moonlit clearing, he couldn't help thinking what a murderous looking bunch of cut-throats the Earl of Edinburgh's men had turned out to be. As soon as he had joined them earlier that day, he had remembered Bothwell's warning and regretted not bringing any of his own men. Still, it was too late to worry about that now. At any moment there would be a signal from the tower that loomed in the darkness ahead, and they would ride down the wooded slope and into the castle of Norham.

On the way to this midnight rendezvous, Gavin had been puzzled by one thing. They had seemed to take a wrong turning at a crossroads, and he had asked Jamieson,

'Surely we should have turned eastwards back there? I have been this way once before, and I am sure it does not lead to Norham.'

'My friend, I fear the night plays tricks on you. Trust me, I have travelled this road a hundred times, and I can assure you we will reach our destination before daybreak.'

Gavin was not convinced, but he bowed to Jamieson's experience.

Now, in the clearing, he felt in his bones that something was wrong. Just then, Jamieson whispered, 'The signal! There is the signal!' And, sure enough, Gavin could see the dim light that glowed briefly from one of the castle windows. Before Gavin could reply, the horsemen began to move off down the hill, with Jamieson in the lead. Gavin spurred his horse and followed them and almost at once they drew up, unchallenged, outside the castle walls.

Now Gavin was sure something was wrong. This castle was no more than a small fortified peel tower! Norham was a massive, ancient border fortress. This could not be Norham. But even as Gavin realised this, he found himself seized by two or three of Jamieson's men and roughly dragged from his horse. As he crashed to the ground, he caught a fleeting glimpse of Guthrie Jamieson looking down at him, a look of devilish triumph in his eyes.

'Guthrie!' he gasped. 'Why—' but he got no further, as a heavy mailed fist hit him full in the face, and the world around him dissolved into blackness.

✢   ✢   ✢

Marie had heard nothing from Gavin for over a week now. This was not unheard of, and she was only just beginning to worry. Who knows what ridiculous adventure Bothwell has dragged him into now, she thought, as she sat warming herself by the fire in the Great Hall of Naughton Castle.

Suddenly, a commotion rose up from the courtyard below, and she recognised the unmistakable sounds of horses clattering across the flagstones and the shouts of their riders. Marie rushed out of the hall and down to the courtyard, fully expecting to greet her returning husband. But Gavin was nowhere to be seen. A motley collection of evil-looking men-at-arms were dismounting from their horses, and in their midst she saw the unmistakable figure of Guthrie Jamieson.

'Guthrie, what brings you here?' she demanded.

'Let us go inside,' said Jamieson, 'I bring news of your husband.'

Together they climbed the winding stair to the Hall, and Jamieson insisted that Marie sit down before he would speak to her. The grim look on his face filled her with anxiety.

'I am afraid the news I bring is not good. There is no easy way to tell you this. Gavin is dead.'

For a moment Marie could not believe what she had just heard. Then, in a shocked whisper, she tried to speak.

'Dead? How can Gavin be dead? What has happened? For God's sake, Guthrie, what has happened?'

Jamieson explained how they had been trying to free Bothwell from his captivity in England.

'Unfortunately, Gavin underestimated the forces we would be up against. As we approached Norham, we were ambushed by Sir Henry Percy's men. We never had a chance, and I was lucky to escape with my life.'

'But Gavin? What happened to Gavin?' Marie repeated.

'He fought like a lion!' Jamieson told her. 'If it hadn't been for him, I doubt any of us would have escaped. I was standing right next to him when he fell. It was a crossbow bolt. There was nothing I could do.' Jamieson paused and the silence of the Great Hall was broken only by Marie's sobbing. Jamieson continued, 'Before he died, Gavin gave me this ring.' He showed her Gavin's signet, a ring Marie herself had given to him. 'And he made me swear on my honour as a gentleman that I would look after you and the children. I told him you would want for nothing as long as I lived.'

'Oh Guthrie,' said Marie, 'I cannot bear it any more. . . .'

Then she broke down completely and Jamieson called her maid, who led her away to her chamber.

✣   ✣   ✣

Alone in the Great Hall, Jamieson reflected on his part in the downfall of the house of McNaughton. He remembered how it had all begun—at the banquet, held so long ago in this very hall, the night he had murdered Machar. First the father, he thought, and now the son! Machar, a greedy, lecherous old man who deserved everything he got, and now Gavin, a naïve young fool who didn't deserve a woman as passionate and spirited as Marie. Still, the success of his schemes had far exceeded his expectations. Now he would have both Marie—after all, who else could she turn to but her dear friend Guthrie?—and all the lands of Naughton. Not a bad day's work, he laughed, as he poured himself a glass of the Duke of Glasgow's wine. Then, in the silence of that vast hall, his voice rang out, as he raised his glass,

'To Gavin McNaughton! Wherever he may be!'

✣   ✣   ✣

Huddled on the bare stone floor of the dungeon, Gavin McNaughton awoke with a start. At first he couldn't remember where he was or what had happened. Then the pain of his broken nose, the dried blood caked around his face, and the fact that his hands were securely tied behind his back, brought it all flooding back.

After he was knocked unconscious, he had been flung into this dungeon. He had regained consciousness, only to find himself face to face with Guthrie Jamieson.

'You treacherous dog!' he had screamed, as he tried to fling himself at Jamieson. But his hands were tied, and a single vicious blow from Jamieson sent Gavin reeling, his

210

head swimming. As he fought to remain conscious, he sank to his knees once more.

'Why are you doing this to me, Jamieson?' he gasped.

The Earl smiled. 'Ah, my friend, why do any of us do anything? Let us just say that you took something that was mine, and now I want it back.'

Gavin had no idea what he was talking about.

'What on earth do you mean?'

'Why your precious wife, of course. Before you came along, she and I had a most amicable . . . how shall I say . . . *arrangement*,' and he laughed as Gavin's face fell. 'I'm sure you know what I mean. Anyway, now that she won't be seeing her beloved husband again, we will be able to take up where we left off. Who knows, I may even take her as my wife—after a decent period of mourning for your tragic death, of course!'

Gavin struggled against his bonds, but to no avail.

'You arranged all this just to steal my wife?' Gavin said in a voice filled with bitter loathing for the man he had so recently considered a trusted friend.

'Not entirely. There is also the small matter of your lands. I believe you have been troubled by the debts you owe to certain moneylenders. Well, I hope this will not be too much of a shock, but I have recently acquired the deeds to your estates from those very same moneylenders. And I am afraid when you inevitably fail to pay what is due, your estates will be forfeit. I will then be the Lord of Naughton. So you see, this little escapade has won me not only your wife, but also your ancestral home and everything you hold most dear.'

Jamieson paused for a moment.

'Do you remember Pinkie, Gavin?'

'How could I forget? You saved my life. Because of that, I had always considered you a true friend.'

'Ah yes, those were heroic times, were they not, Gavin!'

He paused again, looking thoughtful.

'I shouldn't really tell you this, but I see no reason not to

211

now—after all, you will never have the opportunity to repeat this to anyone else. Do you remember how I saved you?'

Gavin nodded.

'Well would it surprise you to know that I saved you for one reason, and one reason only—to hand you over to the enemy in return for English gold?'

Gavin could not believe what he was hearing.

'I see from your expression that you never suspected me. Did you never think it strange that I escaped with ease, while you ended up a prisoner? No? You poor fool! Ironic isn't it, that all those years ago at Pinkie you thought I'd saved you, when in fact I'd set you on the road to ruin. If I hadn't betrayed you to the English, you would never have had to mortgage your lands. And I could never have taken them from you. So now you see how the cards have all fallen in my favour, and how excellently the chain of events I started has worked out for me.'

Gavin's head was spinning. He could hardly take in what he had just heard, but he was also filled with a steely determination—to survive long enough to take his revenge on Guthrie Jamieson.

'Have you nothing to say?' Jamieson continued, as Gavin maintained a stony silence. 'No matter. I expect all this has somewhat overwhelmed you. There is just one last thing. No doubt you're wondering what I intend to do with you. I could, of course, have you killed here and now, but I feel inclined to be merciful and to let you live—just a *little* longer. It will give me great satisfaction to think of you rotting away in this Godforsaken place, while I enjoy all the comforts of your former home. And now I must leave you, for I have much to attend to—after all, Naughton Castle and its mistress await their new master!'

And with a courtly bow, Jamieson turned to climb the dungeon steps, saying as he went,

'Farewell, my Lord of Glasgow, I fear we will not meet again.'

'I'll see you in hell, Jamieson!' Gavin shouted after him.

'Quite possibly, quite possibly . . .' replied Jamieson, as he slammed the heavy oaken door shut behind him, his laughter echoing around the walls as his footsteps faded into the distance.

— XXX —

AT Norham Castle Bothwell waited in vain for the arrival of his friend the Duke of Glasgow. As first weeks, and then months dragged by with no word from Gavin, he realised something had gone wrong, and it wasn't long before his thoughts turned to Guthrie Jamieson. He had warned Gavin against trusting the Earl of Edinburgh, and now he felt sure, if the plan had misfired, Jamieson was responsible.

Fortunately for Bothwell, Sir Henry Percy allowed him the freedom to exercise in the courtyard and converse with those who visited the castle. One day, Bothwell came upon a tall powerfully-built man, his face disfigured by a distinctive scar that ran from his left eye to his chin. In an instant, Bothwell recognised him as Jock Armstrong, a borderer who had ridden with him on many raids into England.

'Jock, is it really you?' he cried out.

'My Lord o' Bothwell! Glad am I tae see a friendly Scots face here in England!'

'I could say the same, my old friend! What brings you here?'

214

Armstrong told Bothwell of his most recent exploits, but he also mentioned how, a few months before, he had accompanied a raiding party led by the Earl of Edinburgh. Bothwell immediately demanded to know more.

'Aye, a strange business that was. The young Duke of Glasgow was wi' us. A bad affair indeed!' And he went on to tell how McNaughton had been betrayed and cast into a dungeon in some isolated tower-house. Once he realised what was going on, Armstrong had wanted no part in such treachery.

'You know me weel enough, my Lord, I have done much that I regret, but I have never betrayed anyone. I never did see such black-hearted villainy. But I had to hold my tongue, or I would have joined the Laird of Glasgow in that very dungeon!'

As soon as he had been paid off, Armstrong had taken his leave of Jamieson's cut-throats. He had been paid well for his trouble, but now the money had run out.

'And that is how ye find me here, my Lord, looking for new adventures to fill my purse.'

Bothwell was greatly troubled by what he had heard, although the depth of Jamieson's duplicity did not entirely surprise him.

'Where is this place that the young Duke is being held?' he asked Armstrong.

'Crookham Castle, a lonely peel tower in the hills no mair than five miles south o' here.'

Instantly Bothwell knew what he must do. If Gavin was still alive, then he was honour-bound to try to rescue him. Bothwell knew the borders as few other men knew them, and he remembered Crookham well. A broken-down tower house that stood alone in the shadow of a windswept hillside. No-one went near it these days, as it was said to be haunted. Jamieson would have chosen it both for its evil reputation and its location—so isolated that no-one would ever have found Gavin there. Bothwell thanked God for the lucky

215

chance that had brought Jock Armstrong to Norham and thus given him the slim possibility of saving his friend's life.

'Jock, I need your help. You say you are looking for adventure and for gold. Well, by God, I'll give you more than enough of both if you agree to ride by my side for the next few days. What do you say?'

Armstrong's face lit up.

'My lord, I like your spirit! I dinnae ken what mad scheme ye have in mind, but I'll be honoured to take your gold. My sword is at your service! When do we leave?'

'Meet me with two horses outside the castle walls at nightfall, and be ready to ride at once for Crookham.'

'Ah, so that's how the land lies! We go tae save the bonny Duke o' Glasgow, do we? A tricky proposition, even for twa such scoundrels as ourselves,' he laughed, as they parted.

✣   ✣   ✣

There was only one problem. Bothwell had not thought it prudent to tell Jock that he was not a guest, but a prisoner at Norham. Even a bold fellow like Jock Armstrong might think twice before aiding a fugitive and risking outlawry. And at night Bothwell was always securely locked up in his room at the top of the East tower. The window was not barred— as it led directly to a drop of about seventy-five feet onto the rocks below the castle walls. So far, even the bold Earl of Bothwell had declined the challenge of escaping that way, but this was now a matter of life and death. Bothwell thought back to that night at Edinburgh Castle. He had defied the precipitous castle rock of the greatest fortress in the land, so why not the walls of Norham?

— XXXI —

AFTER being told of her husband's death, Marie spent the long lonely night on her own. Even Effie could not console her, however hard she tried. Marie wept bitterly as the hours passed, sometimes howling aloud with the intensity of the pain she felt. In the darkness she could see Gavin's handsome face through her tears, could hear his voice, as sweet as the breeze in a summer meadow, whispering that he loved her and would never leave her. She imagined him making love to her, tenderly, and remembered her own passionate responses. He was all she wanted, but now he had left her, and she felt alone and vulnerable in a vast and desolate world. So much had happened to her, and as she lay in the darkened bedchamber her mind raced but the tears would not stop. Occasionally she drifted off to sleep, only to be woken by a horrifying vision of Gavin lying dead with a crossbow bolt in his chest. Other nightmares haunted her—sometimes it was Gavin's father Machar lying in a dark pool of blood, the dagger glistening in her hand, and at other times, even worse, it was the pale, waxen face of the Dauphin, his cold dead eyes staring at her in silent accusation.

But somehow she got through the night, and as the new day dawned she rose to find Guthrie Jamieson already up and sitting beside the fire in the great hall, deep in thought.

'Good morning, Guthrie,' said Marie softly. 'I am so glad you are still here.'

'My dear Marie,' Guthrie replied, rising from his seat. 'How are you? You look so pale.'

'I still cannot believe he is dead. He had so much to live for.'

'And he died a brave and honourable death. No man could ask for more.'

They both sat by the fire and stared into the flames.

'If there is anything I can do to help you, anything at all, you know you only have to ask and it shall be yours.'

'You are very kind, Guthrie. My thanks for breaking the news to my mother last night. I could not have . . . Oh God, my poor Gavin . . .' she began to sob quietly, her face buried in her hands.

Jamieson strode quickly over to her and put a comforting arm around her shoulder.

'Hush now, Marie,' he crooned. 'Gavin was a brave man, you should be proud of him. At least you have the children to comfort you, and Naughton Castle will be young Machar's one day. That is all that Gavin would have wanted. You must be brave, my dear.'

'I . . . know . . . it's just the shock, I suppose. I will miss him dreadfully.'

'Of course you will. But you must think of the children, and let the rest take care of itself.'

'You are right, Guthrie. I must go to them. But first, I have a favour to ask of you.'

'Anything.'

'I could not face the Queen at the moment. Will you take a letter to her from me?'

'At once.'

Marie spent the rest of the morning with the children, trying to avoid Effie. The last thing she needed right now was her mother fussing around, but she knew she could not avoid her forever.

'Oh Marie, I've found you at last,' Effie exclaimed as she swept into the room. 'I thought you had disappeared into thin air! How are you my dear? You look terrible!'

'Thank you mother. You always know just what to say.'

'Oh you know what I mean! Have you been crying all night?'

'Yes—I suppose so. I just cannot believe what has happened. What will I do without him?' A tear welled in Marie's eye, but she refused to cry in front of the children.

'Well, of course, it's a terrible shock about poor Gavin, but I think you're really a very lucky young woman. You still have the children and this beautiful castle and land from here to the Trossachs, and me of course! You know, when your father used that unfortunate business of Gavin's father to pack me off to Orkney, I thought that my life would be over, but looking back it was only just beginning. I was well rid of your father; he was nothing but a scoundrel and a womaniser. . . .'

Marie did not have the strength to argue with her mother, and knew it was hopeless to try when she was in this mood. Not for her a few words of comfort: it was as though Effie didn't care about anything or anyone but herself.

'. . . and at least you have that nice factor Mr McNairn to look after things for you. I suppose you will have to take over some of Gavin's responsibilities, but not for a while yet, and I'll always be here to make sure that the children are properly looked after. . . .'

As the days passed, Marie began to feel a little stronger. She had started eating a bit more, with Effie's constant encouragement, of course, and had even started to sleep better.

There were still nightmares, but they were less frequent now.

A week after Guthrie Jamieson's departure, he returned, bringing with him a letter bearing the Royal Seal.

'The Queen asked me to bring this to you directly, Marie. She is heartbroken about Gavin's death and sends you her sorrow and her love. I'm sure the letter will explain all.'

Marie could hardly read the letter through her veil of tears. She wept bitterly and finally put it down by her side.

'I did not know that people could be so kind. There is so much I have to be thankful for.' She looked up at the Earl, standing beside her. 'You will stay for a while, won't you Guthrie?'

The Earl bowed deeply. 'I am at your service, as always.'

♣ ♣ ♣

The days drifted past, and Marie began to feel alive once more. Guthrie had even managed to make her laugh once or twice, and Effie had stopped fussing quite so much. Days turned into weeks, and although Marie thought of Gavin almost constantly, she could now do so without so many tears.

Guthrie Jamieson had stayed by her side throughout it all, occasionally departing to take care of some business or other, but always returning when he could, and always so supportive. Indeed, he had changed so much recently that she could hardly recognise him as the scoundrel she had known in France. She had always felt that somewhere underneath all his bravado and his plotting, there was a good man. Perhaps now he was mellowing with age.

And he was so good with the children, spending many hours in the nursery with them. He even seemed to be able to cope with Effie's inane conversations. Indeed, Marie began to wonder if her mother had not taken rather too much of a shine to the Earl. After a glass of wine or two with their meal, Effie was often quite flirtatious, and Guthrie seemed flattered by the attention.

'Mother,' said Marie as they sat at their embroidery one afternoon, 'you seem very fond of Guthrie.'

'I am. And if you won't do anything to encourage him to stay with us, then I must.'

'What do you mean?'

'I mean that it is more than two months now since we heard that poor Gavin had been killed, and it's time you were thinking of your future.'

'You surely don't mean Guthrie?'

'And why not? He's rich, handsome, and you've known him for years. What could be a better match?'

'I sometimes cannot believe that you are my mother. How can you say such things, when you know how I felt about Gavin?'

'You and I have always had different ideas about life, Marie, but as I always say, live life to the full and enjoy what you can. You won't get a better man than Guthrie, and he loves the children *so* much. Not many men would be so considerate. And he's been the perfect gentleman.'

Marie remembered so many times past when Guthrie had been anything but the perfect gentleman, and she had been anything but a lady. No, she thought to herself, it can never be, she could never marry the Earl. There had been too much water under the bridge for that.

❖ ❖ ❖

Guthrie Jamieson was relieved that Effie had gone to bed early. It gave him a chance to be alone with Marie. In a few days he would have to leave, and he felt that it was time to test the water.

'Marie,' he said, quietly. 'I know that Gavin's death has been a terrible shock, but I just wanted to say how much I still admire you. Obviously it will be some time before you will think about marriage again, but I must know—do you still feel anything for me?'

Marie flushed a deep red, and lowered her gaze. Her heart was thumping as she replied. 'Guthrie, you have been so kind since Gavin died. I will be forever in your debt. But no, I do not think I shall ever be able to marry again. My only concern is for the children now, and to ensure they are provided for as Gavin would have wished.'

'But you are still young, young enough to find happiness again.'

'No, Guthrie. Please, let us not talk of this again. I am tired now, please excuse me.' And with that, she rose and hurriedly left the room.

As he sat in the gathering gloom, Guthrie glowered at the fire. Very well, he thought, if that is the way she wants it, so be it. There's more than one way to pluck this little chicken.

✤   ✤   ✤

As Marie, Guthrie and Effie sat at the table after lunch one afternoon, the factor knocked and entered, looking concerned.

'Mr McNairn. What a pleasant surprise. Is everything all right?' Marie asked, seeing the worry on his face.

'Weel, my Lady, I've been daein' my best to keep things runnin'. But there's a lot o' money due, and there's them that'll no' wait for it.'

'Do you need me to sign anything?' Marie asked, puzzled.

'Weel, it's a wheen more delicate, my Lady. Perhaps we cuid discuss it in private. . . .'

'It's perfectly all right. There are no secrets among us here.'

'Verra weel, my Lady. I tried to let this lee as lang as I cuid, efter the tragic death of his Lairdship, but, weel, ye see, the reason I cannae pay the money oot is that there isn't ony left.'

Effie leapt up like a scalded cat.

'What?' she screeched. 'What do you mean, you stupid little man? The Duke was rich!'

'Mother, please sit down! Give McNairn a chance to speak.' Marie turned back to the factor, her heart thumping. 'You had better sit down and explain yourself, McNairn. Please . . .' she gestured towards a chair beside the Earl. 'What is this all about?'

'Weel, it's jist as I say, there's nae money left. Efter the old Duke deed, God rest his soul, he didnae leave as much as a'body thoucht—there wis the new chapel, of course, which wasnae built fur naethin', and the guid Duke's own tomb, built wi' *Italian* mairble nae less—and then young Gavin wis taken at the battle. When we found oot he wis alive, there wis nae gold to buy him free—and to this day I dinnae ken what happened tae it a'. So, he had only twa options, tae mortgage everythin' or tae rot in an English dungeon. Ever since, he's worked hard, harder than any man alive, to get the estate even, but the demands o' thae moneylenders jist get worse and worse. . . .' His voice cracked, and his hand drew a parchment from inside his jacket. 'And now this,' he said, shaking his head.

'What is it?' Marie asked.

'It's a demand frae the English moneylenders. They want a thousand gold pieces by the end o' the month, or the castle will be forfeit.'

'In the name of God!' shouted the Earl. 'Surely this cannot be legal?'

'Aye, it's legal a' right. And the money must be found.'

Effie started to wail, 'This cannot be true. I'll wager I know what happened! *You* took the money, didn't you McNairn? Go on, admit it!'

'Mother! Hold your tongue! If you cannot conduct yourself properly you will leave us!'

The factor looked startled and upset.

'I've loyally served this family these thirty years past—' he began.

'You must forgive my mother. Sometimes she doesn't know what she is saying.'

'That's as mebbe, but whit can we do aboot a' this money?'

'Is there nothing left at all?'

'Nothing, my Lady, nothing at all.'

Marie tried to stay calm. Surely there must be some way out of this calamity.

⚜ ⚜ ⚜

'Marie, you must let me help you!' The Earl of Edinburgh looked thoroughly at ease by the fireside.

'No, Guthrie, I must find a way out of this mess myself,' Marie replied.

'At least let me lend you the money you need to hold off these dogs for a while.'

'You are very kind, but I am determined in this. I have decided to seek the Queen's advice on the matter, and I will travel to Holyrood tomorrow.'

'Do you think that is wise, Marie?'

'I don't think I have an option.'

Despite her better judgement, Marie allowed both Guthrie and Effie to accompany her on the journey. When they arrived, her reunion with the Queen was tearful—it was the first time they had seen each other since Gavin's death—and they talked long into the night. But the Queen saw that there was something else amiss.

'You look troubled, my dear Marie? As if you have the weight of the world on your poor shoulders.'

'I am troubled, your Majesty. I am about to lose Naughton Castle and there seems little I can do about it.' And so she told the Queen the whole sorry tale, as well as Guthrie Jamieson's offer of marriage. When she had finished speaking, the Queen said,

'There is something else, isn't there, something about the Earl that you are not telling me?'

Marie was startled. 'What do you mean, your Majesty?'

'I think you are a little in love with Guthrie Jamieson, is it not so? You know you can confess to me. And such a match would not be so bad a thing, perhaps?'

Now Marie felt trapped. She could not tell anyone the truth about Guthrie Jamieson. Yes, he had been kind, but still she did not really trust him. But what could she do? Once more she was being trapped into a marriage she did not want, this time for the sake of her children. Only once had she found true love, and now that love had been taken from her.

❖   ❖   ❖

'Oh, Marie, I think it's wonderful!' Effie trilled. 'This marriage will finally solve all our problems! And he's such a nice man.'

'I haven't told him yet, mother, so don't say a word.'

Later that evening, there was to be a banquet at Holyrood, in honour of the French ambassador, who was one of the Queen's favourites, and Marie had decided to speak to Guthrie.

The banquet was the usual grand affair, and it was very late before Marie finally had the chance to speak to the Earl alone.

'Guthrie, there is something we need to talk about.'

'Yes, Marie?' The Earl sensed victory.

'You know that the children are the most important thing in the world to me now. I cannot bear to think of them without their rightful inheritance, but even that is about to be snatched away from them. I will do anything to stop that happening. For that reason, if you will agree to pay off all the debts of the estate, then I will agree to marry you.'

'A bargain indeed! I have waited for this moment for a long time now, and I accept your terms most willingly. You shall have your money, and I shall have my bride. And I am sure, my dear, that Gavin would have been proud of what you do today for the sake of his heirs.'

They had been standing outside the banqueting hall, and Jamieson suddenly grabbed her roughly by the arm and led her into one of the antechambers nearby. He slammed the door shut behind them and grabbed her round the waist, kissing her passionately, his strong arms tearing at her gown. She was paralysed under this onslaught, and held her eyes tightly shut. He had been such a gentleman these last few months that she was not expecting such lust from him, and now he was pawing at her breasts like the wild animal she had known before. In no time he removed her gown and bodice, and his own richly-coloured doublet, and they were making love on the floor, his powerful chest pinning her to the painted floorboards. She felt herself responding to him, after all this time, and knew that it was wrong—and yet it felt so right.

— XXXII —

HAD anyone been keeping lookout from the crumbling walls of Crookham Castle, they could hardly have failed to spot the two horsemen as they crested the hill. Silhouetted against the rising sun, they galloped over the ridge and down a wooded slope still wreathed in the dawn mist.

But there was no lookout. The Earl of Edinburgh had hardly even considered the possibility of a rescue attempt, and consequently the garrison of the semi-derelict castle consisted of a mere five men-at-arms—all of whom were soundly asleep at this early hour.

Bothwell had hoped to take the garrison by surprise, but even he would have expected to face a far more formidable force. Yet as he and Jock Armstrong warily approached the walls of Crookham, they could only guess at what dangers awaited them within. At least he had the redoubtable Armstrong with him, Bothwell thought.

Only a few hours before, placing his trust in his own skill and daring, Bothwell had climbed out of the tower window at Norham. Climbing down that tower had been a nightmare, as the ancient masonry crumbled under his feet and hands, but somehow he had not fallen. As he sat exhausted in the shadows at the foot of the castle wall, his spirits had soared when he saw the unmistakable figure of Jock Armstrong coming towards him out of the dark. And he had not only brought the two horses, he had also taken the liberty of procuring swords, dirks and a pair of long wheel-lock pistols. What could he not achieve with a hundred rock-solid borderers like Armstrong at his back, Bothwell thought!

As they skirted round the castle walls, Bothwell and Armstrong were careful to make no sound. They had left the horses in the woods at the bottom of the hill and, taking only their weapons with them, they crossed the stream on foot. Coming to the gateway, they were astonished to find the rusting iron gate unlocked, as it swung open with a harsh creak. More importantly, it seemed to be unguarded. For a moment Bothwell began to fear they were too late, that Gavin was already dead and his captors flown. Then, from above came a cry of 'Who goes there!' instantly followed by the crash of musket fire and the sound of a bullet ricocheting off the gate.

Without the slightest hesitation, Armstrong rushed up the steps of the keep with Bothwell close behind, their pistols and dirks at the ready. By the time Bothwell reached the top of the winding staircase Armstrong was already struggling with the man who had fired at them. His musket, now discharged and useless, lay at his feet and the two men faced each other, dirks flashing in the sunlight that streamed in through the narrow windows. In a second it was over, as Armstrong rushed forward and drove his dirk into his opponent's stomach. The man fell in a crumpled groaning heap, but by now his comrades were wide awake and rushing up the stairs. Two died as soon as they emerged into the light, shot clean through the head, as first Bothwell and then Armstrong fired their pistols. The others were not so bold and waited in the chamber below.

Again neither Bothwell nor Armstrong hesitated, they

rushed as one down into the room below. As they hurtled through the door they were met by the shattering report of a musket, as one of their opponents fired at them from point blank range. With a terrible cry, Armstrong fell where he stood, but Bothwell rushed on, sword and dirk in hand, and ran the musketeer through with his sword. As the acrid smoke from the musket cleared, Bothwell found himself facing the last survivor of the garrison—a terrified old man who clutched an ancient sword in his trembling hand.

'Spare me, sir, I beg you! For pity's sake!'

Bothwell looked at the pathetic creature with disgust.

'Put down that sword, old man. Fear not, I would not soil this good sword with your unworthy blood!'

The old man flung his sword away and collapsed, whimpering, in a corner.

Bothwell turned to look at Armstrong. He had been struck in the shoulder by the musket ball, but his wound did not look too bad.

'How goes it Jock? I think yon fellow has made a pretty mess of your sword-arm!'

'Aye, maybe he has,' Jock grimaced, as the pain subsided, 'but I doubt he'll be doing it again in a hurry!' And they both laughed heartily.

After tying up the old man, and binding Armstrong's wound, they set about searching for Gavin. It did not take them long, as the first place they looked was the dungeons.

✤   ✤   ✤

Deep in the bowels of the castle, Gavin had heard the first musket shot. Two more shots rang out, then another, then silence. Gavin strained to hear what was going on. He had almost given up hope of ever getting out of Crookham alive. And now at long last maybe his prayers were going to be answered!

The muffled sound of laughter echoed down from the

chamber above, and Gavin's heart sank. The last time he had heard laughter like that had been when Guthrie Jamieson took his leave all those months ago. If Jamieson had returned, then Gavin knew he was done for.

Then he heard the sound of heavy footsteps descending from above and coming towards the door of his cell. Gavin steeled himself to face his tormentor, but when the door burst open he was astonished to see the smiling face of James Hepburn, Earl of Bothwell.

'Bothwell! Thank God! How did you find me?'

'Ah, that's a long story, my friend,' Bothwell replied, as he swiftly untied Gavin's hands. Looking at his friend, Bothwell was shocked at his appearance. He had clearly suffered much in the last few months.

'For now, the main thing is to get you out of this place. I have no wish to linger here in case any more of Jamieson's lackeys appear. I have had more than enough swordplay for one day!'

Without delay, they climbed the stairs from the dungeon and Gavin emerged into the light of day for the first time in many weeks. Then they hurried away from the castle without a backward glance. Jock Armstrong was waiting for them with the horses at the edge of the woods. He had liberated an extra horse for Gavin from the castle; its former owner would not be needing it where he was going, he told Bothwell with a grin.

From Crookham they rode west to Smailholm, a gaunt fortified tower in the hills near Melrose, and along the way Bothwell told Gavin all about his meeting with Armstrong and the escape from Norham. The Laird of Smailholm turned out to be a good friend of Bothwell's, and he was more than happy to give the three men shelter for the night. After a long day in the saddle, and feeling the effects of his wound, Armstrong quickly took to his bed, leaving Gavin and Bothwell to talk as they sat in front of a roaring log fire.

Gavin told his friend everything that had happened—the

Earl of Edinburgh's treachery, including his plan to ruin him and steal Marie from him, and the desperate privations he had suffered during his lengthy incarceration at Crookham.

'By God, Bothwell, I thought things were bad all those years ago when I was a prisoner after Pinkie. But this was far worse. Jamieson had left word that I was to be slowly starved to death, and his men carried out his orders to the letter. If it hadn't been for one old man amongst them who took pity on me and passed the occasional bit of food to me, I would not be here now.'

Bothwell told Gavin about the old man whose life he had spared.

'Yes! That was him. I am glad to hear he survived. As for the rest, they deserved no mercy.'

'What will you do now?' Bothwell asked.

'I have unfinished business with Guthrie Jamieson, and I must leave at dawn for Naughton. No doubt I will find him there and, God willing, he will never see another sunrise if I have anything to do with it!' Gavin's eyes flashed with hatred.

'I understand your haste, my dear Gavin, but you are in no state for swordplay just yet. I have arranged with our host that we shall all remain here for a week or so. That should give both yourself and Jock time to recover your full strength. Then you will be ready to face Jamieson.'

'Yes, perhaps you are right,' Gavin conceded wearily.

'I only wish I could come with you,' Bothwell continued, 'but I cannot show my face just now, or I will find myself under lock and key once more. I fear I may have to take ship to France and live in exile until I can overcome my present troubles.'

'I would not want you to risk more than you already have for my sake,' Gavin replied. 'And I will never forget what you have done for me this day.'

'Think nothing of it, my friend. Bothwell always keeps his word. You saved me that night in Edinburgh, and I have

231

merely returned the favour. And now we must sleep, for we have all earned a damned good night's rest.'

✤   ✤   ✤

One week later, the two friends parted, Gavin galloping away to the north, leaving Bothwell and Armstrong at Smailholm. As they watched Gavin disappear into the distance, Bothwell turned to Armstrong.

'So Jock, what's it to be? Is your thirst for adventure quenched, or do you ride with Bothwell to who knows where?'

'I think ye already ken the answer to that my Lord!' Armstrong replied, and the two men turned their horses to the south and rode off into the morning mist.

— XXXIII —

AT Naughton Castle everything was being made ready for the banquet to celebrate the betrothal of Marie and the Earl of Edinburgh. The Queen would be there and a lavish feast was being prepared, not to mention the wonderful music and entertainment that had been arranged—all of it paid for by Guthrie Jamieson.

Effie was in her customary state of high excitement.

'Oh Marie!' she exclaimed, 'at long last everything has turned out for the best! I know Gavin's loss was a grievous blow, but that is all behind us now. Once you marry the Earl, we will never want for anything. He is such a fine and generous gentleman.'

Marie wasn't listening, her mind was far away as she thought back over the dramatic changes that had occurred in her life. She thought once more of her childhood at Spynie, the loss of Donald, the death of Machar, and her time with the Queen in France—how long ago it all seemed now. Marrying Gavin McNaughton had closed the door on her past, she had thought; all the sadness and heartache were finished. How wrong she had been. Her life with Gavin had not been perfect, but she could never have guessed that their time together would be so short. She was proud that he had died a hero, but how she wished he had never set eyes on the Earl of Bothwell.

Now, yet again she was making a fresh start. Whatever doubts she might have had about Guthrie Jamieson, they had to be banished from her mind. And anyway, what did her own happiness matter when set against the future security of her children? If she didn't marry Jamieson, they would have no future—Naughton would be lost and they would be ruined. What was past was past. Now, she looked to the future.

'Marie! Did you hear what I just said?'

'Yes, mother. I always take heed of everything you say,' Marie replied wearily.

'I'm glad to hear it. I expect you are preoccupied with the preparations for the arrival of the Queen?'

Marie had hardly seen the Queen since Gavin's death, but even Mary had insisted that marrying the Earl of Edinburgh was the best thing she could do.

'It's what Gavin would have wanted, Marie,' Mary had told her. 'He and Guthrie were dear friends, and was it not your husband's dying wish that Guthrie should look after you?'

Marie could not deny the sense in what the Queen said. But somehow she could not rid herself of the lingering doubts about Guthrie Jamieson. He had certainly done everything he possibly could for her and the children, but she could not forget his old ruthlessness and cunning. He seemed to have changed, cast off his old self, and become the true gentleman he had always pretended to be. But Marie was not sure. How could she ever be sure about a man like Guthrie?

It was too late for doubts now. The Queen would be arriving that very evening and the wedding would take place the following day. The die was cast, and Marie would have to make the best of it, for the sake of the children, if not herself.

The Queen arrived attended by her faithful companions, the four Marys, and her bodyguard of about a dozen men-at-arms. Marie greeted her in the Great Hall.

'Your Majesty, I am honoured to see you here.'

'I am glad to be here, my dear Marie, on so happy an occasion as this. I trust you are well?'

After a few minutes' conversation the Queen was led away to her chamber.

The other invited guests were beginning to arrive *en masse*, including nearly all the great nobles and courtiers. Magnus Hepburn and the Bishop of Moray were there—even though Marie would have preferred not to invite them. But Effie had insisted.

'How can you not invite your own father to your wedding? He may not be the man he once was, but he is still influential. This will be an excellent opportunity to bury all the differences that have grown up between you. And as for your half-brother Magnus, well, he was a close friend of Gavin's was he not? It would dishonour your late husband's memory to exclude him. No, they must both come to the wedding!'

For once in her life, Marie conceded, Effie was right. And she had invited them both.

Soon the Great Hall was buzzing with animated conversation as the guests greeted each other and looked forward to the next day's celebrations. After a while they began to ascend the stairs to their chambers—a good night's sleep would be essential if they were to enjoy the following day to the full. After checking that everything was ready for the next day, Marie too retired to her chamber and fell into an exhausted, dreamless sleep.

✤ ✤ ✤

In his chamber at the opposite end of the castle, Guthrie Jamieson was wide awake. His mind was filled with thoughts of the past, intermingled with eager anticipation of what tomorrow would bring—the culmination of all his schemes. He could hardly believe how easy it had all been in the months since he had tricked Gavin McNaughton into going to Crookham.

Now, here he was, about to become the Master of Naughton and the husband of Marie. He remembered the first time he had ever seen her—the night he murdered Machar in this very room. The irony of it! Machar would surely be spinning in his grave! His charm and cunning had now won her over, or so he thought, and she was to be his. He wondered if he loved her. Had he ever loved anyone? And to his surprise, he found himself unable to answer either question. There was no doubt that he wanted to marry her— but perhaps he just wanted to possess her in the same way he wanted to take McNaughton's lands? Well, what did it matter? If she bored him, if he tired of her, he would soon find a way of disposing of her.

As Jamieson blew out the candle by his bedside, his final thought was of Gavin McNaughton. 'I think by now he has had long enough to contemplate his ruin. Tomorrow I must send word to Crookham. It is about time the young Duke *really* went to meet his maker.'

— XXXIV —

MARIE awoke early the next morning, as the pale autumn sunlight was just beginning to filter through the tapestry curtains of her four-poster bed. It was not long before her maid arrived to dress her in the sumptuous wedding gown of silk and velvet. Effie arrived soon after.

'What a vision of beauty!' she exclaimed as she saw Marie resplendent in all her finery. 'This is going to be a day we will never forget!'

Marie felt numb. It was as though all this was happening to someone else. It felt as though it was nothing to do with her, that she was being dragged along by the tide of everyone else's expectations. It had been so different the day she married Gavin.

The ceremony was to take place in the ornate chapel adjoining the Great Hall. The chapel was lit by elaborate stained-glass windows which overlooked the courtyard. Already the guests, arrayed in all their finery, were starting to assemble in the Great Hall, waiting to follow the Queen into the chapel.

When the Queen arrived, sweeping down the great stair-case followed by her maids and various courtiers, an honour guard of her own bodyguard was waiting for her at the foot of the stairs.

Finally, entering through separate doorways, Marie and Jamieson came into the hall. They knelt together in front of the Queen as she gave them her blessing.

'My two dear friends, what pleasure it gives me to see you here. May your life together be prosperous and happy.'

Then Marie and Jamieson rose and walked together to-wards the chapel, closely followed by the Queen and the rest of the guests, amongst them the Bishop of Moray. In that vast hall, he was not the only one who found himself think-ing back to another wedding celebration at Naughton, one winter's night many years before.

Just as the procession reached the entrance to the chapel, a terrible cry rang out, echoing around the vaulting of the Great Hall.

'In the name of God! Stop!'

Everyone halted in mid stride, looking around to see where the shout had come from.

At the far end of the Great Hall stood a dishevelled, menacing figure. His filthy, tattered clothes and his unkempt beard made him unrecognisable as the former master of Naughton Castle. Sword in hand, his mind filled only with thoughts of revenge, Gavin McNaughton had come home.

As he advanced towards them, the guests hastily moved out of his way. They had no idea who he was or what he wanted, but they could see from the look in his eye that he was a very dangerous man.

The Queen turned to Jamieson and asked, 'Who is this fellow who comes to Naughton in rags?'

'I have not the faintest idea, your Majesty,' lied Jamieson, 'but I will see he is dealt with! Guards!' he shouted. 'Seize that man!'

Jamieson had recognised the intruder at once. How on

earth had Gavin escaped? By God he would have the heads of those idle dogs at Crookham for this! But that could wait. For the moment everything depended on silencing McNaughton before he could utter another word. Drawing his own sword, Jamieson pushed his way through the crowd and the advancing guards, before coming face to face with his nemesis.

The Queen and the wedding guests looked on aghast. No-one moved, their eyes fixed on the strange intruder and the Earl of Edinburgh. Marie rushed to the Queen's side, unable to believe what she was seeing. Can this really be happening, she thought? Her mind reeled from the shock— she was the only other person in the room who had recognised Gavin. She tried to cry out, but no sound emerged from her mouth.

As the two men stood there, barely a sword's length between them, McNaughton spoke.

'I have waited a long time for this moment, Jamieson, thinking how much I would savour tearing out your black heart! If you have a God, then commend yourself to him with all speed. You will not get another chance to do so in this life!'

'Brave words, my friend, but, as a true gentleman, I prefer to let my sword speak for me—*en garde!*'

Then, with a wild cry, Jamieson threw himself at Gavin. Their swords flashed in the light of the hundreds of candles that lit the Great Hall, and the harsh, metallic clang of steel on steel echoed around the walls. The Captain of the Queen's bodyguard held his men back—if the bold Earl of Edinburgh wants some sport with this pathetic ruffian, he thought, then we will leave him to it!

As blows rained down on him, and the two men circled each other, Gavin fell back towards the chapel. Overturning a long banqueting table as he went, capons, pheasants and all manner of other game were sent flying from their gilded platters, while goblets and candlesticks went crashing to the ground. In an instant, the carefully prepared feast was reduced to chaos.

Surprised by the ferocity of Jamieson's attack, Gavin retreated into the chapel itself. In the small vaulted space the fight became even more bitter, the smell of incense and the coloured light filtering in through the tall stained-glass windows lending the whole scene a dream-like, unreal quality.

Then as the onlookers, crowded in the chapel entrance, looked on in horror, the Earl of Edinburgh stumbled over the altar rail and fell heavily. Gavin's sword was raised high for the final blow, but Jamieson was not finished yet. In a swift movement, he flung his dirk at Gavin, striking him a glancing blow on the neck. It was enough to make him pause, allowing the Earl to spring to his feet.

Once more he rushed at Gavin and forced him to fall back. As he defended himself with a fierce desperation, Gavin felt cold marble pressed against his back. Glancing round, he found that he was cornered. Behind him was the elaborate marble tomb of his father, Machar McNaughton; in front, the wild-eyed figure of Jamieson. As Gavin's concentration drifted for one fatal second, Jamieson lashed out and knocked the sword from his hand.

The irony of the situation was not lost on Jamieson.

'How apt, that you should die by your father's side!' he laughed. 'And how appropriate that it should be by the same hand!'

At long last, Gavin had the answer to the question that had always haunted him. It was Jamieson! Jamieson had murdered his father!

As Jamieson drew back his blade for the final thrust, Gavin threw himself forward in blind fury and Jamieson's sword, deflected from its target, sliced through his arm just below the shoulder. Gavin cried out in pain as he fell heavily on top of the Earl. Jamieson's sword clattered onto the flagstones just out of reach, as the two men rolled around on the bloodstained chapel floor, but he managed to break free and turned to run, only to find himself facing one of the great stained-glass windows. Turning round, he felt the point of a sword against his throat.

'It is finished, Jamieson,' Gavin gasped, as blood poured from the wound in his arm.

Jamieson stared at his opponent defiantly.

'I think not!' he said, his voice filled with contempt.

Before Gavin could say another word, he found himself seized from behind by men of the Queen's bodyguard. A look of triumph came into Jamieson's eyes.

'Take this villain away,' he commanded, 'and hang him in the courtyard, like the dog he is!'

As they started to drag Gavin away, a voice cried out,

'Enough! Enough of this. It is I who hold the power of life and death here. No-one else but I!'

It was the Queen who spoke. Jamieson and Gavin had become completely oblivious to the audience who stood all around them. And until now none of the onlookers had tried to intervene.

In the chapel, silence reigned for a moment. Then the Queen spoke again.

'My Lord of Glasgow, how is it that you have risen from the grave?' she said, drawing shocked gasps from the on-lookers. Marie had finally managed to tell the Queen that the ragged man was none other than Gavin McNaughton.

'And you, my Lord of Edinburgh, why are you so keen to see him return to the ranks of the dead?'

Gavin spoke first, ignoring the Queen's question.

'Your Majesty, the crimes of this . . . this . . . monster are legion,' he said pointing at Jamieson. 'He is a traitor, a spy for the English, he betrayed me to them. He has stolen my wife and my estates. God alone knows what else he may be responsible for. And now I learn that it was he who killed my father!'

The Queen turned to Jamieson.

'What have you to say to that, my Lord of Edinburgh?'

Jamieson looked around him at the faces that crowded into that small space. And he was filled with loathing for them all. Then his eyes met Marie's. In that brief moment, he realised he had lost her forever, and he was filled with a bitter sadness. His mind raced to think of some way out, something he could say, a plausible tale that would buy him some time. But he felt suddenly weary. Tired of all the lies, the scheming, the treachery. 'To hell with them all!' he thought. His mind was made up. It was over. But, if he must fall, then he would wreak havoc while he still could.

'Your Majesty, I am afraid there may be some truth in what McNaughton says. But I think he might do well to ask his wife about her own part in the death of the old Duke. And perhaps the good Bishop of Moray and his ghastly concubine, Effie Dalgliesh, might also like to divest themselves of the secrets of that night at Naughton!'

Jamieson's tirade was briefly interrupted by hysterical screaming, before Effie collapsed in a dead faint. The Bishop of Moray's face crumpled, his life ruined in an instant.

Jamieson continued remorselessly.

'And as for you, your Majesty, you might like to ask your dear friend Marie about her role in the demise of your beloved Dauphin. How sad a thing it is to be betrayed by even one's closest friends!'

As Jamieson finished, the chapel was filled with an oppressive silence. No-one seemed to know what to do or say in the wake of his outburst. Even the Queen stood motionless, a look of blank amazement on her face. She hadn't even glanced at Marie. Gavin seethed with impotent fury, but he was still securely held by the guards.

And then Jamieson seized his opportunity.

With one bound he sprang towards the chapel window, and in a shower of brightly coloured glass he crashed through it. Tumbling into the courtyard amidst the shards of broken glass, Jamieson picked himself up and grabbed a horse that was tethered nearby. Hauling himself swiftly into the saddle, he turned to look back up at the astonished faces that stared down at him from the shattered window.

Gavin had managed to break free, and he stood at the window.

'You can run, Jamieson,' he screamed, 'but you can never hide from me! Wherever you go, I will find you!'

Jamieson smiled up at him.

'In that case, it is merely *au revoir* my friend, until we meet again! And be sure to give my regards to your wife!'

Swinging his horse around, Jamieson galloped across the courtyard and disappeared through the open gateway.

As the dust settled in the courtyard below, the chapel was filled with a babble of excited voices, cries of alarm, and the gentle sobbing of Effie and a number of the Queen's other companions.

Gavin was the first to make a move. In his rage the implications of all that had just happened meant nothing to him. In his mind, there was only Jamieson. He would kill him, whatever the cost, no matter how long it took. Everything else could wait—his estates, his children, his wife. He didn't even look at Marie—there was too much to say, and too little time to say it. Picking up his sword, he ran to the door.

'Wait, Gavin!' Marie cried out. 'We must speak!'

'There is no time. Every second wasted takes Jamieson further from me. When I return . . .' And without a backward glance Gavin rushed down the stairs. Moments later, the thud of hooves in the courtyard signalled his departure.

Then the Queen silenced them with calm authority.

'Leave us, all of you. I wish to speak with Marie. Alone!'

The chapel cleared, the guests trooping out subdued and thoughtful, stunned at what they had just witnessed.

Alone together amid the broken glass and torn tapestries of the chapel, Marie and the Queen faced each other. Tears streamed down Marie's face as she struggled to find words to express what she was feeling.

After what seemed like an age, the Queen asked, in a trembling voice,

'Is it true, Marie, what he said about the Dauphin? Tell me it isn't true!'

Marie did not know how she could even begin to explain her actions to her friend. Whatever she said, if she told the truth, it would be an admission that she had betrayed her. It would mean ruin for herself and the children. And what good was the truth to the Queen? To learn that her husband was murdered and her best friend was involved? No, the truth was a luxury Marie could not afford.

'How can you even think that of me, your Majesty? That I could betray you, my dearest friend? On my children's lives, I swear I knew nothing of this until today.'

The Queen sighed.

'How glad I am to hear you say that, Marie. In these difficult times, if one cannot rely on one's friends, then what is left?'

And as the two of them embraced in the quiet of the chapel, Marie swore to herself that this terrible day would be a fresh start for her after all. From now on, whatever happened, so long as she lived she would never again prove unworthy of the Queen's faith in her.

Other Margaret Thomson Davis titles from B&W:

THE TOBACCO LORDS TRILOGY

Beginning in Glasgow during the Jacobite Rebellion of 1745, *The Tobacco Lords* is the epic story of the lifelong rivalry of two very different women—Annabella Ramsay, daughter of a rich Tobacco Lord, and Regina Chisholm, a child of the slums.

Available for the first time in one volume, this is a compelling story of romance and rivalry, and a marvellous evocation of the city of Glasgow and its people in the 18th century—from the wealth and grandeur of the lives of the Tobacco Lords, the city's thriving merchants, to the poverty and desperation of the filthy, overcrowded tenements.

*'Mrs Davis is a justifiably acclaimed portrayer of her city, and
her latest look at it during the '45 Rising is full of gutsy
writing and shrewd observation'*
THE SCOTSMAN

THE DARK SIDE OF PLEASURE

A powerful story of passion and tragedy set in early Victorian Glasgow, *The Dark Side of Pleasure* chronicles the rise and fall of two families—the wealthy and respectable Camerons, and the Gunnets, desperate people who will do anything to escape the poverty of the slums.

Alfred Cameron, the owner of a prosperous coaching firm, his wife Felicity and their beautiful daughter Augusta enjoy a life of privilege and luxury, surrounded by servants and the trappings of success. But the family firm is in danger—threatened by the encroaching railways, and undermined from within by one of their own coachmen, Luther Gunnet, a ruthlessly ambitious man who will do anything to raise his family from the slums.

*'I have the greatest possible admiration for Mrs Thomson
Davis's imagination. She is one author who
seems to improve with every book'*
GLASGOW EVENING TIMES

THE BREADMAKERS SAGA

The Breadmakers Saga is the epic trilogy of a Glasgow working-class community living through the dark days of the Depression and the Second World War. The lives and loves of the people of Clydend are vividly and absorbingly depicted—people like Catriona, a young woman trying to cope with an overbearing husband; the baker Baldy Fowler and his tragic wife; Alec Jackson, the philandering insurance salesman; and a host of other characters who face up to the ordinary challenges of life and the extraordinary challenges of war with honesty, optimism and hope. Available for the first time in one volume.

'All human life is there, laughter and tears together'
THE SCOTSMAN

'Mrs Davis catches the time with
honest-to-goodness certainty'
THE GUARDIAN

LIGHT AND DARK

Set in Edinburgh and West Lothian at the end of the Victorian era, *Light and Dark* is the powerful story of the Blackwood family—Lorianna, a beautiful young woman, married at sixteen to a considerably older man; Gavin, her austere and sanctimonious husband; and Clementina, their wild and wayward daughter who grows up rebelling against everything her parents stand for.

The Blackwoods appear to live an affluent and normal family life in their impressive mansion, but things are not quite what they seem, and the whole family are about to be engulfed in a dreadful tragedy that will overshadow the rest of their lives.

'Mrs Davis is one of my favourite historical writers,
with that rare ability to achieve lightness of
touch and readability without overtones
of superficiality and sentiment'
THE SCOTSMAN

THE HAYBURN FAMILY

The sequel to *Aunt Bel*, and the concluding part of McCrone's ever-popular Victorian family saga, sees the family once more in crisis as their successful shipyard on the Clyde is under threat and the family seems certain to be torn apart by conflict between the generations. A suitably dramatic and moving conclusion to Guy McCrone's sequence of Glasgow novels, *The Hayburn Family* confirms his position as a most vivid and authentic chronicler of life in Victorian Glasgow.

> *'McCrone knows just about everything*
> *a man can know about the Glasgow*
> *of those days'*
> GLASGOW EVENING CITIZEN

Available from all good bookshops,
or direct from the publishers:

B&W Publishing,
233 Cowgate, Edinburgh,
EH1 1NQ.

Tel: 0131 220 5551

If you would like to be included on our
mailing list, for details of forthcoming books,
please write to the above address.